THE
SOUL
NOTE

BY
WINBORN WHITE

The Soul Note is a work of fiction. All places, incidents, and all characters, with the exception of some well known historical and public figures, are a product of the author's imagination and are not to be construed as real. Where real-life historical or public figures appear, the situations, incidents, or dialogues concerning those persons or events are entirely fictional and are not intended to depict the actual events or to change the entirely fictional nature of the work.

Acknowledgements

I would like to express my appreciation to my family and friends for all their support and encouragement.

I also want to say how grateful I am to my wonderful daughter. Her insightful input, thoughtful direction, and unfailing support and encouragement contributed greatly to the completion of this book.

Thank you all!

The ancient Romans called it a *Genius loci*, the protective spirit of a place. We know it more now as the whole spirit of a place, the soul of a place…

Prologue

Summer 1965

The temptation was just too great. Even though the boys had promised to stay put in the pickup truck, the lure not to was getting the best of them. The promise had been easy to keep at first, before they fully comprehended what they were committing themselves to. Now that they were there they could hardly be blamed for succumbing to the siren call so easily. They were not alone.

This was the Soul Note, the legendary "teen" nightclub extraordinaire they had been hearing the older boys talk about for years. And now, after all their begging and pleading, Jack's older brother, Duke, had relented to let Jack and his friend Jimmy tag along, but only after they had promised they would stay by the truck and not wander off. Once Duke had met up with friends and the two boys were left to themselves in the Note's parking lot, they quickly scampered out of the cab and into the back of the pickup's bed.

They propped themselves up onto a couple of hay bales that had been tossed into the truck's bed for added weight. The bales would keep the rear from swerving rambunctiously around during any sharp turns or when the gas pedal was applied too aggressively when a stoplight turned green, which it frequently was. The boys stacked the hay bales one on top of the other making an ideal viewing stand overlooking all the activity in the lot. They were immediately immersed in the sights, sounds, and smells of the parking lot with all the irresistible distractions of a carnival midway. Swept up by it all, they marveled at the variety of coveted vehicles as they passed by, one after the other, each one seemingly more desirable to the boys than the previous one. As their drivers found parking spaces and an assortment of occupants emerged, the place quickly filled with a throng of young people from all over the region. Yelps of greetings and squeals of delight at seeing old friends and classmates rang out over revving engines and through plumes of exhaust, dust and cigarette smoke.

Along with the eye-catching cars, the bevy of girls that streamed by them on their way to the nightclub's entrance was equally as enthralling.

"Geez, did you see her!" Jack, the smaller of the two boys, exclaimed. Both their heads turned in unison, their eyes following a fetching young woman wearing a bright white mini skirt and black knee-high leather boots, which seemed to be the chosen fashion of most. "She looks just like Raquel Welch!"

"Yeah, shoot, they all do!" replied Jimmy.

Others wore form fitted dresses with high heels, while others wore tight slacks and colorful blouses.

"Dang, and they all smell good too!" Jack chirped as he caught a whiff of strong perfume. "Come on, Jimmy." He jumped down from the truck's bed and started to walk in the direction of the pungent fragrance. "Everyone's heading in there! Let's go! Heck, there won't be nothing to look at out here anymore."

"But Jack, what about our promise to Duke? He's your big brother, man. And I sure don't want him pissed off at me!"

"Oh, come on, Jimmy. Duke isn't going to find out. And if he does and wants to pound someone, it'll be me, not you! Besides, Duke never pounds me, he just kind of makes like he will. And we aren't even going to get in anyway!" Jack paused, and upon seeing Jimmy's still lingering hesitation, he added, "Okay, I promise, we'll come right back if you get scared!"

That did the trick.

"Why you little twerp! I oughta pop your little pigeon head off!" Jimmy exclaimed as he jumped down and chased after Jack, catching up to him in a couple of lengthy strides. Jack ducked and avoided Jimmy's half-hearted attempt at a headlock as they fell in behind a covey of gently swaying teenage girls headed toward the entrance. Jack, more than content to follow along behind the girls slowly, smiled grandly with a feigned innocence at their good fortune.

As they approached the entrance, they saw a hulking man outside the entry taking admission tickets, which had been purchased at a nearby window. He saw them too.

"Don't even think about gettin' in here, you little punks!" snarled the giant doorman.

"Heck no, mister, not us. We weren't even going to try to." Jack smiled. "Okay if we just hang out here for a bit, though?"

There was a line of patrons restlessly waiting to enter. The doorman did not look up from his ticket taking, nor did he acknowledge what Jack had said. After a moment, he rolled his eyes and said, "Okay, for a minute! Hop up on top of that wall there so I can keep an eye on you!"

Without hesitation, the boys scrambled easily onto the top of a five-foot-high cinder block wall that encircled the entrance. Jack thanked the doorman, and once the boys were settled in on their new-found perch, he said, "This is cool!"

"Well, don't get too comfortable, and don't fall off! And don't even try to sneak by me when I'm not lookin', you hear?" threatened the doorman.

"Shoot, no, mister, we won't. Promise! Don't we, Jimmy?" Jack said, using his elbow to poke his pal slyly in the rib.

"Yeah, sure," Jimmy agreed. "Beats just sittin' around out in the truck."

"What're your runts names anyway? And whose little brothers are you?" the big doorman asked, still focused on taking tickets and checking to make sure no one was trying to sneak in any beers or other liquor into the place. "I know you're taggin' along with someone. Not like it never happens."

"My name's Jack, and this is Jimmy. What's your name?" Jack asked quickly, hoping to avoid having to tell the man who his brother was, the worst-case scenario of his connivance.

"My name's 'mister' to you kids, but I'm known as Bust Up around here."

"Buster?" asked Jack. "That's a cool name."

"Naw, ain't Buster! It's Bust Up!"

"Oh, Bust Up! That's a cool name too! How'd you get that name?" Jack inquired.

The man's head was as large as a mature pumpkin's, and when he lifted it up he looked straight at Jack with deep set dark eyes. "'Cause I bust things up, kid. Break things up, too, 'cause I'm what's called the bouncer at this place," he said, smiling widely as a group of attractive girls surrounded him. They seemed in a hurry to get inside now that the live band had taken the stage.

"And you boys better mind your manners around these nice, fine young ladies," Bust Up added. "Yes, sir, you better mind your manners with the ladies with ol' Bust Up around." He grinned after the group of girls as they entered through one of the heavy steel doors that he politely held open. As they passed through, the band's rendition of Wilson Pickett's "In the Midnight Hour" blared out an engulfing welcome.

After a while, the line at the entrance had thinned out and with only an occasional glimpse of the inside of the dance club the boys were starting to get restless.

"How old are you little punks anyway?" Bust Up asked.

"I'm eleven, and he's twelve." Jack pointed to Jimmy. "I can't believe we're not old enough to get in. I mean, we haven't seen any naked girls going in there or nothing," he joked.

"Yeah, don't you wish? You know you got to be at least sixteen to get in here. I bet your folks don't even know you're here, do they?" Bust Up said with an intense stare. "Heck, I bet they're thinkin' you're home all safe and sound in your warm little beds holdin' onto your little teddy bears!" he roared, enjoying his creative jesting of the boys. "Can you kids read?" he asked in a serious tone.

"Heck yeah!" Jack responded briskly.

"Okay, then read that sign." Bust Up pointed toward a white sign with plain black lettering on the wall above the ticket window.

"Sure," Jack said. "It says, 'Rock 'n Roll is in the Soul.'"

"Okay, good for you kid. You read good. What's it say below that?'

"Admission, one dollar."

"Do you kids got a dollar on you?"

"No, but I got a quarter, I think," Jack said, continuing to do all the talking while Jimmy just looked on with a peeved look on his face.

"So, you're not just too young to get in, you got no money either. Better start savin' your pennies in your little piggy banks so maybe you can afford this place someday… when you grow up!" Bust Up roared, continuing to enjoy teasing the young boys.

"Hey, Bust Up, where'd the hamburger take the hot dog dancing on their first date?" Jack asked, laughing at Bust Up's joke.

"Ah, I don't know," Bust Up replied slowly with a confused look on his face.

"To the meatball!" Jack shot back, laughing grandly, while adding an exaggerated slap on his thigh for emphasis.

"Ha, ha, kid, very funny! Very funny!" Bust Up chuckled, shaking his head as he let two more girls in through the door. Both giggled at Jack's childish joke. "I oughta just let you little hot shots in with these nice gals just so I don't have to hear anymore of your Jack Benny funny stuff out here no more. You're givin' me cramps, kid! But, I won't! Besides, you don't really want to be goin' in there anyway," he added, looking at the boys wearing a strange ghoulish grin. "Know why they call this place the Soul Note?"

The boys just looked at each other and shrugged. "Heck, we don't know, Bust Up, guess just because they wanted to," Jack said.

The boys laughed at Jack's quip, but Bust Up didn't share their sense of humor. Wearing the same ghoulish grin and lowering the tone of his voice, he said, "It's 'cause people get their souls eatin' up in there!" The grin left his face as he let that sink in and turned to let in some more folks. He held one of big doors open wide enough so the boys could see the band and the packed dance floor, the cigarette smoke so thick it made it difficult to see anyone or anything clearly.

"Looks like fun!" said Jack, wide-eyed.

"Yeah, but what do ya mean it eats up people's souls anyway?" Jimmy asked, his eyes as wide as Jack's.

"Well, look at it in there! It's the Devil's own den of iniquity!" Bust Up said, wearing the same strange grin. "Supposed to look like fun, kid, deceives you that way, tricks you to get you in there, and then gobbles up your soul! Sucks it right up outta ya! That's what it feeds off of in there and it gets real hungry!"

He took a few more tickets from some more unsuspecting victims as they eagerly entered through the opened door. "Ain't so funny no more, huh, kid?" Bust Up snorted. "That's why I ain't gonna let you boys in, 'cause you're way too young to be gettin' your souls all gobbled up!"

"I'm gonna go on inside now to see who's butt I can kick and throw out of here, maybe save a few souls, so you two better just stay right there and don't even think about tryin' to sneak in. You can bet I'll be keepin' an eye out on you! You kids oughta be thankin' ol' Bust Up for savin' your souls!" he added before leaving.

After he left, the boys stayed put on the wall and quietly watched as even more unsuspecting souls entered in.

"Crap, that was weird!" Jimmy shook his head. "Guess we don't wanna go in there now and get our souls eatin' up, huh?" he added, chuckling nervously.

"Yeah, sure *was* weird! Hope Duke doesn't get his soul eaten by nothing in there, though!" Jack said, chuckling, too, but with a pensive look on his face.

"Oh, come on, Jack! Dude's just tryin' to scare us so we don't try to sneak in! He don't know nothin' 'bout no souls gettin' gobbled up or any of that kind of stuff!"

"Well, it's kind of a little spooky, though," Jack mumbled, his head lowered as he stared down toward the ground and watched his feet dangle.

After a while, with the prospects of sneaking in continuing to look bleak with Bust Up keeping a watchful eye on them from inside the door, coupled now with a lack of enthusiasm, the boys were ready to head back out to the truck and find something else to do as they waited for Duke.

"It was your big idea to talk Duke into bringin' us," Jimmy groaned. "Now we're stuck here with nothin' to do but just sit around and wait for him. This place is gettin' borin'."

Suddenly, they heard a loud commotion from inside the nightclub followed by a tumultuous boom as the entryway doors burst open. The sudden crash startled the boys so much they nearly lost their balance on the wall. Shrill screams and someone yelling "Fight! Fight!" accompanied the throng of panicked patrons as they swarmed out of the dance hall.

Then the familiar, but now angry face of Duke appeared mystically out of the mob. He immediately spotted the two boys. "Get your asses back in the truck where I told you to stay put, damn it!" he roared.

He grabbed both boys simultaneously and pulled them down off the wall. He wrapped one arm around each of them and, while crouching, they weaved their way through the crowd. The sounds of breaking glass and people yelling echoed through the parking lot as they reached the red pickup truck.

"Now get your butts in there and keep your heads down! And stay in there!" Duke threatened.

Then he was off, darting back toward the flashpoint of the chaos. The boys, at first, did what they were ordered to do, but couldn't resist peeking up out of the truck's windows to see what they could, though it wasn't much. The parking lot was pitch black, and apart from the glare of an occasional overhead light pole or the headlights of the cars as they peeled out of the lot, the boys heard more than they could see. Screams mixed with muffled thumping sounds, and loud shouts of profanities continued to echo throughout the lot. Some of the words they had rarely ever heard before.

The rowdy crowds seemed to ebb and flow around them, and some of the thumping sounds grew louder as dark, ghostly images continued to appear outside the window and then vanish just as suddenly. The boys could hear the howl of a foghorn and the shrill whines of the sheriff sirens back toward the nightclub, as well as hazily see the blue and red flashing lights. It wasn't until the reinforcements deployed into the maelstrom that things started to quiet down.

A while passed before Duke reappeared and got behind the wheel, starting the ignition. His nose was bleeding and he attempted to staunch the flow with a handkerchief someone had given him. He looked flushed with his tousled blond hair falling into his eyes, one of which looked a little swollen along with a reddened cheek on the same side. He rolled down the window as a passerby slapped the truck's fenders and hood. Other ghost-like figures either ran or walked by, most not saying anything, and instead offered a wave or a thumbs-up sign.

Others stopped briefly, offering their thanks, and one large boy offered to shake Duke's hand, glancing in through the open window at the two young boys. "You kids okay?" the boy asked. "Saw you two out on that wall when we all came bustin' outta there. Damn! Happened fast! Duke, man, thanks as all hell! You and your buds were great to help us out like that! Those pricks! Glad you were on our side! Damn! Hope that nose ain't broke! But the girls ain't gonna care anyway seein' you in action." He glanced at Jack. "Your big brother fights like a hellcat! Owe you and your pals big time, Duke. Won't ever forget it, man! Not ever!" With that he ruffled Duke's hair and took off, anxiously looking around for his scattered buddies.

"Let's split before I get arrested for letting you two juvenile delinquents talk me into bringing you to a brawl at a notorious nightclub." Duke winked at them with his good eye as he shifted into gear, still holding the handkerchief against his nose.

"Who was that guy?" asked Jack.

"Oh, that was BTW. Those guys whose side we were on are from Central High down in Grand River, Dad's old school," replied Duke, cautiously navigating the truck out of the lot.

"What's BTW stand for?" asked Jimmy.

"Big, Tough, Worley," Duke answered. "BTW. Big and tough that's for sure! Glad we were on his side! And enough with the questions, been quite a night! Just don't say anything to the folks, you two, cool?"

The boys earnestly nodded their heads in agreement and fist punched with Duke in solidarity. They could not help but notice the scraped skin and blotches of blood on his knuckles, not to mention his torn shirt, swollen eye, and a crimson-soaked handkerchief covering what looked like a possible broken nose.

"Geez, that sure was a boring place! Huh, Jimmy?" Jack joked, unable to resist the jab as he looked back at the Note as they drove away, it's large ruby red neon note still beaming out majestically in the darkness. "And we didn't get our souls sucked out, either!"

Chapter 1

Chicago, 1988

Maybe it's just a note or two, a chord, or even a stanza. Maybe it's the rhyme, rhythm, harmony, a slick lick, or a memorable riff. Maybe it was "her" song, "your" song, or "our" song. Whatever the trigger, you know it when you hear it. It's the one that pulls and tugs at you, whirling you away in a heartbeat. It can steal your consciousness away from whatever you're doing, wherever you are. It's an innocent thing, a sensory association thing. It's the consequence of being a living, breathing, feeling human being.

It's just a musical note, a written sign denoting a vocal or instrumental sound that when strung together with other notes, creates a song, and that song gives it immortality. That note becomes a small spark that burns eternal, and like a smoldering ember from a bonfire, it bursts out into the atmosphere until, in some mystical way, it embeds itself into someone's soul. It's called a "soul note," because that ember has seared itself somewhere down deep into that soul, that spirit. It doesn't matter what age you are, that soul note can still snatch you up and there's nothing that you can do. It's indelibly imprinted on your psyche like a psychosomatic tattoo, and no matter what you try to do to erase it, should you wish to, it's there, and it's there for keeps. Whenever it flares up, it can take you back in your memory to another place, another time, and maybe another someone.

Maybe it's somewhere back in your subconscious you haven't been to in a while, maybe a long while.

Maybe it's a good place to be, a peaceful, cherished remembrance for your thoughts to dwell in, to escape to if only for a moment. Maybe it brings a wistful smile to your face, a fond memory.

But maybe it's not so sweet. Maybe it takes you with it kicking and screaming. And no matter how hard you try to block it out, no matter how many times you try to wish it away, pray it away, it's still there, deep in your soul, and it's still going to get you, for better or for worse.

Just as The Eagles lamented in their memorable classic "Hotel California," there are those who dance to remember and there are those who dance to forget.

It got Jack Dean as he sat staring out of his office window. Rarely these days did he ever truly listen to the music. It was simply background noise. Though, this Santana song was different. He had not heard it in a long time, but when he did, it got him.

As General Manager for WKIX, or "Kicks," as it was sometimes called, he had the program piped into his office, mostly to monitor the advertising and make sure the young disc jockeys kept to the script and minded their on-air manners. Jack's station had found its niche in a competitive big city market by targeting the now-aging Baby Boomers. The format ranged from tunes of the early sixties through the mid-eighties, sometimes randomly mixed, other times focused by genre, with a Motown hour or classic vintage rock by groups like the Rolling Stones, Cream, The Doors, Jimi Hendrix, The Who, Santana, and Mountain.

Jack's office was a large plush wood-paneled corner office on the thirty-fifth floor overlooking the lake shore far below and most of the city. He gazed off into the distance at a freighter lumbering northward out on a foreboding Lake Michigan. It was another rainy, gloomy mid-November morning. The sun hadn't been out yet all month.

He thought about his date last night. It was more of a business meeting than an actual date. Her name was Elizabeth, not Betty or Betsy or Beth. She was an exceedingly attractive blond with an aristocratic air about her from one of those upper crust little villages up the coast, and she wore it like her full-length faux fur. She was young, hip, and new in the business world with a freshly minted MBA, and she was trying hard to make a positive impression in hopes of selling Jack a broadcasting consulting project.

He had taken her to Le Chat, a quiet little gem he had stumbled into by accident one night. It was near the infamous nightlife section of town. The happy hour with friends and clients had worked its way well into the evening by the time they had all ceremoniously parted. The cool night air had felt refreshing, but he had not walked half a block when a door opened and a tuxedoed man said, "*Bonsoir, Monsieur,* welcome. *Entrer, entrer!* Come in, come in!" The inside was dark, and Jack had to stand just inside the door for a moment or two to let his eyes adjust. A tuxedoed woman took his overcoat, escorted him to a small table, and lit an equally small candle. He was hungry as the meager happy-hour fare had long since diminished, so he impulsively ordered the Coq Au Vin. It was excellent. Afterwards, he had lingered late at the bar in the even darker lounge nursing a Bourbon Manhattan on the rocks, listening to a talented pianist and sultry-voiced diva. Jack had never forgotten the place.

—⚏—

Even though Elizabeth had not yet learned the fine art of mixing business with pleasure and had started right in on how she felt the station needed to reformat and "get more with it" with Rap, Punk, and New Age music, Jack found himself enjoying her youthful energy and enthusiasm.

"Why not be hipper and go after the younger kids?" Elizabeth asked as their main course arrived. "After all, aren't they the ones eager to spend all their parent's hard-earned money, all that disposable income that's so lavishly doled out to them?"

Jack smiled at her, knowing that was something she probably picked up from the marketing or economics courses she had taken in business school. He braced himself in anticipation that her next suggestion would be to undertake both a quantitative and qualitative analysis of the station's listeners, and how they compared to WKIX's competition, marketing practices, and philosophy of the station's management—him.

He didn't give her the chance, though.

"How is your Coq Au Vin?" he asked her after she swallowed her bite. He knew the Coq Au Vin would not disappoint.

"Oh, excellent, thank you," she replied, dabbing a napkin on the corner of her mouth. Realizing his tack, she smiled back at him and paused to take a sip of her wine. "It's delicious, and the wine is excellent as well. A very nice selection, Jack. I like your tastes."

"Thank you," he said, wearing a friendly smile. "Just my tastes in food and wine, but not necessarily in my music?"

"Oh, I'm sorry, Jack," she continued, holding her fork in midair. "It's just that, yes, being a little younger my tastes are…" She hesitated, trying to choose the right word.

"Hipper?" He chose the word for her.

"Well… yes." She laughed, and Jack laughed with her.

He liked—what was it?—her pluck? Plus, she had a nice smile and a sense of humor. All good qualities to have in the rough and tumble world of the radio broadcasting business, as he knew all too well.

Elizabeth took the lead in asking Jack questions about how he had started out in the business and about his meteoric climb up the ladder to become the head-honcho at one of the largest radio stations in the country at the relatively young age of thirty-four. He would have preferred to be the one asking the questions, learning more about her, but he appreciated her interest in him and believed it to be of genuine curiosity.

He obliged in telling her how he'd started out in Detroit, beating the pavement, hustling, and putting in the long days. "The more calls I made, the better chance I thought I had in making a sale," Jack said. "And mostly that was true, just a lot of hard work. So, I did well, made a little money, and found I liked the business." He paused and took a sip of his wine. "I guess I got noticed and had an offer to take a position in a larger station down in Jacksonville. I don't know, it was in March, it had been a long winter, and Florida sounded nice, and it was. Jax, as they called it there, was a great town. Deep South, and I loved it, especially the barbeque—and the music. That was back when those great Southern bands, like Lynyrd Skynyrd, The Allman Brothers Band, and The Marshall Tucker Band, were all big."

He watched Elizabeth as she took another sip of her wine, her eyes looking directly at him as she did so. "You know," he paused and joined her in taking a sip of his wine, "a lot of the early great rock sound. Elvis, Jerry Lee Lewis, and Little Richard all came out of the South where they'd been so influenced by the jazz and gospel music they'd grown up with down there." Not seeing her eyes wander, he continued, "Places like Muscle Shoals and Macomb, and I guess I just started to look at what I was doing differently."

"Oh, that's interesting," she said, still not taking her eyes off him. "How was that?"

"Well, all along I just looked at my job as selling air-time, which was a hard thing to do because air is such an intangible thing to try to sell to someone. I mean it's not the same as selling something like a vacuum cleaner or a copier. People can't touch it or take it for a test drive. So, I would use ratings, various studies, things like that to sell my station's ad time."

"Well, like you said, it must have worked because you were good at it," said Elizabeth.

"Yes, but I was only working hard, not smart, or with any real passion or belief in what I was doing."

"Okay…" she said, her voice trailing off with a skeptical look on her face, not sure where he was going with his story.

Seeing her look, Jack smiled and continued. "And down there I started to see how much my customers loved that music. How devoted to it they were. Their radios would be playing it all day and then they would go out and listen to a live band somewhere at night. It was in their soul and they believed it was in their customers' souls, too, and it got into mine. So instead of simply selling airtime tied into the music, I started selling the dreams, the emotions, and the memories that the songs were all about. Doing that changed everything for me, and from there I went on into some management roles and then to larger stations in Dallas and Denver, and now here."

"Dreams, emotions, and memories," she repeated back to him. "I like that. I think I get it too. They don't really work that well with punk, rap or New Age, do they?"

"Oh, sure they do," Jack answered as he took another sip of his wine. "It's still music and there is definitely a soul and a passion in them, too, but I don't think that matters much to my competition. They're going to go with whatever target listener they feel they'll get the biggest bang for the buck. Like you said, it's all about the money. We like to make money, too, but I'd like to think keeping that classic rock sound, that genre out there on the airwaves alive and well is a noble cause. And we've grown a sizable base of support for it here already." He smiled again as he finished his meal, lost in his own thoughts, momentarily. "Who knows? Nowadays, most of our listeners are mostly those faithful memory ones, but we believe that if we can keep the sound out there long enough, we'll start to win over a whole new generation of... dreamers."

"I like your noble cause, Jack. Now I get your station's tagline mantra, 'Rock and Roll is in the Soul,'" she said, smiling and making quotation signs with her fingers. "I like it! Who knows? Maybe I'll become one of those dreamers too? Perhaps I'll start listening to your station more and join in with your crusade?"

"I'll second that emotion," Jack proposed. Holding up his glass of wine, they toasted to the prospect.

"I do have those, too, you know, Jack," she teased. "But I'm not so sure I'll toss my soul in just yet."

After the dinner, they migrated into the dark lounge for a nightcap. For a while Elizabeth enjoyed the entertainment and the ambiance, but after she finished her Kahlua and Cream she grew restless.

"Let's go over to the Cave," she suggested. "It's new and the place gets packed about now, but I have a friend who's a doorman there and he'll get us right in."

"Sounds... interesting," Jack replied, still nursing his brandy, "but I have an early meeting."

"Oh, come on! The night's still young. I promise I won't tell any of your devotees that you went there!" she persisted, but he still declined.

Jack polished off his drink and fetched a cab for her. "Have a nice time," he said as he gave the cab driver a twenty and watched it drive off, leaving him in a plume of exhaust in the frosty night air.

—⁓—

Jack continued to watch the lone freighter as it made its way further up the coast, growing smaller off in the distance. He wondered what it would be like to be on its deck as it wallowed along out on that unforgiving treacherous Lake Michigan. *Cold out on that deck,* he thought to himself, *nothing but big darkness out ahead.* Yet, there was something deep in him that felt the beckoning of it, that call of it, the challenge of the unknown. Maybe it was just the wistful desire to sail away or that old restlessness in him to start anew and see new places.

His thoughts started to drift off with the freighter, but he brought them back to his dinner with Elizabeth again. All in all the evening had been a pleasant one and he had found himself enjoying her company as it went along. He had wanted to win her over, make her a believer, and perhaps he did. Yet, she was young, and the Cave was her kind of crowd. He understood as he had been that age once not that long ago. *Where did it go?* he wondered.

There was much more he could have told her about the business, even about his life, too, but he was guarded and preferred not to talk about himself as much as he already had. He had been successful by being the one asking the questions and listening to the answers.

Jack could always put a smile on his face and walk in a door. When he shook hands, he looked the person in their eyes. He had confidence. He liked people and a challenge, and selling "air" was definitely a challenge. The majority of his customers were drawn to do business with him by his homespun honesty and easygoing likability. But, in addition to his devotion to help his advertisers prosper, which he had confided in Elizabeth, he wasn't just selling airtime, he was selling dreams, memories, and emotions. What he did not tell Elizabeth was that no one in the business was better at it than he was.

"Excuse me, Jack, Carlton's here," Sally, his secretary, said over his office intercom.

"Okay, thanks, Sally. Have him come in, please," Jack said, speaking into the intercom.

Carlton "Crush" Crusher was his program director and one of his best friends. He was six or seven years older than Jack, but they were kindred spirits, especially when it came to the music. They had first met at the station they both worked for in Dallas. Jack was a new general manager at the time and Crush was one of his new disc jockeys. The country and western sounds were dominating the radio scene and Jack had been brought in by the owners to differentiate them. They wanted to see if he could develop a niche in the listener base to significantly grow their ratings and that sound specifically, as he convinced them, was classic rock.

Jack saw how enthusiastic and receptive Crush was to the new venue, and that he was not just a true devotee of the genre, but that he was a certified aficionado of it, a veritable walking, talking encyclopedia of Rock and Roll. There was virtually nothing Crush did not know about the bands, their members, and their lineage.

In Crush, Jack knew he had found a fellow musical soulmate and quickly made him his program director. Much success followed, and the ratings soared. Higher ratings meant more advertisers that paid higher for those ads, and because of that the station started to make a lot more money. The owners were thrilled and asked the duo to do the same in an even larger station they owned in Denver, and it was a huge success there as well. Then it was onto Chicago WKIX, one of the largest stations in the country. Their listener base was growing rapidly, and the station was steadily reclaiming its former glory of being the most listened to station in the entire Midwest.

In his exuberant youth, Crush had been a one-time self-proclaimed and proud hippie who had lived briefly in a commune near Taos, New Mexico. He also made the pilgrimage to Woodstock on an iconic, psychedelic school bus. He had turned on, tuned in, and dropped out, and after a brief time had got out, leaving the commune lifestyle to take a job as a disc jockey at a small-town radio station back in his home state of Texas. From there he had bounced around to more stations than he cared to count, until he landed in Dallas along with Jack.

"Hey, pard! Mornin'! Brought you a cup a java. Good stuff, authentic Colombian bean!" Crush said as he handed

Jack the cup of black coffee. "You look like you're in need of one of these. Late night?"

"Thanks, Crush, and no, not really," Jack said, standing up. He walked over to the other side of the office and looked out of the window. "Crappy out there, huh?"

"Yeah, and the traffic's nuts. Be glad you don't have to deal with it. Must be nice just to walk a few blocks to come to work. I envy you that, man."

"Yeah, but you've got the life, a great lady, great kids, great big home out in the burbs, member of the club... Not bad. How did you pull that off?"

Crush laughed. "It was all Ellie and you know it! Weren't for my babe I'd still be up in ol' Taos milkin' the goats!" He took a sip of his coffee as he sat down on a plush leather chair next to the window. "Sometimes, though, I gotta tell you..."

"Goats?" Jack asked.

"Yeah, the goats! Oh, hell. Do you remember when I told you about that commune where Ellie and I first nested up? Had a bunch of goats on it and the ol' fella that owned the place let us all live out there on his property, rent free, if we took care of the place and his goats, which of course meant milkin' 'em. Pretty good gig, huh?"

"I suppose... Goats, huh? Well, at least they weren't pigs. Maybe more money in pigs, though? You know, I grew up kind of rural, so I get what pigs can be like. Good money makers from what I understand, though. Had a friend sell a pig he'd raised and bought a motorcycle with the money he got for it at the 4H auction."

"What did he buy, a Hog?" Crush asked.

"Oh, you're quick this morning, Crush! Yeah, he bought a 1938 Knucklehead, I think?"

"He was smart," said Crush as he drank some more of his coffee. "That was a great bike. I'll bet he chopped it up big time, though. We all did with any ol' Harleys that we could find. Nothin' like the sound of one those ol' pre-war Knuckleheads. You know what they say, once you go whole hog... Still got my Super Glide. Love my Hog!"

"Anyway, back to my story," Crush said as he sat his coffee down and cleared his throat. "I guess that ol' farmer must've been doin' okay with all those goats, though, 'cause he never said much about payin' him anythin' for the bunch of us to be livin' there. Worth it to him to have us milk all his goats, I guess, and after doin' more goat milkin' than I ever cared to again in my life, I understood why. They can be dang ornery when they don't like where you touch them! I thought about payin' someone else with my cigarettes or pot stash more than a few times to get out of doin' it.

"Speakin' of which, funny we got on this subject, I got a call last night from my ol' pal Ralph Raglan. He's workin' with some Wall Street investment company now and wanted to sell me some stocks. Shoot, I haven't seen him in years. Anyway, reason that's so funny is that it was Ralph that went with me to live in that commune up in Taos, the one with the goats."

Jack sat down in another of the plush leather chairs across from Crush and continued sipping on his coffee. "So, how did that all happen?"

"Well, we were both goin' to school down in Texas and it had just let out for the summer. So, before we went on home to get summer jobs or whatever, we decided to take a run up to Santa Fe for a few days. You know, for a change of scenery and some of that fresh high-country air." Crush paused to take another drink of his coffee before he continued. "Anyway, first night we got there we ended up goin' out to some run-down ol' night club south of town and wonder of wonders we ended up meetin' these two gals there from Texas also goin' to school in California. They were pretty good lookin' too. They were wearin' these long 'granny-type' skirts that we called them back then, and leather sandals. Real down-to-earth granola eatin' types, I guess you could say."

"Hippie chicks?" asked Jack.

"Shoot." Crush shook his head. "Yeah, I guess so, but that was kind of a cliché back then. I mean, it was Santa Fe, man. They could have been artists for all we knew, and we were just a couple young dudes from down Austin way. Yeah, we'd grown our beards as best we could and let our hair grow out some, so I guess we kind of looked the part, but we really didn't know much about all that Haight-Ashbury stuff we'd been hearin' about or seein' on the news in those days. And they weren't wearin' any flowers in their hair or nothin' like that." Crush chuckled. "Anyway, they seemed friendly enough, so we fooled around with them for a few days and then they asked us if we wanted to go on up to Taos with them. They were goin' to go see some friends of theirs at some commune up there.

"So, to make a long story short, me and Ralph said, 'Sure, let's go!' Sounded just dandy to us. The folks there took us all right in. They were great. We all had to do a lot of work, including milkin' those goats, but we moved in with them and we all got along just fine. We ended up stayin' there all summer. Nicest, kindest folks you ever did meet. We ate a lot of good cookin', smoked a lot of good weed, and got to know those chicks really well too."

"Excuse me, Jack." It was Sally over the intercom. "Call on line two for you."

"Thanks, Sally. Could you please tell them I'm in a meeting right now and that I'll get back to them? Carlton and I are having a deep business discussion."

"Sure, no problem, Jack, good luck with that!" she said, giggling before releasing the intercom button.

"So, how did you end up going to Woodstock?" Jack asked, though he had heard the story at least once before.

"Hopped up onto the damn bus!" Crush exclaimed. "A big ol' school bus everyone rode around on. Me, Ralph, Ellie and… Betsy, yeah that was that other gal's name. A bunch of us got on. We packed it up and off we went. I don't remember much of it, though. I think I ate some bad mushrooms when we got there. Anyway, I was so stoned the whole time, Ellie said she thought I was trippin' durin' most of it, and I probably was. She took good care of me, though, makin' sure I didn't die of dehydration or some-thin'. I even got poison ivy. I was miserable, man.

"That was it for her, though. We got back and Ellie said she was leavin', said she was done milkin' goats and was go-ing back home to this little town down south of Amarillo. She said that if I knew what was good for me that I'd go with her. Said she was the best thing that was ever goin' to happen to me. Thankfully, I wasn't so stoned to know she was right on, so I did, I went with her. And that, my good ol' buddy Jack, and seein' as how you asked me, is how I pulled it off!"

They both laughed loudly, and it took several minutes before they could stop and catch their breath.

"Thanks, Crush. I needed that," said Jack. "So, that's how you and Ellie happened? Unbelievable, she's so refined and out of your league. You must have been a real Lothario back then!"

"Naw, same ol' me. Same beard and still wearin' my hair long, but now I pull it back into a ponytail to make me look more respectable. Shoot, I'm probably still wearin' my same ol' jeans! I tease her that she fell for my good nature and sense of humor. She says that's because she was stoned!"

Both men laughed again.

"So, did you buy any stocks or bonds off your friend Ralph last night when he called?" Jack asked.

"Naw, but we had a good talk, did a lot of reminiscin'. Here we were, a couple of radical hippies, livin' in a commune like you'd see in the movies or on TV, and now look at us, both all right proper, livin' in the burbs and workin' for the man!"

"No, Crush. According to the deejays around here, you are the man! Plus, look at it this way, you were a part of history. Being a hippie, going to Woodstock, and being an integral part of the counterculture revolution and all."

"Yeah, horse shit! Part of history!" Crush scoffed. "Like we were stormin' Normandy Beach there on D-Day, or on Guadalcanal with the Marines like my pop did, or sloshin' through some rice patties over in Vietnam like your brother,

Duke, for that matter? Now they're the real heroes! Poor guy..."

Jack nodded his head in agreement, but not wanting to let his thoughts and feelings for his long-lost brother go too far down that sad path, not just then, he smiled again. "Well, at least you knew all that stuff was going on, I think I was only about fifteen and in football practice, two-a-days, when Woodstock was happening," he said. "I was so tired I don't even remember seeing it in the news back then, it went right by me... Who knows? Maybe you were somewhere in the movie like that Wavy Gravy guy?"

"I doubt it! I was too busy pukin' out in the woods most of the time! Know what you mean, though. I don't think most folks knew that much about all what was goin' on outside of seein' it mentioned in the newspaper or on the evenin' news. I mean, when it was happenin' the world didn't stop turnin'. Fact is, I don't think it made much of an imprint or affected small town America too much at all until the movie came out, what, a year or so later after it actually went down? Then when every kid out there saw it on the big screen, they all wanted to—"

"Be just like you," Jack interrupted. "Long hair, smoking pot, dropping acid, getting the foxy hippie chicks, skinny dipping in the pond... Not to mention eating rancid mushrooms, retching out in the woods, and getting poison ivy on your privates. Like I said, you're a part of history, Crush!"

"Okay, okay, mister wise ass, so we didn't set the greatest example in the world, but we were peaceful about it all."

"Why not?" Jack countered. "What was there to fight about? Someone bogarting your last joint? Looked like there was plenty enough of the stuff to go around!"

They both laughed again.

"Peace, Jack," Crush said, smiling as he held his hand up to make a peace sign. "Speakin' of which, did that pretty gal slay you last night or what? Are we gonna do a consultin' study to prove our movement is takin' off here like it did back in Denver and Dallas?"

Jack smiled. "To both your questions, no, but she was... nice. Way too young for me, but... nice. She was a good listener, though, and I thought maybe I had won her over to our sound, made her a new convert... and then she wanted to go to the Cave! But, who knows? Maybe she will give us a listen sometime."

"Ah, youth!" Crush laughed. "And you ain't even that old yet! What, you're only thirty-four or so, right? Too young for you? You're workin' way too hard, Jack! You should've gone and bounced up and down for a while on the dance floor with her. Would've done you a lot of good! Have some fun for a change! For all you know she could be the one, man! How it happens, you know? I mean Ellie was a fine lookin' chick, but I wasn't thinkin' I was gonna take up with her like we did. I mean, not right off... least I don't recall...

"Young guy like you oughta be paintin' this big city red every night with every pretty gal in town!" Crush laughed again. "I mean, look at me now. Talk about an ol' fart! Married—granted to a great gal—three kids, two dogs, two cats, and who knows what all else is crawlin' around out in the garage. I got Little League, Pop Warner, swimmin' lessons at the Y, dance classes, Cub Scouts... I mean I'm in it so thick I even traded in my ol' Mach 1 on a minivan the other day. Now I got two! Now I really know that the party's over! And you know what, brother? I wouldn't change a thing! I like the party I got now. I'm one fortunate ol' disc spinner!"

They were both silent for a moment.

"You do have a great life, Crush," Jack said, breaking the silence. "And you *are* a fortunate ol' disc spinner!"

"I'm serious, though, Jack. You're old beyond your years, buddy. And you are workin' way too much! Always have since I've known you. When I walked in here you looked like you had been slayed righteously. You looked down, Jack, and frankly that ain't that uncommon with you I've noticed these days. So, if it wasn't her it must have been that Santana I had playin' that got to you. It always does, that's why I don't slot it in that often. I know what just hearin' it does to you. Songs can do that—wrap up around a person's soul, man. And that's a righteous thing! But they're supposed to make you feel good, brother, not bring you down, or we wouldn't be skyrocketing the ratings like we do. Shoot, we'd be... I don't know... moppin' the floors."

"Or milking the goats." Jack smiled.

"Look, I'll hold the fort over the weekend. Why don't you take a ride on over to your ol' hometown? Maybe see some folks you used to know. Who knows? Maybe work some things out. You always said you'd been wantin' to and now we're not that far away. Take you, what, a few hours to drive over there? We've had some good whiskey talks,

Jack, and that's what good buddies are all about. All that happened back then—what all of it you've told me about anyway—needs some kind of resolvin' or you're never gonna be good with it, or worth a damn, for that matter, when a quality gal like my Ellie does come along. Maybe she already has and you can't see it 'cause you're totin' some heavy baggage, man, understandably so. You've been livin' a hollow life, Jack. Maybe that works for some people, the ones that ain't got no soul, but you deserve better, damn it. There, that's my lecturin' for the day!"

"Thanks, Crush. I appreciate your lecturing. I do. You're a good friend, the best. I'll think about it," Jack said.

"Okay then, please do. Well, we got a whole lot accomplished in this meetin', didn't we? I won't tell the owners if you don't." Crush smiled. "Be safe drivin' over there, pard. I'll see you when you get back. Peace out, my man!" He held up the two-fingered peace sign as he left the office. "Hey, brother!" He popped his head back into the office. "Rock and Roll is in the Soul!"

Jack smiled and shook his head as he turned back to gaze out the window, listening to the beginning of another Santana song. The freighter was long out of sight now and dark, gloomy clouds were settling down amongst the tall buildings.

"Jack?" Sally's voice cut in through his intercom, interrupting the background music. "Just a friendly reminder about that luncheon at the club today."

"Thanks again, Sally. Which club?"

"The City Club. You'll need to leave by eleven thirty if you're going to walk, and you may want to take an umbrella."

"Yes, thanks. Looks like I'm going to need it," Jack said, eyeing the dark clouds.

"Oh, and only suit and tie there, Jack. You know the drill," said Sally, reminding him of how formal the club's policy on attire was at its luncheons.

The Santana song came back on over the speakers, and there it was again, that familiar whine. *Crush being devious,* Jack thought. That same song off that eight-track tape they had worn out back then. With those long, slow, baleful guitar riffs that were like a desolate, berserk coyote crying out to something—to somebody… to him. As always, from that first soul note, it had him. It clamped right down onto him, taking him back. Back to those memories, back to that place, that time…

Chapter 2

It was snowing hard, but the big black Mercedes didn't seem to notice. It felt good to get out on the open road. Back in his sales days Jack had spent his life on the road. Though, ever since he'd gone into management he didn't drive much anymore. Especially since his apartment was only a few blocks away from the office, he always walked to work instead. Downtown, big city living, he truly didn't even need a car. If he didn't want to walk somewhere he could just grab a cab, bus, or the subway. And yet he still liked having a car, so he grudgingly absorbed the expense of keeping one, which included the high parking fees at his apartment building. He reasoned it was worth the cost just to occasionally get behind the wheel and the solitude it offered.

Jack had taken Crush's advice and outright prodding and had left the office earlier that afternoon after the luncheon at the venerable City Club. It was a Friday, anyway, and he and Crush usually met up with some of the station's sales reps, some clients, and some ad agency folks at one of their watering holes. Crush assured him that as much as he would be missed and how they would miss his smiling face and the lousy jokes he would tell, they would still have a good time, especially with the station's credit card Jack had given him.

From his early days in the business it had always amazed Jack at how many deals in his business were actually done in a bar, at a ball game, or on a golf course. That was why he liked it so much, though, and why he was good at it. He made it fun and he was honest. He was old school, where a handshake was a bond, his word, and that was it. If the deal was complicated and needed to be in writing, it could be done on a bar napkin, scorecard, or a paper plate. In all the years he had only been burned a few times, with many of the biggest deals in the industry having been consummated with someone shaking hands with Jack Dean himself.

The car's headlights seemed to magnify the flakes of snow as they hit his windshield and ricocheted past him. After he had negotiated all the toll booths around the city's south side, the miles started to melt away, and he gradually felt a familiarity in the countryside. He still kept in touch with his station, listening to the car's radio. The big fifty-thousand-watt WKIX could send its airwaves arcing out from over several hundred miles away. He forced himself to maintain his concentration on the road, but his subconscious still began to wander.

He thought about his conversations with Elizabeth the night before and earlier in the day with Crush, about dreams and memories... and emotions. He braced himself for all those tsunamis as he grew closer to his old home-town, knowing the flood gates would soon be opened wide. It was inevitable now, even though the Don Henley song "The Boys of Summer" tried to forewarn him that he could never look back, never look back…

He had gone so far away, seen so many things that it would be a long look back, but a long look back he was willing to take.

So far away, he pondered as the song ended. He remembered how, as a kid, he had lain awake at night listening to this very same station on a little transistor radio and fell asleep wondering what the world was like in the big city so far away… *so far away*… Now, unbelievably, he was at the helm of that station, which was one of the largest in the country. The youthful wonderment was long gone. He knew all too well now what the world was like in the big city… so far away.

Still, a small part of him could not help wondering what it must have been like to have been in the business back then. When venerable AM stations ruled the airwaves, and the wild, heady days of FM were still just in its infancy.

The disc jockeys were the stars of their own shows, with attention-grabbing names like Moondog, Wolfman Jack, Cousin Brucie, Dr. Don, and Johnny Rabbit. It was rock music mostly. On cold winter nights, Jack would listen to the Beach Boys or Jan and Dean and would dream about warm places. Then he, like Crush and all their youthful counterparts, had been engulfed by an irrepressible wave of the iconic British rock groups: the Beatles, the Rolling Stones, Cream, and so many others. Rock music, wherever it germinated was as much a part of their youth as their youth itself. The imprint those songs had seared into them at their impressionable young ages had made it hard for them to imagine one without the other.

Their entire generation had been exposed to so much so fast. The music had tried to express it, to unleash and uncoil their energies, youthful angst and frustrations. They turned to it in the hopes it would help them make some kind of sense out of it all, or at the very least help them have something they could relate to and hold onto to assure them they were not alone in this big, roaring world they found themselves hatched into. In doing so, they thrashed out in volcanic eruption gusto, trying to grab their share of merriment on life's playground despite all the serious clashes and cultural upheavals that they witnessed going on around them. They did a bloody good job of it, too, living life with the pedal to the metal. They had quite the corker of a party of their own going on there for a while, relishing in the realization they could do their own drugs and do their own sex now too.

Lost in his thoughts, yet still maintaining his attention to the road ahead, Jack reflected back to a late night, whiskey influenced conversation with Crush…

—⟋⟍—

"As far as I'm concerned, it all started to go downhill when someone started playin' disco," Crush ventured. "I'm just sayin', the party started to change. Oh, sure, it was still a party, man, and everyone still had a good time in their

Ziggy Stardust platform shoes and Saturday Night Fever polyester leisure suits, didn't they?"

Jack couldn't help but chuckle at Crush's sarcastic jabbering, joking with him that he had missed his calling. "It's too bad you got so stoned back then, you really should have been a sociologist. You'd have been great at that. I mean with your in-depth and firsthand knowledge of the counterculture, the evolution of the hippies and their music…"

Crush just laughed and took another drag of his cigarette and sip of his whiskey. "I tell you, man, it all started to go downhill from there."

"Oh, I don't know, I think that depends on who you ask," Jack countered. "I mean my parents might have felt it all started to go downhill after Glenn Miller's plane went down during the war or when the Big Band sound they loved started to fade out and Elvis knocked Frank Sinatra out of number one…"

"Well," Crush pondered, "let me think on that… I suppose… when Elvis came along? Naw, there was always good music until disco!"

"You're just an old rocker, Crush, and you are never going to change," Jack laughed. "But that's what makes you such a great program director for a solid gold oldies, classic rock station!"

"I'm tellin' you, man," Crush said, smiling back at Jack. "Somethin' started to change when those great local bands went away, because there weren't anymore work for them in the clubs, we lost somethin' then! After a while, I'm tellin' you, that party started to play out. I could see it, Jack, because I used to work those nightclub deejay gigs to get some extra cash. You could see it happenin'. The lines at the door and on the tabletops started to thin out too." He winked an eye as he placed an index finger against one of his nostrils and snorted. "And, well… shoot. After disco phased out then it was the punk rockers and rappers that took over the clubs and the good ol' radio airwaves too. You could just see it fadin' away, along with all the familiar faces, the local bands, and even the great rock bands just… they all just faded away… our whole youth… just faded away… poof!" Crush animated with an exaggerated opened palmed, ten fingered flash of his hands like a magician would do. "Hey, all's fair in love and the music business, they say," he added, continuing with his lamentation. "The life and times were a-changin', brother. In a heartbeat, or a quarter beat, the beat was still goin' to go on, but it would dang sure have a different pulse to it! Right on! Right, Jack?" He polished off what was left in his shot glass and used it to affirm his last statement, placing it back down emphatically onto the bar.

—␣∿␣—

Crush's perception was pretty much right on. *To each his own*, Jack surmised. He took an exit off the freeway to get some gas. The snowfall was even thicker now that he was on the other side of Lake Michigan and the temperature had dropped noticeably as he pumped the gas, having left his overcoat inside the car.

Back on the road with the heater turned up, Jack knew he was getting closer as he recognized the names of the towns on the exit signs. As he passed by each one, his mind began to wander again. There had been several more of those late night philosophical discussions with Crush over the years. Jack smiled as he recalled portions of them. For the most part in their talks, Jack had contented himself to be the one doing the listening, but sometimes he would toss in his two cents as well.

He thought about what Crush had told him just that morning about trading in his treasured Mach 1 Mustang for a second minivan. Jack smiled thinking that after all the crazy times the Boomers had put themselves through, the survivors, like Crush, had to grudgingly grow up when they started having little ones of their own. Having had their own youth-filled days at the wheel, it was time to trade in their Mach 1's, Camaro's and 260Zs for a minivan, or two.

As Crush said, their party was inevitably over and now the parties had birthday cakes with little candles on top. Like Crush's kids, they were growing up fast, so the grown-ups had to as well and do their best to act like they knew what they were doing. Jack knew that it was hard for Crush and Ellie, and it would be for him, too, should he ever be as fortunate to see those sweet little ones grow up wearing clothes twice their size and get hit with drinking, drugs, and sex. All any parent could do was hope and pray that their own children would somehow handle all the temptations better than they had. That all that love they had showered so much on them would somehow pull them through.

Yet to Crush's thinking, it had become a different world, with even more worries for parents. Although Crush's and Ellie's children were still in elementary school, several of their friends' kids were now older and in high school. Jack remembered the time when Crush told of one of his friends' frustration in dealing with a young teenage daughter...

—⁓—

"Better wear your rubbers if you know what I mean!" Crush's buddy had said while yelling after his daughter from the front porch when she defiantly stormed out of the house one night. He and his wife had watched her get into a car with a scraggly looking boy with a sneer on his face. "Or, better yet," he continued, "just keep that zipper up! And I mean it! There are things out there that can kill you!" Crush recalled his friend saying that he was so flustered and upset that he was just blurting things out. "Hey, don't you know I care? I love you! *We* love you! Please be careful! It's a wild world out there! It's hard... you can't just get by with... false smiles... girl!"

Crush's friend and his wife were so pissed off and flustered that all they could think of to yell out as the kid recklessly screeched his little beater back out of the driveway was some garbled reference to an old Cat Stevens song.

"Poor people," Crush moaned as he slowly shook his head. "I sure don't look forward to those days. Maybe Ellie will handle it okay, but I'm gonna be a basket case!"

—⁓—

Jack thought of another occasion when both he and Crush opined how through it all, like the station's background music Jack had piped into his office, throughout all

41

those times, there in the background, was the music. Both men agreed how connected they felt to the music they had grown up with and why it was the reason their efforts to keep it out there on the airwaves were so successful…

—⟋⟍—

"It's our music, dang it!" Crush said. "And damn it, we're entitled to stake a claim on it!" He theorized it was because as teenagers they could escape to it after watching all the madness going on in the world on a little round black and white television. "We could run to our rooms, turn off all the lights, turn on the black lights, put a Jimi Hendrix album on the Pioneer Turntable, adjust the headphones, and all would be well and peaceful in our little part of the world. Oh sure, crap, maybe the Pied Pipers weren't as clean cut and upstanding as our folks had hoped for—far from it for sure—but whatever creative juices were goin' on, those bands back then made great music. So, that's why we're skyrocketing the ratings, Jack, because there are legions of us out there, and we're always goin' to believe in it and hold onto it until they pry off our old boney hands that are clinging on for dear life. And that will be when they bury us! Me, anyway!

"Shoot, it was Ellie the other night after we'd had a couple of beers and the kids had gone to bed that put it all into a good perspective for me. She said, 'Looking back on everything now that the haze and all the pot smoke has begun to lift and clear away, and now that we're supposedly the grown-ups, we'll naturally try to rationalize and make sense out of it all. And that maybe the simple consensus will be that it had just been a big, wild country out there for us and that we had done our generational best to bust the buttons off its britches.'

"'Ellie,' I said to her, 'Maybe so, babe, but that was me tryin' to bust those buttons off your britches!'" He chortled loudly. "We both just laughed. I said, 'Are you sure you ain't stoned? Generational best? Uh… you mean like livin' in a damn commune and milkin' a bunch of ornery ol' goats day and night, smokin' so much pot folks couldn't remember their own social security numbers, and goin' to some five hundred thousand freak-out party out on a farm in the middle of nowhere?'

"'Oh, shush! We had just been wide-eyed kids then, Carlton,' she said. 'We were just kids growing up, getting caught up in a wild time, and we jumped right into it because we knew they were bound to come to an end one day… But Carlton,' Ellie says to me in that sweet way of hers, 'we still have some nice memories of those times, don't we? And some of them, I believe, are worth holding onto. Folded neatly and stored away like my favorite pair of patched and faded old blue jeans.'

"'Right On!' I said to her, 'You mean the one's missin' those buttons?'" He guffawed, but then grew more pensive. "But I do think she was stoned! She was right, though, they are worth preservin', and it's the damn music we're playin' that's helpin' to preserve 'em! Just like cannin' peaches, huh Jack?"

The two men laughed about that soliloquy, but it did crystalize how they saw themselves in their shared passion.

They were in the business of preserving that music and keeping the sound alive and well. They had taken the lead at the front as the "Crusaders of the Memories Business," playing the oldies and classic rock sounds.

It hadn't started out that way for Jack, though. Not as nobly. As he told Elizabeth, it had just been a sales position at the station where he got his first job. That was all working in radio was ever going to be to him, just a job, until he took the one down in Jacksonville. He had shared the same story with Crush, only with more of the whiskey-lathered detail, after one of those long nights at the bar with an important client.

"There I was, down in hot, musty old Jacksonville," Jack began. "It was one of those muggy, sultry days in August, and I had gone on a picnic with a date. I'd first met her at one of those big disco palaces down there. The kind of place you'd have hated, Crush.

"Yeah, me and ol' Bob Seger!" Crush grunted in reference to Seger's top hit "Old Time Rock 'n' Roll" and started humming a few bars of it. "Yep, just like the man says, I still like that old-time rock and it do still soothes my soul! Hey, man, that's our thing, man, Rock and Roll is in the Soul! That's us, WKIX says it's so!"

Jack chuckled at Crush's animation and continued with his story about his date. "She looked bored, like she didn't want to be there, and I'd seen her turn down all these other guys. I didn't want to be there, either, but I'd gone just like tonight because some clients had wanted to go. Anyway, instead of asking her to dance—which I can't do very well, not the disco stuff anyway—I just introduced myself and said it was nice to meet her. She just stared at me, but then she finally smiled and somehow I managed to start a conversation with her for about a minute before she and her friends left. I managed to get her number, though, and mumbled something about a date before she was out the door." Jack paused. It had been a long day and the last shot of whiskey he had been nursing was starting to kick in. "Anyway, I called her a bunch of times and she finally agreed to meet me for a picnic down in the Five Points area along the river. So, she brought some food and I brought a couple bottles of wine, and we found a shaded spot under this giant Magnolia tree. She had an easygoing way about her and this dewy Southern drawl… I have to say, I had thoughts of the picnic growing into something more until a storm moved in off the coast and we had to beat it into a nearby bar. So, that was when we heard the news that Elvis had died! So much for that big date. I said I was sorry, but that I had to get to the station…"

Jack stared into the shot glass and his memory wandered on him. That storm, as he recalled, wasn't one of those lingering Kentucky rains that Elvis sang about. It was one of those Florida glory be storms, biblical with its lightning and boulder-crashing thunder as if all of God's angels were in an epochal fight for the very soul of man against an army of miscreant serpents from the underworld.

That crushing news of Elvis, the loss of the "King of Rock and Roll," the icon of the postwar generation, made the world pause and believers bow their heads in prayer. The Beatles, the Rolling Stones, they all looked up to him—they *all* did. He was already known as "the King" by the time Jack was born and some of his earliest memories were of hearing Elvis incessantly on the radio or someone's record player. Then there were all the Elvis movies and concerts. He was a force of nature unleashed. With his youthful tragic passing, everyone wondered what life would now be like without him. How could—or even would—the world keep turning?

"So, that hit me like a brick," Jack continued. "And there I was, right down deep in the midst of it all there in ol' Jax. Right in the epicenter of that great Southern rock music, and you could almost feel it oozing out over that big St. Johns River and down through all the old parts of the town, wafting up into the atmosphere with all the cigarette and barbecue smoke billowing up out of the nightclubs back then. You could just feel it during a thunderstorm, too, sparking out onto the airwaves with each flash of lightning and ricocheting out all around the rest of the country. I could just envision all those disc jockeys as they ladled that sound into the steaming caldron of gold-plated hits with all the other immortal songs of Rock and Roll…"

"No more for you, buddy. You sure you never dropped any acid?" Crush said as he patted Jack on the back. "Time to get us a cab, brother!"

"So, where were you when you heard Elvis died?" Jack asked.

"Oh, hell, I was in the can!"

"In the can?" Jack raised an eyebrow in disbelief.

"Yeah, I was on a shift at the mike at this station down in Lubbock and I put on one of those long Moody Blues tunes and went to the can. So, here I am takin' a break, sittin' in there readin' *The Hobbit*, havin' a smoke, and I hear the news come on over the speakers. Yeah, that place even had the sound piped into the bathrooms! It floored me too! So, I get on the mike and just start playin' Elvis tunes the rest of the night. Probably for all the rest of the week too!"

"So, that was when I decided to fight the fight, man," Jack said, cutting back in. "That's when I said I was going to wage the war and hold the line against all those other stations and program hotshots who wanted to blast away with disco, or punk, or grunge, or whatever else happened to be the hot-selling sound of the day."

"I'm with you, brother! Whatever you're smokin' pass the bong, please! We're kindred souls, ain't we? Because we figured out that if we stopped playin' it, they'd stop listenin', stop hearin' it, and then it would all just fade away... Just go away, swept somberly, quietly away with the refuse of the mornin' after. Just like Kansas prophesied, brother, we're all just dust in the wind, and boy howdy, all that dust would settle down upon and smother out all the decomposin' old albums we never took down off the shelves or spun around on the turntables anymore."

On a different occasion, Crush told Jack another one of his stories, and like all the others, Jack never forgot it, even when under the whiskey talk haze...

"So, here we are on this ol' school bus I told you about headin' to Woodstock," Crush continued, "and we'd seen this nice lookin' young gal hitchhikin'. You know, wearin' this tie-dyed T-shirt and these faded bell-bottom blue jeans. So, of course we stopped and gave her a ride the rest of the way there with us. I mean, here she was, this nice, polite, young, innocent gal. What were we gonna do? Let her keep on walkin' all the way there by herself and maybe get picked up by some bad characters? Anyway, she was kind of quiet and shy, but seemed real nice. We lost track of her when we got there. I mean, there was over half a million people there! It weren't hard to do! In the garden like that Crosby, Stills, Nash and Young song, you know, 'Woodstock! Gotta get back to the land, set the soul free! Get back to the garden!' But man, we didn't just nibble at the apple there in that garden, no sir. We took these great big voracious bites out of it… Man, did we ever!

"So, like I've told you before, I was so sick from eatin' those rancid mushrooms and I was just wanderin' around lookin' for one of those plastic outhouses they had put around. And there she was, this same gal wanderin' around aimlessly in the crowd, lookin' all lost. She looked messed up, too, you know, all disoriented. Maybe some bad acid or somethin', I'm thinkin'. Her smile was gone and she didn't look very innocent anymore, either. I wanted to help her, so I asked her if I could… help her, that is. She just looked at me strangely and said she was lookin' for somethin'. I asked her what it was she was tryin' to find. I mean, I'm thinkin' she was tryin' to find an outhouse, like I was, or some guy, or one of the aid stations. But she just said she didn't know what she was lookin' for, just that she was lookin' for it.

"And she just kept wanderin' on. I was so sick I needed to find me that outhouse quick myself, so I lost track of her in the crowd. All these years later I often still wonder whatever happened to her and if she ever found what that 'it' was she was lookin' for… Ellie said 'it' was probably her innocence." They were shooting pool that night, and Crush stopped long enough to take a shot, which he missed. "Yeah, I used to tease Ellie about what she said about that, about that gal lookin' for her lost innocence and all. Shoot, I told Ellie that she probably went on to evolve into one of them disco diva's that used to flock to the clubs. Who knows? Maybe she morphed into one of those painted ladies in leather and lace who used to give it up so lively out there on that cocaine-laced, refractin', reefer fogged dance floor."

"You're a born philosopher, Crush. I guess no one could tell you didn't like disco!" Jack chimed in as he went to take his shot.

"Hey, I'm just prattlin' along here... And then, in her worn down high-heeled stilettos, she'd silently slink away, and after a while all remnants of her time would be gone..." Crush concluded his dissertation and took a bow.

"But not if the one and only, the best rock disc jockey in the land, could keep the sound alive." Jack picked up on Crush's philosophizing as he, too, missed his shot and settled for a swig of his beer. "And if the noble deejay could keep the music playing, the sound alive, we'd always see her again on down the road! On the beach at Surf City, waxing her board, or down a dark desert highway, living life in the fast lane, slowing down in her flatbed Ford. She'd be wearing those faded blue jean cutoffs, her brown skin shining in the sun, long hair slicked back, and sunglasses on. We'd still see her out there on the beach, glistening against a never-ending sunset. Her summers would all be endless. There would always be a flower in her hair and she would always be forever, forever young!"

Jack took another swig of his beer as he watched Crush miss another shot and continued, "So this one goes out to the dreamers, and those who remember they once had those dreams. This one's for you! And the great deejay would bark, 'Here's a little old Cream coming at you, man! That pure, sweet Cream so thick you could make butter out of it! Can you dig it? Can you still dig it, man? WKIX can! Kicks still can! We will, we will, rock you!'"

Chapter 3

The miles had somehow melted away, yet the snow continued to come down heavily. After one missed exit and a wrong turn, Jack drove through the main street of his old hometown, the Jackson Browne song "Running on Empty" fading off his radio, it's poignant lyrics leaving an impression on him. He hadn't been back since his high school days years ago. The memories flooded back. They were mostly innocent ones. They wrapped themselves around him like a child's favorite blanket or a quilt with patchworks from every street corner, traffic light, and building.

Lakewood was a small town and the county seat of Lake County. Jack noted that it did not look like it had changed much since he had last cruised through the familiar main drag. There still were only five or six traffic lights on the entire main street with a couple of two-story bank buildings, a hardware store, a furniture store, a department store, two or three cafés, a big three-story courthouse, a drugstore, and a movie theater, all still as he had last seen them. It seemed to his recollection that he had some kind of connection to all of the buildings at one time or another back then. He had washed dishes, swept floors, painted storefronts, hung out with friends, and walked or cruised those same streets a thousand times. Maybe it was just a small town, but it had made big memories.

The evening cruising was beginning in earnest. Pickups and muscle cars from Jack's era seemed to outnumber the smaller, more contemporary domestic and foreign imports. Even after all these years some of the old rides still looked as good as they did back then. Occasionally he would do a double take on a driver, thinking he recognized someone. He had been so out of touch with his old hometown, and now being back and engulfed in its familiarity, just driving through, was akin to a spiritual experience for him. He wanted to see those same old familiar faces glancing over at him from inside the cars he passed by or pulled up next to at a stoplight. He wanted to see their smiles and hear their voices, shouts, and laughter.

Jack and his friends had a lot of good times just cruising around back then and they had devoted a large portion of any available idle time they had doing it, but there had been other things to do and they did them all. Maybe the kids in the cars he was passing by now had other things to do too. Perhaps they had their favorite places and haunts they would head out to later. *But it sure couldn't be any better than it had been back then*, Jack contemplated as he sat at a stoplight waiting for the light to turn green, almost anticipating when it would and listening for that inevitable screeching of tires and the smell of burning rubber. No, these young ones weren't so lucky, no way. Jack, his buddies, and a whole generation of young people from all over that part of the state had been the fortunate ones. These kids would probably argue the point with him—defend their youth, their own generation. But they would surely lose if they ever heard all the real stories of what it had been like back then and not just the partial truths or fabrications their parents and those who survived those times wanted them to know.

Slowly, and almost reluctantly, Jack passed through the town and continued driving down a narrow two-lane road that eventually began to meander and wind its way around the big Lake Kit. Some of the old landmarks started to look familiar to him. At one point he thought he had just passed Old Mik Point, but he couldn't be sure as daylight was beginning to fade and it was still snowing hard. It had always been Old Mik Point that was the best hangout place any group of friends could have had. Reluctant to turn the car around in the fading light and the narrow, treacherous road, Jack drove on.

Up ahead he slowed as he saw a dimly lit sign heralding the words "The Lodge at Camp Kit," "Guest Cabins," and "Vacancy," and pulled into the entrance. When he was a kid, Camp Kit had been a summer camp for girls, then a fish camp for a short while. But with its rustic log lodge and wide sandy beach, it was a natural in its reincarnation as a vacation destination or weekend getaway. For some reason, he was surprised and yet relieved to see it was still open in early November. Large pine trees, freshly frosted with the early November snow, lined the winding lane up to the lodge. Low, muted lights edged the dark slate walkway leading up to the equally muted front entrance. As he rang the doorbell, he could hear the deep, rich-sounding bell echoing from inside.

Before too long a middle-aged man wearing glasses and a red and black plaid Mackinaw shirt answered the door. He was accompanied by two friendly and inquisitive Labradors, one jet black and the other a light cream color, each vying between the man's legs to see who the stranger at the door was.

"Hi there. Looks like kind of a wicked evening starting up out there tonight," the man said with a smile.

"Sure is. Been driving in it for a while now," Jack said as he shook the man's outstretched hand. "Afraid I don't have a reservation, but I'm hopeful you might have a spare room for a couple of nights."

"Come on in. Getting cold as heck out. Nice and toasty in here, though. Got a big fire going. We're all booked up here in the main lodge, but I got a nice little cabin down by the lake. I can have it all set up for you in no time."

"Sounds great, thank you. That'll work fine," Jack said, stepping inside.

"Dandy! I'm Nick. Nick Morrissey. Welcome to Camp Kit. My wife, Carla—she's back in the kitchen—and I are the owners. These two here are Elvis and Buddy." He gestured to the two dogs. "They're brothers. Last two of the litter and we just couldn't bring ourselves to separate them by picking just one. But we love them. Guests say they do too."

"My name's Jack. Jack Dean. I'm a dog lover too. Bet they love being right here on the lake." Jack surveyed the large room. He had been in it briefly a couple of times way back when it was still a camp. The big timbers were still there, as well as the impressive stone fireplace with its huge hearth, ablaze now with a welcoming warmth. Instead of the austere emptiness he remembered, the room was populated tastefully with large dark leather chairs and thickly pillowed couches and rocking chairs. Classical music emanated throughout the room, adding to the ambience.

"Oh yeah, fun to watch them practically fly off the end of the dock. Lake's got a little too nippy for them now, though. Say, we're all about to eat dinner. We're like a bed and breakfast here so meals are included in your room rate. Meatloaf tonight. Guests rave about it. Some even call to ask when we're serving it when they make their reservations. Wife uses an old family recipe, puts a little of our local sweet sausage in it. Adds just a nice little kick to it. Of course, I'm a little biased. Truly blessed, too, to be married to a wonderful cook. Guess it shows a little too much," Nick said as he proudly patted an impressive middle-aged girth.

The meatloaf was delicious, as was the rest of the meal. While slightly reluctant at first to break bread with a group of strangers, Jack was warmly welcomed by all the other guests and enjoyed their conversations. After excusing himself and extending his compliments to Carla, he followed Nick, who was accompanied by Elvis and Buddy, down the winding slate walkway to his cabin.

"It's just a little one bedroom, but it's cozy," said Nick as he escorted Jack inside the cabin, directing the two Labs to sit quietly on the front porch. An inviting fire was glowing in a small fireplace and the furnishings were similar to those of the main lodge.

"Nice and warm too," said Jack. "This is nice, very nice. Sure didn't expect this." He marveled at the metamorphosis the place had undergone since the last time he had been there it had been just an old, very rustic fish camp.

"Thanks," said Nick, smiling as he nodded his head and looked around the room. "The place was a little forlorn when we took it over. I'm a city guy. Carla's from here originally, but we both worked for the same CPA firm in Chi-Town. We'd vacation over here every chance we could. Always wanted to stay right here on the lake, but there just wasn't any place to. One day we were coming from the state park beach and saw a 'For Sale' sign out by the main road. We pulled in and drove down this little path overgrown with weeds. When we saw the lodge building our jaws just dropped. We couldn't believe our eyes." He paused, petting one of the dogs and then the other one that nuzzled in, wanting his share of affection too. "We made our minds up right then and there to do the craziest thing—quit our jobs, buy this place, and fix it up. Been eight years now. Guess you could say it's been a labor of love and it's all worked out well. Guests keep coming back year after year and it's all grown into one big family, as you could probably gather from the folks at dinner tonight."

"Yes, I did get that feeling," Jack responded as the dogs both swarmed cordially around him. "Everyone sure seems happy to be here. So, it wasn't just the meatloaf?"

They both chuckled. Nick encouraged Jack to feel free to ask for anything he should need. They shook hands again. Then Nick made his way back up to the main lodge with Elvis and Buddy agreeably tagging along.

After Jack unpacked and settled in, he walked back out to the parking lot and started up the big cat, trying his best to work the thick layer of the heavy wet snow off the windows to create some visibility. Back out on the main road, he gathered his bearings and drove back to Old Mik Point. Cautiously, he made his way down the two-track lane that led up to a cottage. Since it had grown dark, he had the full bright-beamed headlights on. The giant oak and maple tree canopies overhead, however, only added to the darkness along the lane. Emerging out into a clearing, he saw the familiar rustic cabin. The old place looked much the same. It amazed him how little it had changed at all.

The cabin was deserted and appeared to have been boarded up for quite a while. It had never been a palace, but as Jack looked down over the big, dark lake from the bluff where the cottage stood, he realized it had been a young man's heaven on earth. It had belonged to the grandmother of one of his good buddies, Joe McVay, who never used the place after Joe's grandfather passed away. His grandmother had just let the boys use it, happy that they enjoyed it so much and took care of the place for her. They cleaned up after themselves, did yard work, and any maintenance projects that may have come up. In those days, it seemed they spent more time there than they did in their own homes.

It had always just been a rustic old cottage. Its location down in a cove on the southeastern side had gifted it with a sandy shoreline and those big trees that the boys could pull their cars under and work on in the shade on a hot summer afternoon. Someone had set up a weight bench there in the shade, too, and some old picnic tables to hang around on. Then, at some point on a lazy afternoon, they would bound down the wooden stairs leading to the lake and plunge into the cold, clear deep water at the end of the dock and it would feel so good.

There were always other friends and assorted characters coming and going which kept the days lively. Some would bring food and drinks while others just came to hang out. Inevitably, after all the activities and commotion of the day wound down, evenings consisted of grilling burgers and hot dogs, slapping at mosquitoes, telling jokes, and talking about girls, cars, and sports, all in the hazy orange glow of the sun settling down over the lake.

The core group of friends comprised anywhere from four to over a dozen of the boys, all good friends who had known each other since they were kids and had virtually grown up together. In addition to Jack and Joe, there was Bobby Hughes and John "Big Schuler" Schuler, who were the semi-permanent house guests, while the others provided the constant ebb and flow of the not quite so regular visitors.

They all had part-time jobs of one kind or another. Jack worked mostly at the local Feed 'n' Seed store on the edge of town, along with any other kind of jobs he could find. Joe worked at a local grocery store, Bobby for his dad who had a plumbing business, and Big Schuler at the county fairgrounds doing odd jobs. They all supplemented their incomes by helping the area farmers, mostly hefting hay bales during the summer or working for the fairgrounds with Big Schuler when the carnival was in town and the county fair was on. They were good workers and made enough spending money for gas, parts for their cars, and an occasional date and movie.

Eventually, as the weekend neared, they would all make it back out to Old Mik Point, looking forward to one of those long days of summer that included fishing, water skiing, and messing around with their cars. Then, toward evening, they would plunge into the cool lake, scrub themselves up, pile into somebody's ride, and head out.

Chapter 4

Those were good times. They really were the best, Jack thought as he climbed back into the Mercedes and drove back out onto the main road, which wound its way precariously around the lake.

The road was narrow and he drove cautiously around the hairpin curves, treacherous now from the wet snow—as treacherous as they had always been. Even in the best of conditions they were bad. Some of the curves were still familiar to him. He had hated driving them back then, and he still did now with the pelting snow.

Suddenly, the bright lights of an oncoming car blinded him momentarily, and in that moment, he froze. He quickly dimmed his lights, as did the other driver, but it was almost too late. If Jack had not been driving as slowly as he was and able to react as quickly as he did, it *would* have been too late. Way too late to avoid a collision as the other driver had veered onto his side of the road. Sweat broke out on

Jack's forehead and he gripped the wheel harder, his heart pounding.

Finally, up ahead he saw in the headlights what it was that had held onto him for all these many years. As he neared it, his heart sank. It was a dismal sight, but there it was, the Soul Note, or "the Note," as they only called it back then. The old place looked like it had been abandoned for a long time. Tall weeds now took the place of what had once been an unpaved parking lot. The two-story outer cinder block walls, which used to be brightly whitewashed, were now a naked peeling gray. Even the sign was a lost cause. What was once a glimmering neon beacon, was now dark and broken and barely visible in the gray, fading twilight. The fabled ruby red neon note had broken off and was dangling upside down, twisting forlornly in the wind, saved from falling off completely by a lone strand of wire, making an eerie, faint screaming sound.

The Soul Note, the infamous and legendary under twenty-one nightclub, was the only one of its kind in that area of the state. It was once a solitary, gleaming oasis, located at a crossroads, miles from anywhere, with just Lake Kit to draw a circle around on a map. But on a Friday or Saturday night in the middle of a sweltering summer, it didn't matter if it was out on the moon. From the small towns and big cities from all points of the compass, young people between the ages of sixteen and twenty would make their weekend pilgrimages there. Oh, sure, there was always cruising, going to a show, or the drive-in, but if you wanted to be where everyone else was going, be where it was happening, meet other kids, see friends from all over the region, dance until the sweat poured off, and maybe be one of the fortunate ones to meet someone special and spark up a little good old-fashioned romance, then "the Old Soul," "the Note"—the Soul Note—was where you needed, wanted, and had to be.

After all, this was the dawning of the Age of Aquarius when Jupiter aligned with Mars and young people had been mashing the potato, doing the Twist, the Watusi, the Locomotion, jukin' and jivin', and gyrating there since the fifties. No one could remember how the old place came to be so far away from any major city, sitting practically out in the middle of nowhere. Legend and old-timers said it was originally a speakeasy or a juke joint just down the road from the Kit Lake Casino where the big bands jammed out back in the thirties and forties. Then after the casino burned down in the early fifties, young people still needed a place to go let off some steam and the Soul Note was always steaming.

It was a classic nightclub, an *American Bandstand*, *Soul Train*, and Wolfman Jack's *The Midnight Special* all rolled into one. How many future generations would populate the world as the result of a long slow magical dance under the glittering, revolving, all-knowing orb that ruled the night there in the dark, smoke-filled cavern of the Soul Note?

During the summer with the vacationers crowding the lakes and the state parks, the hot sun simmering and shimmering in its own mystical way over Lake Kit, and the Top Fuels and Funny Cars screaming down the quarter over at Darden Dragway, the Soul Note was the place to be. The radio disc jockeys would shriek incessantly over the airwaves like some kind of maniacal carnival barkers of old, "You better be there or be square! It's a dare! This weekend, man! It's happenin'! Badlands is jammin' out live! And they will rock you out! Be there! Get there! The Note, baby! Yeah, you know the place! I'm talkin' at you, baby! The one, the only, the Soul Note, baby! We got the rock, you bring the roll. Rock 'n Roll is in the Soul! Be there! Friday, Saturday! The Soul Note!"

That was back then, and this was now. All these years later it sure did not look like anything had rocked or rolled there in a long time. Jack left the door open and music on as he got out of the car. He pulled up the collar of his long, dark overcoat, tucked his scarf in, and stuck his hands in his pockets. It was snowing harder now and he felt the wind whipping around his ears. He walked around the lot as tunes from a Santana cassette whined eerily in concert with the wind. He had known this place so well, had thought about it so often over the years. It sure didn't look like it used to...

Summer 1971

Chapter 5

The fight could have been larger than it actually was, if you could even call it one. They had just pulled into the parking lot of the Note and were getting out of the truck when it happened. It was just one of those things. They had parked next to a beat-up old four-door sedan with roughed-in Bondo all over it. When Bobby hopped down from the back of Jack's truck, he accidentally kicked over a half-drunk can of beer someone had placed on the ground.

Before Bobby had hardly realized just what he had done, he was pushed hard from behind, nearly knocking him down, by the owner of the beer can. If he had been given half a chance, Bobby would have smiled and apologized. But now, as he recovered and turned to face his adversary, Bobby Hughes was mad, and that was all it took. He pushed back and got pushed back again. A couple of wild blows by both boys missed their mark when Big Schuler stepped in.

That changed the game. The other kid just stood there looking up at Big Schuler and the dispute was over, except for a few choice words and some harmless taunting. These other boys were from Torville, one of the toughest little towns around. They just seemed to have a chip on their shoulders and didn't get along with anybody, especially now with a bunch of uppity punks from Lake County High, one of their long-feuding archrivals.

After the ruckus, the Torville crowd had moved off. The boys hung around Jack's truck for a while, polishing off a remaining beer or two someone had handed them and taking in all the sights, sounds, and smells. The collective kinetic energy as stimulating as a carnival midway.

Jack's ride was a well-worn 1949 Ford pickup truck he had bought from his older brother, Duke, when Duke had been drafted into the Army. Duke had bought it off a farmer who lived down the road from the Dean's. He used to help the farmer with various chores whenever the old fella needed some extra hands around his place. It was still a working truck and had been well cared for. Duke had always made a point to comment how much he liked the truck, and one day the farmer mentioned that he just might be willing to let it go. It, like him, had seen better days, and it was going to need some new tires and probably some new brakes too.

Duke had been saving up his money and offered the farmer two hundred dollars. The farmer hemmed and hawed and wanted three hundred. After some more give and take, they agreed on two-fifty and shook hands. Duke hadn't had much time after that to do much upgrading to it except put on new tires and replace the brakes. Then he was off to the army. Though before he left, he made a deal with Jack that when Jack turned sixteen he could buy the old truck from him for the same deal the farmer had given him plus the cost of the new tires, and Duke would throw in the new brakes. But as an additional part of the deal, Jack would have to work on fixing it up as best he could afford and swear to always drive it with care, and never get behind the wheels after drinking any booze. Plus, Jack had promised that he would help the old farmer around his place too. So he had saved up whatever money he could, working odd jobs and helping the farmer and the other big farms in the area just as Duke had.

Even before he had his license, Jack and the boys had started working on it, and with the help of the school's auto-shop teacher, Mr. Hansen, they methodically reconditioned or replaced each vital part as much as Jack's hard-earned dollars allowed. Taking advantage of the auto shop, the boys pulled the engine, bored the cylinders, and added new headers. Mr. Hansen found a refurbished transmission and helped Jack put it in along with a new long Hurst shifter stick. They also added a new exhaust with chrome pipes that arched up around the back of the cab and replaced the worn-out shocks with more robust ones and, as a finishing touch, added a glistening cherry red paint job. The old truck had been given a new life. Jack had mailed his brother pictures of her new looks and even Duke was impressed. The boys, with Duke's approval, had christened her the Sweet Cherry, or just "the Cherry," after the Tommy James and the Shondells' song "Sweet Cherry Wine." She quickly became the envy of all and their favorite ride.

In the haze of a sultry summer evening, the lot was filling up. Music blared all around them as they gazed dreamily at a parade of Chevelles, Camaros, Mustangs, GTOs, and a variety of colorful eye-fetching Mopar trophies of Dodges, Chryslers, and Plymouths while they slowly cruised by looking for friends, places to park, or just riding around for the show of it.

There was a red 389 GTO with its four-barrel carbs, a red '67 Chevelle SS with a 396 under the hood, followed by a black Oldsmobile 442, a bright orange Dodge Challenger with hemi-heads, and a lime green Plymouth Road Runner with a 440 six-pack. Mixed in the procession were a couple Mustangs, a green Torino, and a dark blue Nova. Even a yellow '66 Barracuda and a '69 Trans Am Firebird cruised loudly by. The guys loved these cars and put about every dime they earned into them, but only a few of their peers drove such beauties as these. Most of the guys still in high school, like Jack, just held out hope to somehow get an older car off a friend, neighbor, or relative and fix it up enough to make it into a respectable ride. Only a fortunate few, and the older guys with good jobs, could afford one of the late model muscle cars they all envied.

A black '67 GTO slowed to a stop in front of them. Jay "Fletch" Fletcher sat in the driver's seat with sunglasses still on, even though the sun had almost set. He wore a big grin and looked a little full of himself. No one could blame him, though, when they saw the bleached-blond beauty draped all over him, dressed in a low-slung halter top and wearing sunglasses too.

"Howdy, boys! Your mamas know you're here? Heard you got the shit kicked out of you by some Torville clowns!" Fletch said.

"Screw you, Fletch!" Bobby lashed back as he flicked him the bird. Everyone laughed, including Fletch.

"Now, now, Bobby. No harm meant, just givin' you a hard time. Have pride boys, give 'em hell now," he prodded as he, the blond, and the GTO slowly edged on by. He smiled as he cranked up his radio.

"Darden! Darden! Darden!... Dragway! Dragway! Dragway!... Saturday! Saturday! Saturday!... Don "Big Daddy" Garlits and his Top Fuel, Tom "Mongoose" McEwen, Don "The Snake" Prudhomme..." the radio roared.

"Hey, Jack," Fletch yelled. "How about it? A little grudge run? Come on, now, let's see what that ol' truck of yours can do. Come on, now..."

They all liked Fletch. He had been a star quarterback a couple of years earlier. After graduating, he stayed around town like a lot of the guys did and got a job at one of the local factories. He might have played college ball if his grades had been better and they most likely might have been if he had ever paid any serious attention to them. But he made good money in the factory, and as he still lived at home, he could afford the beefy, impressive GTO. It was known as one of the fastest street rides around and Fletch had proved it many times while running the quarter-mile open stock— or "grudge," as it was called—over at Darden Dragway, and he was always eager to take on all challengers.

Just then a deep rumble electrified the still evening air, making the neck hair of the nearest bystanders stand up. Choppers! But these cycles were not the long, low, and gleaming Captain America ones that everyone had seen in the movies. It didn't matter to the onlookers, though, as the machines that growled into the parking lot had an even more menacing look about them. They were plenty loud, and their rough-hewn look made a lasting impression with each one having been chopped and fabricated to maximize their look and performance in one way or another. The bikes were more cobbled together than chopped, but all of them had their own unique, intimidating, and raw look as they cruised through the scene slowly, their riders looking every bit as surly as the bikes they were riding. Even the boldest, most boisterous among the crowd sobered up and minded their antics as they cautiously eyed the bikers passing by.

As the line of choppers neared the contingent of Lake County boys, the lead rider, a rangy, hard-looking young man veered his bike off the run and pulled up in front of where Jack was casually sitting on the truck's lowered tailgate.

Everyone knew who it was. Jimmy Meeks.

He left his old Harley rumbling as he lit a smoke and then kicked the stand down on the big bike. It had been chopped so that the handlebars curved back around more toward the rider and the front fork extended out more aggressively than its original alignment. The others of the pack stopped in the middle of the run, backing up the flow of traffic all the way to the entrance. Jack smiled and stood up from where he sat on the tailgate and walked over to the biker who remained standing next to the loud popping machine. A plume of exhaust smoke engulfed Jack as he reached out to shake hands with his longtime friend. Jack, now seventeen and nearly six feet tall with an athletic build, looked up into the eyes of Jimmy Meeks as the two shook hands firmly. Both of their hands were thickly calloused with knuckles the size of acorns and the blue veins that wrapped around their forearms bulged like nightcrawlers. Not only was the biker ruggedly intimidating, he was all lean muscle from a lifetime of hard farm work. He wore only a leather vest with a white T-shirt and faded jeans.

"You workin' tomorrow?" he asked.

"Yep, but probably not until after ten," said Jack. "Old Mr. Smith wants me to stack a load of posts the trucker just dumped off onto the lot."

"Maybe I'll stop by. Want to catch up with you about balin' this week. You got some workers to help us out this year?"

"Why, hell yes," Jack answered as he gestured grandly at his buddies all standing around in the background.

Jimmy nodded at Big Schuler. "Well, I know Big Schuler's a worker. I just hope some of your other buds are too. You know how the ol' man is about workin'. I'll see you, pard... Oh, hey, we're lookin' for some of those Torville clowns. Word is they been tryin' to run bikers off the road just for the fun of it. Rafe swears it was them who tried to take him out down on M-37. Pricks! Someone gets hurt, man, their ass is grass."

"We just had a little run-in with them ourselves. Ol' Bobby here just about kicked the crap out of one of them. Didn't you, Bobby?"

Bobby just stood there not saying anything, while Jack, all relaxed and easygoing, was grinning from ear to ear.

"That right?" Jimmy Meeks asked, looking right at Bobby. "Well, if they're the same ones, they're toast. I'll save you a piece, Bobby boy." He glanced back at Jack. "See you later." With that, he backed the big bike up and slowly yet loudly cruised off, each loud pop of the Harley startling those close by and further grating the nerves of onlookers throughout the lot.

Jack recognized several of the other bikers as they moved past him. One of them was Randy Hobbs. Good old Randy. Jack hadn't seen him for over a year. Like Jimmy, he had dropped out of school. Unlike Jimmy, who always seemed so serious, Randy was all smiles and laughs. A little too wild sometimes, but Jack had always liked him. They nodded and scowled at each other but broke into big grins as Randy rolled by. Rafe Bailey followed Randy on a low-slung, chopped-up, pre-war Indian, looking just as snarly as the others, but he also smiled and pointed at Jack as the old Indian growled wickedly past. A few others Jack recognized passed on by and Charley Taggert brought up the rear. Charley was the real deal. He not only looked hard, he *was* hard. Jack had always thought Charley had a chip on his shoulder and wore it like a crown, but he had never had any problems with him. But that may have been due more to Jack's long-standing friendship with Jimmy, which Charley was keenly aware of.

Charley had dropped out of school the day he turned sixteen, but unlike Jimmy who worked hard and long on his family's farm, Charley spent most of his time hanging out at the pool hall, smoking, drinking, and doing whatever drug was cheapest and readily available. Jimmy let him hang with him from time to time, mostly for old times' sake. Sometime back when they were kids in middle school, Charley had made the wise decision to side with Jimmy instead of some of the schoolyard hoodlums, and that cemented their friendship and loyalty. And it wasn't as though Charley was a mean kid, he just had a darker personality that didn't blend well with the easygoing group Jack hung with. Jimmy didn't like the drugs and all the negative vibes Charley had draped all over him, but Jimmy understood him, and they got along. And Charley could be a good guy to have on your side when trouble was around. The problem with him was that trouble always seemed to be somewhere close around.

"Holy shit!" said Bobby. "That Jimmy's sure gotten to be one mean-looking dude. Glad he's not after me."

"Oh, shoot," Jack said casually. "You guys know ol' Jimmy. He's a good guy. You just haven't known him for as long as I have. Heck, I've known him, Randy, and Rafe, and a couple of the others since we were kids, before I even knew you guys. We all went to the country schools out here in the sticks. Me and Jimmy went to the same one. He's always been a tough dude, but he doesn't go looking for trouble unless he has a good reason, like the time that hood kicked that little dog in the head. You guys know he comes from good people too. He went through a rough time when his mom died of cancer a couple of years back. Who wouldn't take that hard? She was one of the nicest lady's ever, man, always laughing and cool. His dad kind of went off the deep end after that, but they still do all right. He's got sisters, and grandparents too. They're good people. You'll see when we help with their baling next week."

"Yeah, that Jimmy's a major dude all right, and that grandma of his cooks up the best fried chicken there is," added Big Schuler. "It's almost worth the two dollars an hour and all the work just for the eatin', man. Better all be there Monday 'cause nobody wants that dude pissed at them for not showin' up!"

Jack's thoughts started to drift back to when he and Jimmy were kids, going to that one-room country schoolhouse. A couple of snot-nosed, patched-jeans, and T-shirt kids practically fighting and wrestling during every recess and lunch break they had. Jimmy was a little older and bigger, and though they fought all the time, it was rarely due to any real animosity. It was mostly just for something to do and to let off energy. However meaningless it was, they always had a good tussle and grudgingly grew to admire each other's tenacity. After a few such tussles, and once they had been made to shake hands and wash up, they gradually came to the conclusion that they liked each other after all and had grown to be best friends back then.

Then later, when the state shut down the country schools, they all rode the school bus together to the city school with all the other rural kids. That's when things started to turn sour for Jimmy. He did not adjust well to the bigger town school with all its diversity. He fought all the time, always justifiably by his own reckoning. Jimmy didn't like hoods or any kind of bully. He would watch for them to pick on some unfortunate smaller kid, then step in and pick a fight. Or he'd track them down later and wait for them after school somewhere. He liked fighting them and roughing them up, and after a while no one messed with Jimmy Meeks.

All that time, Jimmy's mom was dying of cancer, and for quite a while, only the immediate family knew. The school didn't know, and even Jack's mom, who was one of her close friends, didn't know how bad it was. And while Jimmy had his family's love and support, it was hard for him. Soon things just went from bad to worse for him at school, so eventually he dropped out to work on the family's farm and to help take care of his mom.

He and Jack still saw each other now and then at Feed 'n' Seed. And every year since he could remember, Jack would help with their haying. Jimmy always appreciated and never forgot his friendship and the now-distant idyllic rural youth he had shared with Jack Dean.

After a while, outside the Note, things seemed to settle down around them as cars parked, friends found friends, and the tranquil twilight faded into darkness. The glow of the ruby red neon quarter note above the entrance ushered in the crowd. Walking past a big sky-blue Cadillac on their way to the entrance, the boys were captivated by a group of some of the best-looking chicks they had ever seen, with long hair and tight-fitting bell-bottom jeans. The boys smiled and gestured grandly as they held the car doors open. They bowed formally and generally blundered about. The girls all thought they were so clownish, even if in kind of a cute way, as they made their way flirtatiously to the entrance.

From the outside, the Soul Note was just a nondescript two-story whitewashed cinder block building with a large walled outdoor courtyard. On the inside, though, it was a world apart from anything they had ever seen at their high school dances. As they entered, they made their way around a crowded, sunken dance floor separated from the bystanders that milled around it by a waist-high wrought iron barrier. The dance floor itself was large and elliptical with a stage for live bands. A revolving mirrored globe overhead reflected hundreds of light rays around the room. Off to the side of the main room, there was a large sunken area with a round hearth fireplace in the center. Low intimate couches encircled the pit. In the back was the game room with pool tables and pinball games. There was a bar, too, except that since the Soul Note was an under-twenty-one club, it could only sell soft drinks. No alcohol was allowed on the premises. Of course, that didn't mean there wasn't any. There were a number of creative ways that rule was routinely circumvented, to the frustration of the management. It also meant that there was a whole lot of generalized partying that took place out in the parking lot before anyone even entered the building.

Jolly Rogers saw it all, knew them all, and had seen it all. He had been the lead deejay at the "old Soul," as he affectionately liked to call the place, since the early sixties, and he'd been a kid in the crowd himself before that. Somehow it had just kind of fallen on him in addition to his deejay gig to keep an eye out on things and try to police it as best he could with help from a couple of off-duty deputy sheriff's. To say the place was a melting pot would be an understatement. It was more like a volcano, steaming and boiling, working itself up to a cathartic eruption. And it would erupt, it always had. The question was when, not if. After all, it was the Soul Note, and it always had a rambunctious soul, sometimes even a tempestuous one.

Not tonight, though. It was too early in the summer. There were too many new faces and new factions feeling each other out. Even the familiar ones from their own backyards with their own turf grudges were watchful to see how things would play out in a neutral venue. It was just a matter of time, Jolly Rogers knew, before the inevitable combustible angst of young guys and gals mixing it up came to a head.

Jolly and his off-duty deputies had seen the fight, or the minor eruption between Bobby and the Torville boy, as they checked out the pregame action of the parking lot. It was a preemptive and strategic part of trying to maintain some sort of security on the property by trying to identify the bad actors before they even entered the building. But it was an impossible task. There were far too many players and moving parts to keep track of. Though, it did give them a good idea of who was who. After all these years, just like a well-seasoned bouncer, they had developed somewhat of a sixth sense, an intuition, or just the feeling of something combustible in the air when the "big T," the big thunderhead overhead or the simmering volcano underground—or both—was going to burst. Predicting it was all they could try to do. Preventing it was virtually impossible. But they could try…

WINBORN WHITE

"All right, all right!" Jolly shouted into the microphone from up on the stage. "You're in the Note now! The Soul Note, man! The coolest place you've ever been. So, listen up! You all better be cool! No drinking in here! No rough-housing, either! This is the place of 'the soul'. You dig? Like spiritual! Peace, baby! I'm Jivin' Jolly Rogers, your ever-so-hip deejay, and I'm stackin' 'em up, rackin' 'em up, and flippin' the hits here tonight. This *is* the Soul Note, baby! Like we say, we got the rock, you bring the roll! Rock 'n Roll is in the Soul!"

The place was packed as Jack and his friends worked their way around and through the crowd. They saw several familiar faces, including some kids from other towns or schools, rivals, and except for the Torville crowd who just didn't get along with anyone other than themselves, there was generally a mutual respect and friendship. After all, everyone was there, for the most part, to meet people, see old friends, and have some fun.

"Yo! Hayseed!" Remo Jones called to Jack, who turned and high-fived him. Remo was an all-state linebacker from Central Valley, one of the best teams in the state the year before and probably again this year. They had defeated Jack's team from Lake County in the playoffs last year. Jack had been a captain that game and had met Remo at the coin toss. He had called Jack "Hayseed" then before the game. After a close and hard-fought game, Remo had sought out Jack and said, "Hayseed, you guys were the best we played all year. We just had a little more luck tonight. You guys are tough, man!"

"You too. Congratulations, man, and good luck," Jack had said as they shook hands before walking off the field.

Now in the dark, smoke-filled nightclub they laughed and joked with each other as they milled around near the dance floor. Out of the corner of his eye, as Cream's "White Room" pulsated out over them, Jack noticed a beautiful dark-haired girl, dressed in white pants and a white blouse, out on the dance floor. Mesmerized, he watched as she danced in a sultry, somewhat provocative, playful way he had never seen before. When "White Room" ended and "Somebody to Love" by Jefferson Airplane blared out, the crowd parted slightly to give her a little more room. It seemed to Jack that she was looking right at him whenever he caught a glimpse of her. He even shyly glanced around behind him to see if maybe she was looking at someone else.

In all his seventeen years, nothing had ever affected Jack Dean the way this fascinating girl was. A minute ago, he hadn't a care in the world except having some fun and winning some football games. He'd been having a good time of it too. Now he just stood there, his eyes following her like a child would follow a colorful butterfly. It was goodbye to the old Jack Dean. Little did he fathom that he would never be the same again.

After the song was over there was a slight pause as the room tried to compose itself and get back into a calmer groove. The beautiful dark-haired girl in all-white clothing had caught the attention of many in the crowd, not just Jack. Most had never seen anyone quite like her. The combination of her exotic look and her alluring movements were definitely eye-catching, and for Jack, entirely captivating.

As the next song began to play, there were fewer dancers on the floor. Gradually, and somewhat sheepishly, it began to fill up. There was a perceptible increase to the overall beat of the place.

The beautiful girl had disappeared. Jack stood there next to Remo searching the crowd for another glimpse of the apparition who had so powerfully changed him forever. He was a little boy lost, and an overwhelming sense of despair, disappointment, and insecurity had engulfed him.

"Who? Him? Shoot, this here's Hayseed. I'm Remo Jones. Big Remo. You sure are somethin'! Where you from? You dance almost as sweet as the sisters do!"

Jack turned to see who Remo was talking to, his eyes stumbling upon the exotic girl from the dance floor.

"Very nice to meet you both," she said with a distinct Spanish accent and a smile as white as her outfit. "My name is Alejandra Maria Rodriguez, and I thank you for the very nice compliment. I love to dance, especially to this wonderful American music. Hayseed? What an interesting name!"

For the first time in his life, Jack was completely tongue-tied and could hardly move, let alone carry on a conversation. Fortunately, Remo picked up all the slack.

He laughed. "Oh, Hayseed ain't his real name. We just call him that 'cause he's kind of a country kid, you know? Like rural, a good ol' farm boy. His real name's Jack."

"Jack?" She tried to pronounce his name correctly, but in her native Spanish accent the "J" sounded more like a "Ch," or "Ch-ack." She smiled sweetly at him and asked, "Does Jack like to dance, maybe?"

Still in shock, unable to speak or move, Jack just stared at her in disbelief. Mercifully, before he knew what was happening, Alejandra had taken his hand and was pulling him out onto the dance floor as a Steppenwolf song started to play. He was not a good dancer, preferring instead to mill around and socialize like most of those in the packed crowd surrounding the dance floor. More than grateful for her taking the initiative, he welcomed her enthusiasm, hoping it would help him overcome his anxiety over how unskilled a dancer he was. Painfully, he knew he was in way over his head. But now, here he was, in the middle of the dance floor with the most amazing girl—and the most amazing dancer—he had ever seen. Adding to his discomfort, he could see Remo and all his buddies staring in disbelief with wide grins on their faces, just as stunned by what was happening to him as he was.

Feeling every bit the hayseed, he managed to shuffle his feet around somehow, transfixed again by her sultry movements. To his great relief, she seemed not to notice his ineptness and smiled at him frequently, helping to ease his nervousness. But then, just as he was gaining a grain of confidence that he wasn't going to trip over his clodhopper feet and fall down, the raucous Steppenwolf faded off and the most unnerving thing happened: a slow song by Santana began to play. Not knowing again what to do, Jack just stood still. He caught a glimpse of his gawking friends out of the corner of his eye and felt the anxiety returning. Then Alejandra moved closer to him. He took her hand and gently pulled her even closer. The measured lead guitar solo whined achingly, as if saying, "Hold me... hold me so close," while the bass guitar added a low primal beat, adding to the seductive ambience of the song.

By this time the room had darkened, and the night mood was on. Jack could still hardly move, but Alejandra seemed born for the song. She moved even closer against him. Somehow he managed to shuffle his feet once more, terrified he would step on hers. He felt her hips pressed against him as they swayed to the slow, deep pulse of the bass. Jack was oblivious to the rest of the world now; a meteor could have struck his truck and he would not have noticed. Whatever the causal effect, whether it be chemical, biological, or mystical, Jack didn't care. He was mesmerized by her and all that mattered to him was that he was holding her next to him. Her perfume mixed with a faint musty scent of her sweat was intoxicating and he could feel her moist skin through her blouse.

He started to mumble something about what a great a dancer she was and ended up staring down into two of the deepest, darkest eyes he had ever seen, and lost his train of thought. He never wanted the song to end. He just wanted to keep looking into those eyes and holding her like he was. Nothing else mattered but the feel of her warmth and her slow, imperceptible movements against him.

When the song ended, Alejandra stepped back and stared up at him. Regaining some composure, he managed to blurt out a thank you and tell her what a great dancer she was. Still gazing into her eyes, his thoughts went blank again, and even though he wanted to say something more, he was speechless. Seeing his hesitation, she smiled and thanked him for his complement, and said he was a very good dancer too. But still his tongue was tied.

"Whew! It is warm in here, is it not?" she asked.

Grasping thankfully for the opportunity, he asked if she would like to go outside and gestured toward a back wall where large doors opened onto an enclosed courtyard garden of trees, walkways, and small fountains. To his surprise, she agreed, and they made their way outside.

The night air was cool and refreshing. It helped Jack recover a little of his old self, his good old boyish self that seemed to be swiftly drifting away from him, becoming less and less familiar. That fun, uncomplicated, innocent self that was swiftly fading away, gestured now in the distance with one last wave of farewell and saying, *"Good luck, old pal. Go ahead and take those big steps. You're growing up now, young fella. Go on, it'll be all right. Maybe see you again sometime, play a little ball, catch some frogs... Go ahead on, old buddy, be seeing you, maybe..."*

"Oh! This is nice. This is my first time to visit here. How very nice this is," Alejandra said as they wandered down one of the narrow, dimly lit pathways.

They paused by one of the small fountains and sat down on a bench half-hidden by the plantings surrounding it. Her knee touched his leg, and there was something about the touch that said to him that she needed to touch him. It was a little touch, but it was reassuring to him, and it helped him to relax. Jack noticed he was breathing easily again.

The music from inside drifted out to them. They looked at each other, and he found himself staring into her eyes once more.

"So, Hayseed—Jack—it's very nice to meet you. Where are you from? What school do you attend? What is it that you do?" She flooded him with questions. Then she smiled, a warm smile. Not a challenging one or a flirtatious one, just a nice warm smile with bright white teeth framed by dark red lips. She listened attentively while he managed to tell her about himself and maybe a little more than he intended. And then he asked her the same questions.

She was from Spain, a small city along the coast of the Mediterranean Sea. It was very old and very historical with very beautiful beaches. She was an exchange student and was only in America for a semester, a very short time. She had been in America only a couple of weeks but had already made many new friends. She liked many things American, like hot dogs, American Rock and Roll music, and Dairy Queen. And, oh yes, she liked the Soul Note very much. She loved her host family, the Canon's, especially her wonderful new friend and their daughter, Cassie Kay.

Jack smiled. "I know Cassie Kay. She's great. I've known her since middle school. She's really something."

Cassandra Kaylyn "Cassie Kay" Canon was truly something. If God were to bounce little souls on His knees and bestow blessings on them before He sent them off to begin their earthly lives, then He truly gave an abundance of blessings to Cassie Kay.

Cassie Kay was intelligent, beautiful, and statuesque with an athletic figure. But the most striking feature about Cassie Kay was Cassie Kay herself. She had an engaging yet modest and poised personality and seemed to be the only one who did not acknowledge her stunning physical appearance, which served to increase her appeal that much more. If Jack and his friends had been asked to name the seven natural wonders of the world, Cassie Kay Canon of Lake County would easily have been one of the first they would think of.

Unbeknownst to Jack and Alejandra, Cassie Kay had watched it all develop. She and her friends, Dawn Peralta and Sherrie Shands, had strategically positioned themselves on a platform against the railing along the backside of the dance floor. They had all seen Jack and his buddies as they entered the Note, along with all the rest of the girls in the place.

How could you not? Cassie Kay thought. Jack with that smile, that shock of wheat-like hair, bleached lighter by the summer's sun. He was tanned and muscular, with a raw, congenial magnetism that seemed to draw in all those around him.

But they're all like that, she continued to ponder. Joe, stockier than the others with his mop of blond curls and his ruddy good looks. Bobby, dark-haired, brown-eyed and smaller, but with a running back's abundant confidence. Then there was Big Schuler, the big guy, *Mr. Big Stuff,* Cassie Kay mused as Jolly Rogers, the deejay, spun up the Jean Knight song of that name. Big Schuler, with his Super-man physique, but with a self-control and understanding of the carnage he could create if he ever lost his cool.

Just then, a blacklight engulfed the room, ultra-illu-minating everything in white. A tall boy wearing a white

T-shirt and a leather vest standing by the entrance caught Cassie Kay's eye. Jimmy Meeks. Now there's a *Mr. Big Stuff,* if there ever was one.

Unbelievable how this guy breaks the mold, she thought, imperceptibly shaking her head. But he still captivated her with his relaxed, almost predatory manner. *He sure is something, though,* she mused. *Just take your mind off that one. Take a miracle of God to ever make him yours, girl, not to mention to ever get him to settle down someday. And then what would you do with him?*

She managed to tear her gaze away from him and refocused on following Jack and the others. She watched them casually weave their way in a single file deeper into the crowded room, smiling and greeting friends along their way. And yes, girls, they were her boys, or *their* boys, glancing at her friends and seeing their eyes following the boys too. They had known them almost all their lives, so in a way they had a right to lay claim to them. They were their own hometown boys. Oh, sure, maybe they were willing to share them. *But what was it about all of them?* Cassie Kay wondered. She watched Jack's face light up from across the room when Remo called to him, watched as Jack greeted Remo with that all-American smile, and good-natured, easygoing, genuine way of his. She smiled to herself and shook her head as she saw Alejandra lead Jack out onto the dance floor and knew perceptively right then that Cupid's arrow had found its mark.

Dawn saw it too. "Jesus!" she said. "Did you see that? Unbelievable! I've had a crush on that Jack since seventh grade, and in one split second she nabs him. Look at him. He looks like a little lost puppy."

"Yeah, a cute little lost puppy," Sherrie chimed in. "Know how you feel, though... Jack Dean. Only since seventh grade?"

They all laughed.

"Hey, don't blame her," Cassie Kay said, defending Alejandra. "She didn't know you all had a lockdown on him. And I know *Jack* sure didn't. You snooze, you lose, you know? Well, enough of feeling sorry for yourselves. This sure isn't a homecoming dance in the gym."

Cassie Kay made her way over toward a mock rendezvous with Big Schuler and the boys. Dawn and Sherrie quickly followed. Their proximity was all the boys needed. As Jack was already out on the floor, it didn't take Bobby, Joe, and Big Schuler long to pair up with the familiar girls from Lake County. Familiar they might be, but ordinary they weren't. Each wore skin tight bell-bottom jeans, and with no back pockets, they looked like they were painted on. The flared bell-bottoms served to accentuate the curve affect. Each wore colorful blouses with flared short sleeves and revealing tanned midriffs. Other girls wore blue jean cut-offs or high-waisted pleated shorts. Some wore casual white painter pants or the new colorful form-fitting bodysuits that were just becoming popular due to television starlets like Farrah Fawcett. Anything she wore she made it look great, and even her hairstyle was creating a fashion.

From the dance floor, Cassie Kay kept an eye peeled on Jack and Alejandra as the two new lovebirds walked out into the courtyard. She smiled to herself. *Only a matter of time—and a short time at that—before some girl was going to snatch Jack up,* she thought. *Some very lucky, very special girl named Alejandra…*

Jack was entranced with this newfound wonder of the world: Alejandra. The whites of her eyes and teeth seemed to glow in the darkness and the muted lights around them. She was poised and composed, but there was also a presence about her, a vibrancy and essence that he had never encountered. As she spoke, she looked directly at him, into his eyes. And though he tried to avoid staring into hers for very long, she seemed to will him to hold his gaze until he almost felt lost again. He found it hard to concentrate on what they were saying to each other, and this troubled him. Even though she was the most beautiful and exciting girl he had ever met, she was also interesting and intelligent. He wanted to know all about her. He also just liked sitting next to her there in the dark.

Instinctually, he wanted to kiss her, but he dared not. He had been raised to be respectful, and kissing her now or attempting to, having just met her, would not have been courtly of him. In fact, he feared it would be a disaster. After only a few minutes with her, he knew this was a young woman who would expect him to be a gentleman around her. But if ever there seemed like a time and a place and a girl to kiss, this sure seemed like it. Somehow, though, he knew the right time would come. At least more than anything he hoped it would. And when that magic moment happened, he knew he would never forget it.

A band was playing inside on the stage now, and even though he could have just sat there next to her forever, they decided to walk back inside. While they were navigating through the throng of people, he let her walk in front of him briefly, still managing to hold her hand. He happened to glance down, and just as he did he saw a hand reach out and pinch her rear. In one swift movement, he grabbed the hand's wrist and yanked at it. Another one of the Torville boys was attached to it, and he had a big grin on his greasy face. He was still grinning when Jack's fist smashed into it. Jack let go of the boy's wrist as he fell hard to the ground, looking down at him as he held his hands over his mouth. It had been a disrespectful thing to do and Jack had made him pay for it.

Jack pulled him up, wanting him to apologize to her. The boy mumbled an apology and looked hard at Jack, who had pulled his fist back to crack him again. He would have, too, if Remo, Big Schuler, Fletch, and some of the others who had seen the commotion hadn't grabbed Jack and pulled him away. Now a crowd had gathered, and he lost her for a moment.

Then there she was, looking up at him with those big, dark eyes. It had all happened so fast, but her look was timeless. She was his. Now it would be up to him to understand what it all meant. But for seventeen-year-old Jack "Hayseed" Dean, that would take a metamorphosis.

That metamorphous took place the rest of the evening. They sat quietly close to each other on one of the sunken couches around the big, round fireplace. Cassie Kay found them and would join them periodically in between dances, which wasn't often, as she was the most popular girl there and was always being asked to dance. That was just fine with Jack. He liked just sitting there cozily next to Alejandra. Occasionally, though, she would coax him to dance to another slow song, which he didn't mind at all. It let him be that much closer to her, to touch her, and that was what he wanted to do.

They danced to the last song of the night, Procol Harum's "A Whiter Shade of Pale," which he hoped would last forever. But it didn't, so he walked her out to Cassie Kay's car, holding her hand. He didn't want to let go of it as he looked down at her in the darkness of the parking lot and gently pulled her close to him. With car lights flickering and engines revving to life, she let him know it was the right time, and he boldly yet gently kissed her. And he had been right. It was magic, and he would never forget it.

Chapter 6

It was a lazy Sunday morning. Already the day was warming up. A slight breeze and the shade from a couple of old maple trees helped to ease Jack's labors as he bent over to pick up another fence post. By mid-morning he had already made a creditable dent in the large haphazard pile of fence posts. He would have liked to sleep in this morning out at the cabin, maybe wander down to the lake and take a refreshing morning dip or go fishing—or just about anything except what he had to do. But he had promised Mr. Smith he'd stack these posts today, and he needed the money. Even if it was only ten bucks he was going to earn for the half-day's work.

He heard the bike from a distance long before he saw it, as he always did, and he knew it was Jimmy. He was coming from down south of town. When Jack looked up, he made out the bike as it rounded a curve, and he could hear it as the biker geared down. It wasn't long before the bike pulled into Feed 'n' Seed's dirt parking lot. The bike popped and growled as it shut down. The biker stood and used his fingers to comb his hair back off his forehead. Jack took a swig of the gallon jug of ice water he had brought along and used it to wash the sweat off his face, letting the cold water wash down his back and chest.

"Better get used to it. Dad and Grandpa are out balin' already this mornin', gonna have the whole south field ready for us by tomorrow," said Jimmy.

"Sounds good," Jack said. "Can't believe I'm so out of shape."

"Yeah, no kiddin', but you're gettin' taller. Used to be I was a whole head taller than you."

"Yeah, well, I don't think I'll ever be bigger than you, Jimmy. You're bigger than life!" Jack laughed and playfully punched Jimmy in the stomach.

"No, you won't. You'll always be a scrawny little shit." Jimmy grabbed Jack in a mock headlock and rubbed the top of Jack's head with his fist.

They laughed and pushed away from each other.

"Here, you wuss, I'll give you a hand. If I don't, you'll have to come back here tomorrow, and I need you out in the field," said Jimmy.

"Man," Jack said. "Some day to look forward to—this or balin' hay out in hundred-degree heat!"

"Oh, quit your bellyachin' or I'll make you split your pay with me!"

"You and who else?" Jack laughed.

Jimmy, grinning, looked up from his work and stripped off his T-shirt. "Better watch out or I'll get you in another lock and pop your puny little head off. Then maybe that gal won't be so sweet on you. You won't look so pretty without that fat head of yours!"

Their friendly banter made the work seem easy, and with Jimmy's help they were done in no time. They plopped themselves down in the shade of the loading dock and swigged more of the cold water, again letting it splash over their faces and swirl down their bodies, using their T-shirts to wipe off their faces. It was a quiet day with only a rare car or truck driving by them down the main road leading south out of town. Every now and then there would be a short, friendly honk if it was someone they knew, and they would exchange waves with the drivers.

"So, you got you, Joe, Big Schuler, and Bobby. And I got me, Rafe and Randy. That oughta work. We'll have two trailers, Grandpa'll drive one tractor, so that'll make three guys a trailer. One stackin', two walkin'. Oughta be easy, huh?"

"Oh yeah, piece of cake!" Jack said.

"Yeah, that's if your city dude friends can work a lick!"

"What about Charley?"

"No Charley," said Jimmy. "Said he's got to work on his bike. He's been hangin' out more down at Hank's garage. Hank's been kind of trainin' him to work on bikes and payin' him a little to help him out. Mr. Hansen's down there a lot too. He's always helpin' Hank with somethin', so he's been helpin' Charley too. Keeps Charley out of the pool hall and puttin' a little cash in his pocket, so it's all cool for him. He's gettin' to be a good mechanic to boot. Just as well, man. Balin' hay isn't Charley's thing, if you know what I mean."

"Yeah, I do. Shoot, I'm just glad he's got something good going on for him for a change."

"We'll see. Just hope he doesn't take the cash and spend it all on booze and pot. Vices, man. Hopefully it will settle him down some and not just light him up more."

"Yeah, right. Hey, bunch of us are going to the drive-in tonight. Want to come along?" Jack asked.

"Naw, stuff to do around the farm later. Besides, what's the movie? That hippie one again, with everyone runnin' around barenaked, droppin' acid, and humpin' each other out in the weeds?"

"*Woodstock*, man. I know it's been out for a while now, but it's just something to do. Plus, the music's cool, man."

"Naw, not for me. Think I'll do some work on the bike later too. You're the one that goes for those hippie chicks, man, not me," Jimmy said, laughing.

As Jimmy mounted his bike and kicked down on the starter, Jack drew an invisible square and pointed at Jimmy. "Hey, aren't you going to help me paint creosote on all these logs now? I'll never finish up in time to make your favorite hippie show tonight," said Jack.

"Hippies! Shit, nobody 'round here even knew 'bout hippies till that movie came out last year. Now everyone wants to look like 'em, act like 'em, smoke pot, and drop acid like 'em. Everybody thinkin' they're cool, man."

"Well, hey we're living in the age of mass communication now. It's the Age of Aquarius, Jimmy. Better get hip! Too bad we can't all be naturally cool like you, man. So, don't blame the rest of us for wanting to!" Jack yelled, laughing as the biker roared off, kicking up dirt and gravel in his wake. Jimmy glanced back briefly and, wearing a wide grin, casually flipped Jack a peace sign.

Chapter 7

Monday morning rolled around all too soon. They were all gathered under one of the big walnut trees in the front yard of the Meeks' farm. The house itself was a massive, white three-story farmhouse with an impressive veranda that wrapped around the entire perimeter of the house. The main barn was monstrous with two towering silos. The barn had to be large to handle nearly a hundred milk-producing Jersey cows, several horses, and an assortment of chickens, goats, and rabbits. It was a large farm, worked by people who loved farming, appreciated their land, cared for and treasured their animals, and devoted all their energies to making a living from it.

Jack had always loved it too. As a kid, he was here practically as much as he was at his own home. Neither he nor Jimmy had brothers near their own age, and out in the country, buddies were special. It wasn't like in a town or city where there might be dozens of kids to hang out with, play games, or whatever. Out in the country, friends were few and lived some ways apart, and that made it different. But it was never just play. Whenever Jack visited, he would help Jimmy with his chores: milking the cows, pitching hay bales, carrying water buckets, and mucking out the stalls. There was always lots of work to be done and everyone had to do their part. Jack never minded it and was always willing and eager to help any way he could.

This endeared him to the Meeks family, who thought the world of him, and he felt the same affection for them. They were warm, good-humored, and loving people, and Jack always felt welcome and part of the family whenever he was there. Grandma Meeks was always in good cheer, and Jimmy's mom was too. They were always working at something—baking, cooking meals, canning fruit—but there was always laughter and song. Both women sang in the church choir and had beautiful voices, so they were always singing or humming hymns or some other songs they were fond of.

Grandpa Meeks was grand, also. He always liked Jack's good nature, manners, and eagerness to help with any chores. Jack liked him too. He was always whistling some tune or telling a joke or funny story. It was easy to see how much he loved this farm and his life on it. Jack noticed that he knew each animal on the farm and talked to them all the time, be it dog, cat, horse, or cow—especially the cows. Each one of the precious lady Jerseys had a name, and he would speak affectionately and pet each one as he inspected them from head to hoof before they made their way into the barn for their twice daily ritual of morning and evening milking. Jack saw how hard the old man worked, how robust and energetic he was. And then he would see him lying down, resting easily under some shade tree out in the field, chewing on a stalk of grass or smoking from one of his favorite pipes, of which he had many. He'd be surrounded by the family dogs, all of them licking his face, laying their heads down on his lap, or vying for his affection.

Then one day, Jimmy's mom got sick. She had cancer, and as expected, the family met it head on with all their will and energy and prayers, but it took her. She was in Glory now, as Grandma Meeks would say, with the Lord whom she loved so much. She was devastated at the end that she was leaving her darlings, who were still so young, but she was so thankful they would have their father, grandparents, church, relatives, and friends.

"Be strong now. I will be with God, with Jesus. I love you so much, *so* much. Let us pray. Our Father who art in Heaven…" she'd said while on her deathbed, her family gathered around her.

Jack had been in a haze over Alejandra since the Note. The boys had gone back to the cabin that night, staying up to play cards and talk. Jack was on the outskirts of it all, his mind not wanting to let go of her. A couple of the other guys had met some special girls, and their worlds were changing too. When they all finally turned in and rolled up into their sleeping bags or bunks, sweet dreams came quickly.

The morning was already warming up, and the day promised to be a hot one. Off in the distance, the boys could hear the guttural popping of a big tractor and the monotone churning of the baler it pulled as it gobbled up a row of hay that had been cut and raked into neat rows for about as far as the eye could see, one rolling hill after another. It was a familiar and comforting sound to Jack as it helped to keep his thoughts on the here and now, and not wandering off in a daydream of Alejandra, which he had been prone to do since meeting her. As delicious as they were, he knew he had to get his mind off her and keep his focus. There were too many opportunities to make a mistake on a farm, and all with bad consequences.

They lounged on picnic tables in the shade of a big tree. It was a motley crew for sure. There was Jack, Joe, Bobby, and Big Schuler. Randy had showed up, along with Rafe, who looked the part of a rogue biker, and even as young as he was he easily could have been in any of the outlaw biker movies that were popular that summer. He was as large as Big Schuler and had let his hair grow long enough to tie it back into a ponytail. And he even had started to grow a beard. Like Jimmy, Rafe had been a promising ballplayer until one of the coaches caught him smoking a cigarette outside the local pool hall one day and he was suspended from the team. As hard and as wild as Rafe looked, though, he was easygoing and had a friendly nature about him.

Randy, too, was a good guy when you got to know him. He had long, dark hair and an easy smile. There was an edgier, restless, rambunctious mood about him that seemed to get him into frequent mischief, so it was a good thing he had fallen in with Jimmy, who kept him under control as best he could, but still had to bail him out of trouble more than a few times.

The boys had missed the big breakfast, but Jimmy's grandma and his older sister, Katie, were still filling coffee cups and offering the boys biscuits and sliced bacon. Jimmy's little sister, Jessie, was walking around showing everyone one of her prized pet rabbits. Only about ten or eleven, she was a pretty little girl with big green eyes and a bee hive of honey-colored curls that were all put up with ribbons and bows.

"Hi, Jack Dean! See my pretty bunny? Isn't she just so cute? Her name's Flower." Jessie beamed as she gently held the little rabbit.

"She sure is, Jessie," Jack said, smiling down at the little girl. "She's a real lucky bunny, too, 'cause you take such good care of her."

"Thanks, Jack. I like you and Flower likes you too. Grandpa says she's the prettiest bunny we've ever had, and I'm gonna put her in the fair this year. Grandpa thinks she'll win a blue ribbon for sure!"

Just then, a tractor pulling a flatbed trailer growled around from the other side of the barn. It was a vintage four-cylinder Farmall Super M. Jimmy looked like he'd been born on it and probably just about had been as women on a farm always had to do any job a man could do. Another tractor, driven by Jimmy's grandfather, followed close behind. It was a squat, faded-orange Allis-Chalmers with a wide, front-wheel axle, and looked like it had seen its share of hard labor over the years.

Grandpa Meeks wore an old pair of bib overalls and a white T-shirt. He had a full white beard that covered most of his face, along with a head of wavy white hair that was as long or longer than how most of the boys wore theirs. His shoulders were the size of ham hocks, and his arms were heavy and massive. Even seated on the tractor the boys could see he was a huge man. At first impression, the boys were stunned at the similarity he bore to a rough-hewn Santa sitting on top of a tractor instead of a sleigh, or even that of an ancient Thor or Poseidon they had seen on the front cover of comic books. His hands, the size of bear paws, moved dexterously. One hand worked the various levers of the gearshift, choke and throttle, while the other thick paw lightly clamped over a sizeable portion of the tractor's steering wheel.

As Jimmy pulled up and stopped in front of the boys, he scowled. "You dainties ready to get some work done here today?"

With that, they all hopped up onto the trailers and sat down quickly as Jimmy and Grandpa Meeks rumbled off, little Jessie waving them goodbye. Jack sat on the back edge of the trailer as they bounced off down the lane. He watched the little girl grow smaller as the dust and hay chaff swirled around him. Vainly trying not to think of Alejandra, he couldn't help but to reminisce about their kiss. He had called her house last night and was nervous when he politely introduced himself to her host mother and asked to speak with her. When he heard her cheerful voice, he was glad he had called. They talked about all kinds of things. About her home in Barcelona and her family and how much she missed them. But she was having so much fun and was enjoying her new experiences here in America. He said he hoped to see her again soon. Maybe at the Note, again, this Saturday? Yes, she would like that. She hoped that it could be so and told Jack that it was so very nice of him to call.

A shrill whistle whipped through the still morning air, pulling Jack away from his daze.

"Yo, Jack!" It was Jimmy. "Why don't you, Randy, and Rafe go with Grandpa, and I'll take the rest of you. We'll see if you boys can work. Put some muscles on you so's you can knock someone down in your big football games."

And they were off. As they came to the top of a low ridge the tractors came to a stop. Here they looked out onto a large alfalfa field with its bales of newly hatched hay bales in neat rows stretching far out into the distance.

"All right now, fellas, listen up," Grandpa Meeks said, his voice loud enough for all the boys to hear over the sound of the idling tractors. "Looks like a damn lot of bales out there, don't it? Well, there are. And there's a lot more of them than just the ones you can see from here. And there are more fields beyond this one. Here's the thing—and this is my best advice I can offer you—don't look at the whole damn thing. Let me do that. Just think about heftin' up one bale at a time. If you can keep your focus on just doin' that, we'll have all them bales bedded down in the barn before you know it." He took a swig of water out of a jar and spat it out, then took another and swallowed it. "Do that and you won't slip and fall off the trailer and go under a wheel or bust your crotch or blow out a knee liftin' up a bale, or worse, stickin' a hand in the baler. And pay attention to where you are around all this machinery and don't touch no parts that are still movin'! Got all that fellas?" He looked at each of the boys as they nodded their agreement. "Good, damn it. It's gettin' hot as hell already so let's get after it!"

Randy took the trailer first. He stood and balanced on the flatbed of the trailer as it slowly weaved its way around and through the bales. Jack and Rafe walked alongside and tossed the bales up onto the trailer's bed. Randy stacked the bales in a deliberate, methodical order, reversing each row back and forth as he layered one on top of the other. They'd go along this way, trading places as each would learn that stacking the bales on the trailer was no picnic—it was just as hard and as hot as walking.

Finally, they had loaded up the two trailers. As they surveyed their work and looked out over the vast field, it seemed like they had hardly made a dent in the hundreds of bales still scattered about as far as they cared to see. They could almost see the morning's moisture evaporating off the field as the temperature had now risen into the upper eighties and the humidity clung in the air. They pulled their loads up under one of the few shade trees out in the field. The big tractors were left idling, their deep grumbling still loud. The boys lay on top of the stacked trailers. Water jugs were passed up to them. The cool water brought instant relief as they washed it down their throats, splashing off their faces and bare backs and chests, their T-shirts long since discarded.

"How you boys doin?" Jimmy called. He had traded off driving the old Farmall with each of the boys in his group. This way, Jimmy taught each of them about the tractor: where the throttle was, how to use the clutch, how to shift it and handle the big gears, and to always respect the big machine. It was a welcome break from hefting the bales and gave everyone something to look forward to when their turn came. It also increased everyone's appreciation for Jimmy. He was just as willing to work as hard as—if not harder than—any of them. It was good for him too. As the boys proved they were hard workers. Jimmy relaxed more with them and took part in their good-natured bantering and complaining as he walked along, easily hefting the sixty-pound bales up onto the trailer's bed.

After a while a large, regal-looking John Deere rumbled up, pulling the hay baler. It was Jimmy's dad, Arthur. As he let the tractor idle, he pulled out a handkerchief to wipe the sweat off his face. Jimmy walked over and handed him a water jug. He took a long swig and poured some water out onto the handkerchief and wiped his face again.

"Thanks, son, looks like you all are makin' some good progress," he said before turning to Jack and his gang. "Howdy, boys! A little warm out here today, ain't it? Good of you fellas to help us out. We sure appreciate it. Hopefully, we'll beat out the rain this year, huh, Jack?"

"Yes, sir, Mr. Meeks, but a little shower sure would feel good about now," Jack replied.

"I know what you mean, but let's wait and pray for rain after we get all this sweet alfalfa bedded down nice and snug and dry. Thanks again, boys, time to get back at it." He let the big tractor growl loudly back to life from it's short slumber as he engaged the clutch, adjusted the throttle and headed back to his baling.

"That's some ol' 'Popping Johnny', ain't it?" Grandpa Meeks said as he saw their eyes following the big 3010 John Deere as it rumbled off.

"What the heck is a Popping Johnny, Grandpa Meeks?" Bobby asked.

"That's what they used to call one of those back when I was a kid. They didn't have a key you could just turn to start 'em up. Oh, no, that would've been too easy. They had this big heavy flywheel on the side, and you had to turn it over hard and fast with your hands, and hopefully, if you did it just right, it would catch ahold of the engine and get her poppin'. Problem was, it hardly ever worked just nice and easy like that. Sometimes it took a hell of a lot of tryin'. Let me tell you, it could flat wear you out just to get one of those ol' Johnnies going in those days. But once you did, they had a sound you wouldn't believe… Just the sweetest sound there ever was. Yep, I sure do miss that sound sometimes. Well, anyway, it was kind of a rite of passage for us farm boys back then, to see how soon a boy could get that flywheel to crank up an ol' Poppin' Johnny! A feller had to get a Poppin' Johnny poppin' before he could start thinkin' about poppin' anythin' else, if you know what I mean." He gave them a big wink, and chuckled and grunted as he stood up and stretched.

The boys all looked at each other and started laughing as it dawned on them what Grandpa Meeks had meant. The break helped and soon they headed back to the big barn. The boys enjoyed the little journey and even a slight breeze as they lay on top of the bales. Jack stared up at the blue sky, occasionally dotted with a few white puffs of clouds.

He thought of Alejandra again—her smile, her laugh, her voice, seeing her once more. Then there they were, staring up at the old monster barn. After the boys had scrambled down from their perches, Grandpa Meeks pulled the old Case IH tractor and its load up into the middle of the barn's interior. Pigeons and sparrows made a racket in the rafters, upset that their midday naps had been disrupted.

It was dark inside, with only an occasional beam of light inching its way through the cracks between the old wood siding. With their eyes adjusting to the darkness, it felt cool to the boys to look around and get a feel of the area. The barn had that sweet, musty smell of hay, mold, grain, cattle, horses, fowls, pigs, excrement, lime, oil, leather, grease, and about everything else that made a home in the place. It was a world unto itself, and for many of the boys, as alien a place as the moon.

They didn't have much of a chance to acquaint themselves with their new surroundings, though, as Grandpa Meeks and Jimmy had a plan for stacking the bales up in the rafters, so work unloading and restacking got right underway. There wasn't a lot of science to it, but it did need to have a good plan. It was a building project that started with a solid foundation and eventually would fill the high rafters with enough hay to feed all the livestock for another year. One or two boys would throw the bales off the wagon while the others would stagger themselves at intervals and pass one bale on to the next boy and the next until the last one placed the bale in its final resting place. At first the boys thought this work was preferable to being out in the field, but as they tired, the heat, dust, and chaff gradually became so oppressive that they needed to take a break to walk outside for some fresh air and some water or iced tea little Jessie had brought down from the house.

Even though Grandpa Meeks was an old man to the boys, he worked right along with them, and the boys began developing a friendship with him. Outside the barn, while they were all lying around in the shade enjoying a much-needed respite, Bobby noticed a large scar on the old man's left forearm.

"What the heck happened to your arm there, Grandpa Meeks?" he asked.

"Well, I'll tell you," Grandpa Meeks said, smiling as he lit his pipe and then took a sip of his iced tea. "The war's what happened to it. World War I. The *first* big one. Just one of the souvenirs I brought back with me from that hell of a hole. Wasn't much older than you fellas when I thought I wanted a little adventure. It sounded good at the time. My folks sure weren't none too excited about it, though, 'specially my ol' man. Meant he and everyone else had a lot more work around here with me off chasin' French girls over there—Skirts, as he called them. He didn't have to worry much about that, though, 'cause I was settin' my sights seriously on this pretty gal whose people had a place yonder. Thing was, they were all a big German clan. And they weren't none too wild about me goin' over there and shootin' up their cousins and kinfolk back in 'da faaderland'.

"But off I went, though not before Gerda and her mama cooked me the best fried chicken dinner I ever ate. And that apple pie!" He paused to take a draw of his pipe and another sip of his iced tea. "Well, next thing I knew I was hunkered down in some slop hole trench somewhere right on the front lines tryin' not to get my head blown off. And let me tell you, we were in one hell of a fight. Our allies, the French, Brits, and Belgians welcomed us with open arms and seemed more than happy to have us come over there and help 'em out. They were all tough, by God, and had been in a real slugfest with those Germans long before we went traipsin' into the fight. Just look up places called Verdun or the Somme in your history books. Anyway, we go steppin' in all rooster like and took it right on the chin. Even though those German fellas had already been fightin' a couple years, too, and had already lost a ton of men, they were still loaded for bear and damn good at what they did."

"Hey Gramps, what's an ally?" Jimmy asked.

"Oh, good question," Grandpa Meeks replied, "they're like friends. Friends that have the same goals. That think the same and want the same thing, like winnin' a war, and so they get together to be stronger. Like see, this one finger isn't all that strong by itself, but with all these others I can bring them together to make a fist, and bam! And that's what we done with our allies. How we won that war and how we won the next big one. Yep, they needed us, and we needed them too…"

"Anyway," he continued, "this happened just after my first month or so, piece of some kind of flyin' junk! Hardly felt it when it happened. Really wasn't much when I saw all these other poor wounded guys all blown up. I felt guilty there in the hospital. Guy on my left had lost a leg, and the guy on my right had got hit in the head, and I don't think he made it… A whole lot of 'em in there didn't… Well, 'nough of this jawbonin'. Didn't mean to run on. Ready to get back at it?"

And so the day went. Out in the hot open field, they loaded the bales up, and back in the steaming, oppressive barn, they unloaded them. For many of the boys, this was probably the longest, hardest working day of their life. But as they finished unloading the last trailer of the day, they all shared a sense of accomplishment, and a friendship and bond had begun to grow between them all.

"Okay, men, job well done for today. Let's wash up," said Grandpa Meeks. "Grandma's got a spread ready. I know I've worked up a little appetite, how 'bout you all?" All heads nodded in agreement as they walked back out into the late-day sun.

Grandma Meeks, Katie, and little Jessie had set up supper on the picnic tables out on the huge back veranda. This was the favorite place of all the family. It stretched out in a wide arc across the entire rear of the big house. From its elevated perch on a high knoll, the view encompassed most of the sixteen hundred acre farm: it's large main barn and outbuildings off to the left, a pastoral panorama of open fields with an assortment of cattle and horses grazing peacefully, expansive fields of corn, wheat, soybeans, and cucumbers interspersed with woodland, and the rich alfalfa fields, now dotted with hundreds of hay bales waiting their turn to be loaded onto trailers, broken up only by shaded groves of oaks and maples. The view stretched westward, almost as far as the eye could see, all the way to the shores of Lake Kitanoah—or "Lake Kit," as the locals called it—off in the distance.

In the near foreground, located in the backyard of the farm, was a neatly groomed herb garden, lawn, and flower beds under maple, oak, and black walnut trees, as well as assorted groves of apple, peach, and cherry trees. At the edge of the lawn there was a large multi-acre garden with neat rows of sweet corn, carrots, green beans, cabbages, and lettuce. Additional rows of various other assorted vegetables and herbs were fringed with patches of rhubarb, raspberries, and vines of strawberries and tomatoes. The farm had been in the Meeks' family since before the Civil War. Jimmy's great-great-grandfather had settled on it back when he had had enough of working for the lumber barons, cutting down the old-growth forests of the region's giant trees. He'd drawn his pay, married his gal, and bought a plow. The big farm had been well managed, cared for, and cherished by subsequent generations for all these years.

As the sun lowered, the evening began to cool, and a slight breeze felt good. Everyone sat and marveled at the tables filled with platters of fried chicken, mashed potatoes, gravy, green beans, peas, a salad of lettuce and tomatoes, fresh-baked bread, and pots of rich honeycombs from the beehives a neighbor kept.

Before eating, Grandpa Meeks said an eloquent grace thanking the Lord for his many blessings, and all agreed enthusiastically as they said in unison, "Amen."

It was a grand meal, and the boys ate like it was their last. Each expressed their gratitude between bites to the women. As a final treat, shortcake was brought out, and fresh strawberries as big as golf balls were liberally ladled out. They finished their meals after second helpings, and sometimes third helpings. The boys were filled to near bursting. Remembering their manners, they helped carry their empty dishes into the kitchen, still commenting on how that was the best fried chicken ever, the best of *every-thing* ever. And they meant it.

Grandpa Meeks had settled himself down into one of the big wicker rocking chairs out on the large porch over-looking the fields and lit up his pipe. A passel of the family dogs lounged lazily around him with their tongues hang-ing out, exhausted after the long day running along next to the tractors. The boys all gathered around, too, some just sprawling themselves down on the wooden floor.

"Boy, I see what you mean about that fried chicken, Grandpa Meeks," said Bobby.

"Me too," echoed all around.

Grandpa Meeks winked grandly, and he caught Grandma Meeks' glance as she carried more dishes into the kitchen through the screen door. "Yep, sure hits the spot, don't it?"

Arthur had gone into the living room and turned on the television to catch the nightly news. With the windows open, the distinct voice of Walter Cronkite—who the boys had all grown up hearing every evening—could be heard detailing all the recent updates on the war in Vietnam.

"How's your brother Duke doin' over there, Jack?" Grandpa Meeks asked.

"Oh, I guess he's doing good," replied Jack. "We got a letter from him a few days ago. Says he's in some kind of special unit thing that he really likes, and he's not out in the boonies all the time like a lot of the guys. He says his group trains to do a mission, and then they go in and do it, and then try to get back out as quick as they can. But that's about all he can tell us about what he does, I guess. He never writes much about how things are going over there, like what's on the TV. Sure does look like it's all a big downer. He did say he misses home and the States, and like all the other guys over there, they hope they'll start pulling out soon. He said in his last letter, though, that he has to stay over there longer now with this new unit he got orders to join up with. So he doesn't think he'll be getting back anytime soon. I'm sure he's hoping he can come home soon as they let him. He said it all depends on what happens with this new unit if he has to stay longer now."

"Well," said Grandpa Meeks, "I know how he's feelin', and so does Arthur. Damn good thing they've started pullin' us out of there. They're all frettin' that if they pull out of there too fast that the whole thing will just collapse. Then it will really be bad for the ones who can't get out. Sounds like they don't feel the South can handle it on their own. It'll all turn out to be just one big sad deal, maybe."

He paused momentarily as he drew on his pipe. "That's a bad crapper we got ourselves into over there. Don't understand it at all. When we went into World War I and II, we went in to kick ass and win. A sad thing all right. Our guys, like Duke, fightin' their behinds off with leaders that just really don't seem to know how to win the damn thing. Not a way to fight a war, by God! Now we've gone and got all these young fellers shot up and killed with nothin' to show for it, and this country's makin' 'em all feel like it's their fault or somethin'. I tell you, it's a bad deal, and this whole country oughta be ashamed of itself."

He paused again as he inspected the smoldering tobacco in the pipe. "Next time you write Duke back, Jack, you be sure to tell him how proud we all are of him and all his buddies too. Sure doesn't surprise me that Duke's doin' somethin' special over there. He's a special young fella, that Duke. Goddamn good worker too. Always pitched in to help whenever he was over here. Just like you, Jack, and all you fellas. Must be all that good cookin'. Sure works for me." He chuckled before growing pensive and somber again, his voice becoming stern. "Shoot, when we came home there were big parades, and they made us all feel like heroes, and these boys comin' back from that place oughta be treated the same way. Anybody who puts their butt on the line, gettin' it shot at for this country, is a hero and oughta treated like one. We'll come to regret all this someday. This country's too great of a place, and too many have sacrificed everythin' they had for it to let it go to the manure pile like it is."

"Now, Joseph dear, you're getting yourself all worked up," said Grandma Meeks. "Maybe a visit to church this Sunday will help calm your soul." All the women inside the kitchen giggled gleefully, breaking the old man's tension, knowing how infrequently he attended services. "Here, dear, have a little of this Madeira." She handed him a small crystal cordial glass that looked like a toy in his large hand. It was half-filled with the amber liquid. She then turned her attention to Jack, saying, "Jack, please know we hold a special place in our prayers for Duke's safe return. We can only imagine how worried your dear mother and father are for him. We pray for all of the boys over there and pray they won't need you young boys to go over there either." Her eyes started to mist as she smiled and smoothed her apron, looking out over the panorama of the farm.

"I remember the first time I saw you, Jack," she continued. "I was washing the dishes one afternoon and looking out through the kitchen window like I always do. It's one of my favorite views, looking out over most of the farm's back pastures off in the distance. It was about that time of day when Jimmy would be coming home from school and I would often see him cutting across one of the fields on that high ridge out there..." she paused and pointed to one of the hills far off. "So I started to watch for him, glancing up now and then from the sink. And I saw him walking alone, as usual. Then I saw this other smaller boy tagging along behind him and I wondered, *who is that?* And then, all of a sudden, I see him run up from behind Jimmy and tackle him, and all I could make out was the two of them wrestling and rolling over and over on the top of the ridge.

"After a bit, I see Jimmy on top of the boy, and he swings his fist down and hits him. He just sat on top of him for a little, then he stood up and walked off, not even looking back. Then the smaller boy got up, and without even hesitating, he ran right after Jimmy and tackled him again! They started rolling around once more, until I saw Jimmy hit him with his fists a couple more times. Then, after a bit, he got up and walked off, again, but this time he looked back just in time to see the boy starting to run after him. So, he stopped, and I could see him hold a fist up as if he was going to hit the boy, but the boy stopped in his tracks, too, and watched to see what Jimmy was going to do. Jimmy just started to walk away and the smaller boy started to walk after him just like when I first spotted them and they disappeared on the other side of the ridge...

"That was when Jimmy's mother called to me from the living room. 'Gerda, come quick, you need to see this!' So, with a dish towel in hand, I hurried into the living room. She was looking out the big window into the front yard. I saw the school bus heading off down the lane. Then I saw Katie walking down the driveway, carrying her books, with this handsome young man walking along next to her and trying to get her to let him carry her books for her, and she wouldn't let him.

"Next thing you know, here they were in the house. Ellen and I both just stood there waiting for Katie to introduce him, but she didn't say a word. She just stood there, too, with this perturbed look on her face, the little princess! Well, let me tell you, he was one of the nicest looking young men. For a moment, Jimmy, I thought it was your grandfather's look-alike from when he was a young man, tall with all this blond hair and the bluest eyes. 'Real nice to meet you ladies,' he said with this big smile and the whitest teeth. 'My name's Duke Dean. We just moved here down the road from California. I don't have a car yet so I had to take the bus home. I noticed Katie was sitting by herself and looking out the window, so I kind of invited myself to sit down next to her. She's a little shy, isn't she? But she seemed real nice, so when she got off I figured I should, too, and help to carry her books. She wouldn't let me, though.'

"Well, here I am trying to fix my hair with the dish towel still in my hand, so I say, 'It's nice to meet you too. Would you care for some pie?' And he said, 'Oh, yes, ma'am, that would be great!' So, he came into the kitchen and we got him a piece of rhubarb pie and a glass of milk. Well, you'd have thought it was the best pie he had ever eaten, and that's exactly what he said it was!

"Just then, the back porch screen door bursts open and in ran Jimmy with that same little boy I had seen him tussling with out on the hill. 'Hi!' the boy says right off with this big smile and covered in dirt. One of his eyes looked puffy and there was this trickle of blood dripping out of his nose that he wiped at with the back of his hand. Then he spied Duke eating a slice of pie at the table and says, 'Gee, that looks good! Can I have some? My name's Jack. I'm his brother.' And that is how you and Duke came into our lives that day. And you've always loved my rhubarb pie too."

"Nothin' much has changed, huh, Jack?" Jimmy smiled and held up one of his fists.

"And the two of them have been best of friends ever since," Grandma Meeks said, concluding her story.

"Grandma Meeks, I have always loved that rhubarb pie!" Jack exclaimed. "I love all your pies and all your great cooking too!"

Grandma Meeks smiled warmly at Jack's compliment. Her gaze drifted to the horizon, and all was quiet, for a moment, except for some cows bawling out in the barn.

"Oh, Gott im Himmel," she said, smiling, and used her apron to dab at a tear in the corner of her eye. "Look, isn't that a glorious sunset? It's as though the Lord himself is painting it for us. It's His way of reminding us to count our blessings at the end of this day. It's His beautiful everlasting light and His way of saying all will be well, all will be good…"

Grandpa Meeks sipped at his wine and slowly relit his pipe. "She always starts up with that 'Got em schnitzel' stuff whenever she sees one of these sunsets. Which reminds me, did the cousins come over and get the milkin' done?" he asked her.

"Yes, dear. They're down there now, such a big help they are with you men being so busy. Jessie went down to the barn and helped them too. And then she came back up and helped us prepare the supper. Such a big help *she* is!" She smiled lovingly at her versatile helper, now drying the dishes.

"Didn't they want to stay for supper? They always seem to have a hearty appetite, especially for that chicken of yours." He chuckled and sipped more on the wine.

"Sister Heidi is a fine cook as well, you know." She winked at Jessie and the little girl giggled softly. "She will make sure they have some, and as a special treat, she is going to make her meatloaf for us for supper tomorrow. You know how you always love her special meatloaf with that sweet sausage she adds to it. And she mentioned something about bringing over some of her fresh-baked apple pie too."

A wistful expression crossed the old man's face as he sipped at his wine and puffed a contented smoke ring that drifted heavily over the porch and out into the still evening air. After their long day, the boys were content lounging around on the veranda, listening to the older folks, and letting their own thoughts wander as they watched the sun go down.

After a while, it was time to settle in. Since most of the boys were camping over, Grandpa Meeks supervised the traditional setting up of the camp. A large old army tent had been set up in a clearing near one of the farm's Pole Barns that housed the tractors and assorted implements. Inside the big tent were several old army cots with enough sleeping bags for the boys to use. The canvas sides of the tent could be rolled up and tied off, and mosquito netting could be lowered down into place. The sides could also be stretched out and anchored by poles to create a shaded awning all around. In the middle of the tent was a picnic table that the boys could play cards on. An assortment of playing cards, comic books, *Sports Illustrated*, *MAD*, *Field & Stream* and *Hot Rod* magazines were strewn around on it. An added luxury for the campers was a modern bathroom—or a "latrine," as Grandpa Meeks called it—conveniently on the side of the Pole Barn near the tent. It even had showers that the boys had already used to wash off the days' chaff and grime before supper.

They settled into their camp. Their new home away from home for the next few weeks. Even though Jack's home was close by and he could have easily gone home every evening, he enjoyed this summer ritual too much to miss out on it. Besides, it was akin to a rite of passage at the Meeks' farm.

When they had washed up, most of the boys were so exhausted they welcomed just collapsing onto their cots, looking forward to a good night's rest.

Jack propped a transistor radio up on a stool next to his cot. "Everyone cool with some tunes? I can pick up WKIX's FM out of Chicago this time of night."

With a few nods of approval, Jack turned on the radio to his favorite station, grabbing a flashlight and a magazine from his bag. He shined the light as he slowly flipped through the pages.

"Hey, what's that you're lookin' at Jack?" Bobby asked from a nearby cot.

"Yeah, what the hell... Jack!" Big Schuler barked. "Where'd you get that *Playboy*?"

"What? A *Playboy*? Let me see!" Randy pleaded as they all eagerly jumped off their cots and surrounded Jack.

"Oh, shit! Look at that!" someone exclaimed.

"Is that fabulous or what?" someone else chimed in.

"It's not a what, it's Miss October," Jack calmly replied.

Randy, though, was much more enthusiastic. "Oh, man. She's so beautiful. Look at those—"

Just then, Jimmy ducked into the tent with his arms full of tin cups and a pitcher of Grandpa Meeks' home-brewed beer. "Look at those *what*?" he asked.

"Those!" Randy said, pointing at the centerfold.

"Oh... damn, Jack!" Jimmy exclaimed. "You're growing up so fast this summer! Wasn't it just last year you brought your new *CARtoons Magazine* to show us all, or was it your *Archie* comic book?" That got a good chuckle out of everyone, but Jack remained calm.

"Well, I guess one of us needs to grow up, Jimmy, but there's still some comic books for you over on the table." Jack couldn't resist the jab back at Jimmy. There were some muffled chuckles, but Jimmy, to everyone's amazement and with his arms still full, let it slide with just a sarcastic smile. "This is one of Duke's," Jack continued matter-of-factly. "He was going to throw them away when he was shipping out, but I talked him out of it. He said the same thing you just did, Jimmy, about growing up and all, a rite of passage or something like that... But, hey, I'm looking forward to having some of Grandpa Meeks' home brew!"

Jimmy patiently filled each cup, trying not to pour so fast that there would be more foam than liquid in them. Satisfied that he had filled each one equally, he passed them around. Once everyone had a cup, he proposed a toast to a good day's work, and each boy gratefully sipped down the stout, dark malt in agreement with Grandpa Meeks that it was the best they ever had.

Jimmy said the hops Grandpa Meeks used in the batch were home grown in a little grove over near the barn. Rafe chimed in asking if maybe there was any pot growing over in that grove too? Jimmy wadded up one of his dirty socks and threw it at Rafe's head, which just missed and landed in Joe's half-full cup. Seemingly unperturbed, Joe lifted the sock out, stepped outside the tent and vigorously rung it out. Then he placed it down ceremoniously at the end of Jimmy's cot. Without hesitating, he picked his cup back up and drank what remained of the lager, licked his lips, smiled, and sprawled out on his cot with his eyes closed. Everyone got a good laugh out of it to end the long first day, but there were still some who wanted another look at the magazine.

"Hey, Jack, did Duke have one of those mags with Barbi Benton?" someone mumbled just as the last flashlight was turned off. "Bring that one next time, will ya?"

Chapter 8

The next morning dawned all too early. Farms woke early; roosters crowed; dogs started barking. Off down a lane, a bell started clanking, growing louder and louder the closer it got.

"What the hell?" moaned Joe.

"That's just Sweetness comin' in for milkin'. She's a bell cow. They're all followin' in behind her. Time to roll out, you wimps. Come on, roust up, Joe. I'll teach you how to milk a cow. Tried to tell you all last night to shut the hell up and get some sleep. Come on, Bobby boy, rise and shine!" barked Jimmy.

Jack was already up. He knew farm life and knew the mornings started early. He and Jimmy headed for the latrine as the herd meandered past them, heading into the barnyard. Each one took its turn bellowing, and at times they seemed to croon in a chorus with each other, helping to insure the whole farm was awake.

Gradually, all the boys roused themselves. Some went down to the barn to help with the milking while the rest helped with other early morning chores. Breakfast was as big as supper the night before. There were piles of scrambled, sunny side up or easy over eggs, fried potatoes, bacon, ham, fresh-baked biscuits with a slab of the home-churned butter and assorted fresh berry jams and hive honey. Afterwards, the boys had a restive reprieve while the sun burned the morning's dew off the hay bales lying out in the fields from the day before. Lounging around in their tent, they could hear a far-off tractor begin baling anew, ensuring them another long hard work day.

"Hey, Jack, what do you think ol' Duke will do when he gets back?" asked Big Schuler as they lay on their cots.

"Don't really know. He never writes about it. He may just stay in the army. Who knows? I think he likes what they have him doing. If he does get out, I don't think he'll come back here, though. He always talked about going back to California. That's where we moved from. Duke was sixteen then. He made the best of moving here, but he missed it out there, surfing and stuff. I think he's always wanted to go back. I was only nine, almost ten, so it didn't bother me all that much."

"Yeah," chimed in Bobby, "bet he missed those California girls too."

"Yeah, he had a girlfriend, real pretty and nice," Jack said. "I think he missed her a lot, man. Who knows? Maybe the army will move him there. He'd be cool with that, I bet." He started to think about Duke and how much he missed him, something he tried not to let himself do that often.

Yep, good ol' Duke. He's always been more of a good friend than a big brother, Jack thought.

Not that Duke wouldn't lay down the law, though, when he thought he needed to, but that was mostly when it involved Jack's safety and well-being. He always seemed to wear a smile and be in good cheer with his perpetually sun-bleached blond hair and tanned good looks. He was a gifted athlete as well, but he never made Jack feel like he had to live up to him. He just tried to set an example for Jack of what it was to be a good guy, a good friend, and how to someday be a solid, responsible, and honest man, just like their dad. *Sure hope the army takes good care him,* Jack thought. Then he prayed silently for his brother: *God, please watch over and keep ol' Duke safe. Please bring him home from over there. Please let him come back and surf again and be okay, Lord, please.*

Before long Jimmy and Grandpa Meeks pulled up with the wagons, and the work began all over again. By midmorning the sun had worked itself up and the heat was becoming oppressive. They took a break under one of the giant oak trees that had mercifully lived on over the years. Grandpa Meeks continued his story with all the boys. They were grateful for the restful story time.

"Well, where was I?" Grandpa Meeks started in as he lit his pipe.

"You were telling us about goin' over to the war back when you were young," Bobby reminded him.

"Oh, okay. So, all that time over there I kept thinkin' 'bout that pretty gal back home and that fried chicken of hers. Now you had some of that tasty meal last night, so you know what I'm talkin' 'bout. Should tell you, though, I thought about who else she was fryin' up that chicken for with me wallowin' away in that muck over there. We were all feelin' pretty low, with the shells always burstin' everywhere, day and night. Then they blew that whistle again, which meant *here we go*, and away we went, screamin' like banshees, scared shitless, I can tell you!" He paused and took a draw on his pipe and exhaled a large plume of the pungent smoke and watched it drift off.

"That smoke out on that field was so thick you couldn't see but the length of your own arm," Grandpa Meeks continued. "The next thing I knew, there was this big wild-eyed, riderless horse comin' right at me, just plowin' right through us. He hit me like a ton of bricks and went stompin' right on over me. That's how I got my other souvenirs. Knocked me out cold, he did. When I came to, they were rollin' me over 'cause I was face down and lucky I didn't drown in the muck my face was planted in. Anyway, when they rolled me over I could feel my shoulder pop back into its socket. That hurt like hell, let me tell you! Then they put me on a stretcher and carted me off to an aid station. Broke this other forearm, busted up all these ribs on this side, punctured a lung, and broke this leg right at the shin." He patted his right shin where the break had occurred.

"So that time they figured I'd had enough, and they shipped me back home. Everyone met me at the ol' depot like I was some kind of hero, even though I never did a damn thing but wishin' to be back home and feelin' sorry for myself. She and her whole clan were there, and everyone gathered around me. Her old man said, '*Gott im Himmel,* poor Joseph, we were so worried you would shoot up our cousins over there, and here it looks like they were doing the shooting up of you!' And my own old man, when he'd heard my story, just shook his head and said, 'God damn, boy, here you are, raised on a farm, great big animals all around your whole life, and you had to go off clear on the other side of the world just to get run over by a horse? We got plenty of 'em right here crazy enough to run you over!'

"But seein' her with that pretty face and tears in her eyes… She cried that I had come back, that I was so busted up. She hugged me good, tryin' not to knock me off my crutches, and held onto me and locked me straight in my eyes and said, 'All will be good now. You are home, and all will be good for you, Joseph, you will see.' She was even prettier than I'd remembered her, let me tell you. She cooked me up that fried chicken again, and before I even got to the apple pie, I'd asked her to marry me. I tell you, my Gerda's the best thing that's ever happened to me. I sure ain't perfect by a long shot, but for some reason my faults have never seemed to bother her much. And the older I get, the more of 'em I seem to get." He chuckled. "I've been real blessed by her. Anytime she sees me gettin' down over somethin', losin' a calf or a bad crop, she cooks me up that fried chicken or somethin' else real special. Always seems to help. She's always had a good sense of humor too. Always cheerful and all. Yep, I sure been blessed. Tell you what, too, she could out work any of us out here: drive these tractors, heftin' these bales, birth animals, doctor up everyone. And then do the cookin', cannin', tend the gardens, and do the bookkeepin' too! Yep, I surely been truly blessed…

Well, enough of me jaw bonin' and carryin' on again, let's get back at it."

Soon they found their rhythm again and continued to whittle away at the bales one by one. The dark barn was stifling, again, as they stacked the bales higher and higher into the huge loft. Lunch, or "dinner," as it was called on the farm, came none too soon. After the boys washed up the best they could, Grandma Meeks and the girls set up a smorgasbord of salad with fresh tomatoes, onions, green beans, and cheeses, along with sandwiches of sliced ham, roast beef, and potato salad. The boys dug in, surprised by their appetites and how hungry they were. After an hour of rest out of the midday sun, the tractors pulled up again, and back out into the hot fields they went.

And so the long afternoon went until Grandpa Meeks blessedly called it quits. But instead of hitting the showers, Jimmy had the boys grab their cutoffs and they all piled onto one of the empty trailers. Jimmy worked the tractor down a winding two-track road all the way to the back of the farm where a wooded grove ended at the edge of Lake Kit. A few of the boys had been to the far end of the lake, and Jack knew it well from his childhood days spent fishing and swimming with Jimmy and the past baling years at the Meeks' farm. A long, old wooden dock stretched out into deep water, and the boys took turns cannonballing off the end of it, luxuriating in the lake's cool and welcoming darkness.

This was, in Jack's mind, the mystical shore of Lake Kit. Heavily wooded, it had never been developed, and there were no cabins within sight. It was still as much as it had been ever since the Algonquin's, Potawatomi's and Chippewa's freely roamed and hunted in the surrounding forests.

A rowboat with a small, ancient motor was tied up to one side of the dock and rocked back and forth violently from the waves created by the boys' thrashing around. But soon the waves grew calm as they all pulled themselves back onto the dock. The stillness of the evening began to engulf them almost reverently. After a while, though, the mosquitoes and deer flies also began to engulf them and they quickly flopped back down on the trailer's bed. Some of the boys even napped on the way back to the farm.

After another large supper and their home-brewed nightcap, sleep came earlier than the first night with the knowledge of how early the sun would come up the next morning, and all would repeat itself. It would repeat itself the next day and the next, until Friday finally rolled around and the first week of baling came to an end. The boys said their goodbyes and headed off to their own homes, bushed from the long week. Jack's home wasn't very far away, just a mile or so down the road, set back down a lane of tall pines and surrounded by several acres of woods of various oaks, apple, walnut, elms, and weeping willows.

The house itself was a modest split-level brick. Jack's dad was in the radio business and commuted an hour each way to work. He worked long hours and lived each moment for when he could just be out on his "farm," doing all the small jobs that needed to be done, such as working in the garden, pruning trees, and mowing the yard. He himself had been raised during the Depression in a tough, cramped apartment building in a tough, cramped neighborhood in a tough, cramped city. So, this was his Shangri-La, his green acres, like the popular television show by that name.

World War II had come along not too long after he graduated high school and off he'd gone to serve his country. It changed his life, as it had changed everyone's then. He'd prayed many times, every day: *Please, God, see us through this, help me and the guys get back safely. I'll find a quiet place, oh please, God!* Miraculously, he did make it back, and married a beautiful young girl he met at a USO dance on one of his last postings back in the States before the war ended.

She was a big city girl with a background similar to his. She was an only child and was raised in a little house on a quiet street lined with other little houses. She was studying bookkeeping and dreamed of someday having a new life, maybe traveling and having some adventures. A girlfriend had talked her into going to the dance. She had been to several during the war and was happy to meet and dance with "the boys," as the girls called them. At first, she had not wanted to go. She had an exam the next morning and wanted to get some more studying in.

They had just walked into the large ballroom, and the big band had just started up with the Glenn Miller song "In the Mood" that they all were so crazy over. Before she knew it, she was out on the dance floor, whirling and twirling and falling head over heels with a handsome and dashing "fly boy," with a smile that made her swoon.

It was a whirlwind romance and marriage, and she was as game for her new life as he was. The years right after the war were heady ones for them, as they were for their whole generation, the "Greatest Generation," that had somehow pulled through the misery of the Depression, and fought and won two wars, helping the world rid itself of Fascism and Totalitarianism and the hatred and horror they fostered. When the war had finally ended, they had traveled and worked their way across the country until they hit California and decided to stay. For the first time in their young lives, life was good, and all their friends and loved ones who had not made it through the nightmare, looking down on them from their peaceful eternity, would have wanted it to be that way for them.

They were good years there. The boys growing up in a neighborhood packed with hundreds of kids playing out in the streets. But the fun wore out as the crowds grew. So many people, the traffic, the freeways—it all became too much, like the crowded cities they themselves had grown up in. Then a job offer came that gave them the opportunity to move to a place in the country, to that quiet place that they had prayed for back during the war. When they made the big move, it was hardest on Duke, as he was in the midst of high school by then. He was at a tough age to have left friends, the old neighborhood, the school—the girl. But he was a resilient kid and made the best of it. So did little Jack in becoming a rural kid, going to a one room country school with just seven or eight other kids in the same class. It was such a big change, but they had all adjusted somehow. They made new friends and carved out a new life about as far from the old one as they could be.

Jack had come along a little later than planned. Duke, now in the Army, was six years older, but he welcomed having a baby brother and took to the big brother role. He was Wally to the Beaver, and it worked well. Duke seemed to be a natural at anything he tried. He excelled at sports and in school, as well as made and kept friends easily. He set a good example for Jack, and Jack tried hard to emulate him and thought of him as the greatest big brother ever.

But now Duke was on the other side of the world. How did it happen? One day he suddenly announced that he had joined the army. He said that it was the "right thing to do," that he "wants to do it," and that "other things had to wait." So now the "other things" waited while Duke was doing what he felt was right, so far away in a very dangerous place doing a very dangerous job. His family worried for him. Memories of World War II, the sadness of it, haunted them. It was hard, but not hearing from him, except the occasional letter, was the hardest. Prayers were all they had, a lot of them.

Now it was just Jack at home, if you could call it that with all his hanging out with his friends, or at the lake, or working at his various jobs. But that was all just part of his maturation. One day Jack would be out on his own too. So now it was almost just the two of them again, and even though they loved the old farm dearly, without the children it would maybe be a little too quiet, and even a little too lonely. Maybe one of these days it would be time for another adventure, another life chapter.

She was proud of her boys, each one so special. And now, almost overnight, her baby was practically a man. As he walked through the door that night, he looked every bit a grown man, a grown and tired man. *How quickly they grow!* she thought. Wasn't it only yesterday they were running around all over, wearing her out? But she had loved and treasured every minute of it. She watched her grown-up little boy as he stood in the kitchen, drinking a glass of iced tea. *Still so young,* she thought. *But then how old were we during the war? Jack's not much younger than cousin Jackie when he was shot down, or all our poor boys lost on that nightmarish death march in the Philippines, or Donnie Daughtry at Normandy, or John's copilot, Duke Arnold, killed right in the cockpit next to him by a piece of shrapnel.* Tears started to well up, but she quickly blinked them away.

"Hot as heck out there today," said Jack. "Always seems like the hottest days ever are when we're baling. But we got most of the big fields in. Lot more still out there, though, and poor Mr. Meeks is fretting that it's gonna rain."

"That was so nice of the Meeks' to feed and take care of you boys the way they do. I hope you thanked them and remembered your manners."

"Yes, ma'am, the food's always great. The guys all really like them. Well, think I'll go shower and hit the sack. Little tired tonight. I thought I'd do some work around here this weekend. Night, Mom, love you." He kissed her cheek.

"Good night, darling. I love you too," she said. But before he left, she added, "Say, we should put some ointment on all those scratches on your arms from those hay bales. Looks like you've been in a fight with a bunch of wild chickens or cats." *You'll always be their mother,* she thought to herself and smiled.

Chapter 9

The second week was more of the same: long, hot, hard-working days and big, bountiful meals of meatloaf, smoked hams, baked chicken, roast beef, gravy, and mashed potatoes. The boys liked these people they were working so hard for and each day grew closer to them. The grind of the repetitive physical work was all made easier with trips down to the lake to wash and cool off, hearing more of Grandpa Meeks' stories about the lake's old Indian superstitions, and the ritual treat of his home-brewed nightcaps. They felt good about their hard work and were feeling a proud sense of accomplishment each time they gazed out over the vast sprawling fields and saw a dent in the fewer and fewer bales lying out there.

During the first day back, they began to get into their old rhythms, and as they did, the work didn't seem quite so hard and the days didn't seem quite so hot. That deep plopping sound of the tractors almost seemed like the machines were old friends, groaning, heaving, and sweating right along with them. The goal was to fill the big barn up to the rafters with the remaining bales before the rain hit. And it would be done. They just knew it would, because Grandpa Meeks said so. He said he could feel it in his old bones.

The last wagon was loaded with the final bale on the last day of baling, and the fields were bare. The clouds had been bunching up and growing darker all day. The race had been on, and now the sky let loose with a gusher. The boys laid back on top of their loads, loving the cool rain as it drenched them, washing off all the sweat and chafe, and wishing it could have been like this after every load. It felt so good. Even Jimmy, his dad, and Grandpa Meeks had to admit that the rain felt good as they coaxed their full wagon loads into the newly formed hay bale canyon down the center of the barn. Renewed and refreshed, the boys made quick work of the last bales, stacking them up into the highest rafters.

Then they all just collapsed on the cool, bare cement floor near the big doors of the barn where the rain's cooling spray could still reach. Grandpa Meeks, too, laid his large frame down and stared up at the high rafters.

"Tell you what too," he began, "that ol' German dad of Gerda's turned out to be quite a guy. 'Papa,' they all called him. Everyone did, me included. I never saw nothin' that ol' man couldn't do. I learned a lot 'bout things from him—farmin', animals, machinery. He could take apart a tractor and rebuild it. Same with windmills, leatherwork, carpentry—anything. Loved and took care of his livestock like they were his babies, and that's just the way he thought of them. Plus, he made the best home-brewed beer I've ever had. He gave me that recipe before he passed. Course, you boys that've had some can judge for yourselves. He only had the two girls, my Gerda and her sister, Heidi, so I was like a son to him. He and my ol' man knew each other a little before I married Gerda, but they got to be real good friends. He was the hardest-working son of an ol' Kraut as there ever was, and I say that with true affection, and both me and my pop grew to truly love that ol' fella.

"I never will forget this one freezin' frickin' bitter November day. Wouldn't you know it, that ol' big windmill right out there that used to pump our well water up to the house tank just seized up. I was still an invalid right after the war, dealin' with pain like you don't want to know and hobblin' around tryin' just to piss on my own. And my ol' dad, who never was sick in his whole life, came down with the flu that all us servicemen brought back home in 1918 as a welcome-home gift. That was a bad one, worst ever. Well, he was a tough ol' bird, too, but that one got him down bad. Fortunately, by some miracle, he was the only one that got hit by it out where we were. Anyway, here's us two strappin' Meeks', never needin' nothin' or nobody, were so laid up you'd think we'd make an ol' Kraut giggle. But not ol' Papa. No, sir. He come ridin' over on this big ol' common plow horse of his he called Boss. Giant equestrian mutt! Some kind of an oddity, part Persian and some other big breeds in him.

"That day a blizzard came in like we never saw that early in the year and like we ain't seen since. Papa hitched that big ol' Boss up and started pullin' up rods, one after the other all day, wind whippin' like Hades screamin' for your firstborn child. And here I was laid up all snug as a baby in my bed yonder, feelin' like a worthless, spoiled piece of you know what, hearin' through the wind Papa's tools clankin' and Boss snortin' and pullin' at his harness. Anyway, come 'bout twilight, I seen him out my window, up on the platform, way up there, right up at the top on that little platform, what?—forty feet up? I could hear him workin' away on one spent gear then another. Probably had his rasps up there with him like he was a watchmaker, filin' those gears smooth, makin' them all mesh just right. And then I'd see him climb back down off that little ledge and down that narrow ladder and watch him coax that ol' Boss, like they were one machine. He had let down one rod patiently then the next over, what—a couple hundred feet?

"They ever give out a medal for that? Probably never, but if they ever did, that ol' Papa oughta get a gold one. And do you think he ever even mentioned it? Nope. Just a big hearty dinner Gerda made him to eat with some mugs of that home brew of his. After makin' sure it was all up and runnin' smooth come nightfall, he just popped up on ol' Boss and ambled off down the road toward home. I have to tell you, I cried hard to myself that night. Here we were, the big, rough-and-tumble Meeks men, don't need nobody for nothin', and that one ol' humble German had, without even ever bein' asked to help, got us our water back pumpin'. The army had tried to drill into me to hate German's for all I was worth, but that man didn't have one ounce of ill will in him towards nobody. Ol' Papa was somethin', that's for sure.

"Oh, and sister Heidi married a good man, but he'd had enough of farmin' as a boy and became a banker. They still live out yonder there on their ol' farm, and we all try to help 'em take good care of it just like that ol' man would have wanted. That last field we just finished was one of his. So you fellas would have done him proud, hard as you all worked. Yep, I'll bet ol' Papa's spirit was right out there with us with ol' Boss, too, helpin' us bringin' in those bales. He would have liked to have known you all, and I sure do wish you could have known him too. Welp, how 'bout we hump it on in? I'm gettin' hungry!"

The rain continued to come down in buckets as they dashed onto the back veranda where Grandma Meeks, Katie, and Jessie had another huge supper on display. Everyone was in high spirits as they bowed their heads as Grandpa Meeks, or "Grandpa," as they now called him, said the blessing over a delicious meal of smoked ham, baked chicken, scalloped potatoes, green beans and tomatoes, applesauce, fresh-baked rolls, homemade butter and fresh hive honey. It was another eloquent and moving prayer, thanking God for all His blessings.

After he finished and as the boys were about to start in, he stood up. "Men, the end of the harvest is always a special occasion, and so I would like to propose a toast." With that, Grandma Meeks, Katie, and Jessie walked onto the veranda with big pitchers of lemonade and iced tea. Each boy raised his glass as Grandpa said, "Fellas, there is no way we can really thank you enough for all your hard work. But we want you to know how much we appreciate it. You're all darn good workers, and if any of you ever need anything, you are always welcome here. We hope you'll come on back to do this again, or just to say hello. From all of us Meeks' we say, 'thank you.'"

Chapter 10

After the meal, everyone said their goodbyes. The women all gave the boys warm hugs. Piling into their cars, the boys, with their hard-earned pay and a large unexpected bonus, headed over to Joe's cabin. Changing into frayed cutoffs, they dashed down the stairs to the dock and, with loud whoops, leaped off the end of the dock into the refreshing lake.

"Man, did I get ripped!" exclaimed Big Schuler, ogling his own physique as he stood in the shallow water.

All the boys felt it too. After only a couple of weeks of hard work and huge regular meals, they were all tan and muscular.

"Yeah, man," said Bobby. "I bet I put on ten pounds!" He struck a Charles Atlas pose.

"You're all wusses!" a distinct voice yelled from somewhere above them.

Startled, they looked up. Jimmy was standing like some kind of Greek god at the top of the stairs looking down on the mortals. Randy and Rafe were with him, roaring with laughter.

The boys had been so preoccupied with themselves, splashing around, they had not even heard the big bikes coming down the lane to the cabin.

"So this is where the motley crew luxuriates?" Jimmy asked, half in jest, half for real as he handed Jack a beer from one of the six-packs they had brought along. They wore cutoffs and sat down on the dock to take off their heavy biker boots. None of them had worn a shirt.

The lake felt good to everyone. It was good just to swim in the cool water, drink a beer, and relax after another hot, hard week of work. Even Fletch showed up with a couple of other older guys that everyone knew from school. They had brought some food and a couple of six-packs to make themselves welcome.

"What brings you exalted ones to our humble abode?" asked Joe.

"Oh, we were just feelin' lonely and neglected, so we thought we'd just stop by to catch up with you, little brothers. Hope you don't mind," Fletch chided.

"Not at all, as long as you're willing to part with some of those beers."

"For sure, Joe. You guys just have to promise no drinkin' and drivin' out on these roads around here. Shit, I swear, whoever built these roads out here were drunk themselves. Lucky more people don't end up drivin' right off into the lake."

"Naw, man, we're just hangin' out down on the dock. We're all wiped out from balin' hay over at Jimmy's."

"That's cool, man, glad to see you guys puttin' in some physical labor for a change," Fletch said, continuing with his chiding banter.

They lazed around on the dock, talking about cars, bikes, football, and girls, in no particular order. Fletch was stretched out, listening to the conversation when the talk turned to football and of glory days past. "My favorite game memory was durin' our senior year when they brought Jimmy, Rafe, Big Schuler, and Jack up to varsity," he said. "You guys know what a tough year that was. We had all those injuries, so we needed you young runts to step up. Homecomin', man, biggest game of the year, we played that undefeated West Central team. Damn they were good. But we had 'em, what?—fourteen to thirteen with eight seconds left? You guys remember it. They were on our four-yard line, fourth and goal with the whole season on the line. Everyone thought they would run it, pound it in on us, and there I was, middle linebacker, thinkin' they were gonna run it right over me. So their quarterback, who was starin' right at me, faked the handoff to their back, and we all bought into it. Then he looked up, and I go, 'Oh, shit man, it's a pass!' I remember lookin' back over my shoulder and seein' their end open out to my right. My gut just sank. I thought we were toast. It seems like it was all in slow motion, man. Saw that ball sailin' right to him. Then, out of nowhere, there's Jack, flyin' through the air, and *bap*! He knocked that ball clear out of bounds. Game over! We win! Everyone went wild! Jack, man, I'll never forget that play for as long as I live. That was the best feelin' ever. Yep, my best game memory, ever."

All grew quiet out on that dock except for the lapping of the waves against the shore as each boy reflected on their own cherished memories of that moment. Then, quietly, Jack spoke up. "My best game memory was our freshman year. Think we were playing Plankton. It was one of the last games of the year. It was cold and raining. They had this big goon who thought he was this real boss dude. This one play, he smacked me from behind. Knocked the crap out of me. Saw some stars for a bit there for sure. Ate some grass too. He just grinned down at me like some kind of lunatic. Anyway, late in the game—we're winning—I was in on a tackle, and when I got up, for some reason, I looked back across the field. It had started snowing, and the clouds had settled in low, right down onto the field. It was eerie. Way across the field I saw Jimmy in the fog, going at it with that same big goon that had leveled me, knocking his head back and forth between his forearms until the guy's helmet flew off. He just went down on his knees, wavering, just looking up at Jimmy. Then Jimmy walked off like it was just business, man, and disappeared off into that cloud."

For a while, no one spoke, except for the creature sounds of the early summer evening around the lake and the occasional smack when someone slapped a pesky mosquito.

"Sure wish you were still playin' ball with us," Big Schuler said to Jimmy. "Man, you were good."

And Jimmy had been good. He was a gifted natural athlete and one of the fastest guys on the team. He could play any position, but he liked playing defensive end where he could use all his size, speed and strength to control the whole world on his side of the field. Without a doubt he would have been an all-state player if he had stayed in school. Probably would have been recruited and given a full-ride scholarship.

Jimmy's friends knew how much he had loved those games. They guessed it had helped him get through all the rough times of his mother's illness and passing. It had been good therapy, Jimmy's kind of therapy, thumping heads.

"Well, then I would have to go back to school with all you wusses, and it would take a miracle for that to ever happen," said Jimmy. Everyone laughed, but they couldn't stop thinking about how good they had been and could be again with him. "Hey, Jack," he said, almost wistfully, "'member when Duke took us with him to the Note that time? We begged him to take us with him. He made us promise to stay put in the back of the truck, back when it was just his ol' beater."

Jack laughed, recalling the fond memory. "Yeah, and we didn't! Soon as he and his buddies went in, we popped right out, and went and hopped up on that block wall outside the entrance and watched everything going on. All these real pretty chicks going in with their hair all puffed up and wearing a bunch of makeup. All of them back then wore high heels and Miniskirts.

"Duke and his buds were all cool dudes too. Place was so packed, man, seems like way more than it gets nowadays. The smoke would just billow out of the place, like it still does! And we could hardly see inside the place, just hear all the music playing and only getting a glimpse inside when someone opened the door and came out." Jack paused in thought for a moment. "Jimmy, remember that bouncer

guy? What was his name? Buster? Something like that...
Anyway, he was thinking we were going to try to sneak in
the place when he wasn't looking, which we were. So we're
just sitting on that wall, joking around with him, and he
starts trying to scare us, talking about how we really didn't
want to go in the place 'cause we'd get our souls sucked out
of us. He said that's why it was called the Soul Note 'cause it
would eat up people's souls and all... huh, Jimmy?"

Jimmy didn't say anything right away, seeming lost in
thought. "Yep, a regular devil's den suckin' up souls. Scared
the shit out of poor little Jack so much we never did sneak
in!"

"Yeah, look who's talking!" Jack shot back. "Wonder
whatever happened to that guy anyway?"

"Who knows?" Jimmy quipped. "Probably got his soul
gobbled up! Gobble! Gobble! Gobble!" He laughed and
made a half-hearted attempt to get Jack in a headlock, but
Jack deftly ducked away just in the nick of time. Jimmy
teetered on the edge of the dock but couldn't stop himself
from plunging off into the deep end. When he surfaced,
to everyone's surprise, he was still laughing. "Damn, Jack!
You're good at duckin' trouble!"

Jack, laughing as well with a combination of relief and
amusement, launched himself in a cannonball off the dock.
The others all dove in after him.

After a while, Jimmy pulled himself back up on the
dock and grabbed someone's towel. "Welp, enough of this
kumbaya stuff," he said as he stood up. "When we gonna
eat? 'Bout time we get somethin' on the grill, ain't it? Rafe
here's gettin' hungry." He stretched his arms out over his

head and looked at the rest of the boys still bobbing around in the dark water. "Thanks boys for the help with the balin'. Like Grandpa said, me and my family really appreciate it."

Jack pulled himself up onto the dock to shake Jimmy's hand. "Anytime. Happy to help out, Jimmy. Your family was great to us."

As Jimmy turned to walk off the dock, he feigned another attempt at a headlock at Jack. "Hey, buddy. You wanna take on ol' Fletch here over at Darden? You let me know. I'll want to see that. And you better watch out, Fletch, Jack might just smoke you."

And with that, they all jovially bounded back up the path to the cottage to get the grill started.

"You were right, Jack, Jimmy and those guys are cool, man," Bobby said as they lingered behind the others. "Pretty strange about what that guy said to you, though, about the Note eating souls and all. Wonder where he ever got that idea from?"

"I don't know... As I remember he looked like kind of a strange dude anyway," Jack said. "Like Jimmy said, he was just trying to spook us. And he probably did... even Jimmy! But don't ever tell anybody I said so!"

Jack had seen something in Jimmy out there on the dock and knew the others had seen it too. It was a glimpse of the old Jimmy, before the loss, and it was good to see again.

After a while, they had the grill heated just right, and the burgers and hot dogs were sizzling. The boys were proud of their handiwork in building the large fire pit on the bluff that overlooked the lake. Encircling the pit were an assortment of old picnic tables and several hefty tree stumps that providing rustic seating. Along with the burgers and hot dogs, Jimmy had tossed a pile of sweet corn from the Meeks' garden, still in the husks, on the grill.

With everyone gathered around the pit, some seated and some standing, Fletch cleared his throat to speak. "Listen up, everyone. In case you haven't noticed, it looks like we got a serious issue with that Torville crowd. Anyone can see they're wantin' to start trouble, and it sure isn't hard to see who they want it with. Jack, Bobby, you're right in their cross hairs, so I hope you're bein' watchful. You need to be watchin' your backs, for sure."

"We've got 'em in our sights, too, Fletch," said Jimmy. "We've been watchin' 'em. A bunch of idiot low-lifes, man. Know they were the ones that played chicken with Rafe and tried to run him off the road that night. Oh, yeah, we've been watchin' 'em. They keep growin' too. Every time we see 'em over at the Note there's more of 'em."

"Yeah, I've noticed that too. That's a strange bunch of people, man," Fletch concurred. "I sure think somethin' bad is gonna happen with them, any night now and probably right out at the Note. Things have been brewin' with them for a long time. We've had issues with them for years. Nothin' big, just run-ins like Jack and Bobby had, but it's different this year. They've gotten bad, real bad. Maybe it's the drugs they're all doin'. Who knows? But hey, we wanted to let you guys know we're with you. Somethin' breaks out, it'll be big the way they're growin'. So, it'd be a good idea to try to get as many guys as you can to join us. We're not the only ones they've been pissin' off, so maybe we can get some other crews in with us. And listen up, stay watchful! They're gonna try to get you when you're not lookin' and got no help around. So, you guys stick together. We'll be around, too, but stay together best you can. Jack, ol' Duke was a cool guy. Took me under his wing when he was a senior and showed me what it took to be a quarterback, even how to hold the ball and whip it out like he could. He was cool, man, so I know he'd want us to be backin' you guys up. But, I'm still gonna beat your ass when we race."

That lightened the tone, and after more of the guys spoke up and things began to quiet down, Jack grabbed one of the ears of corn and a hot dog and wandered over to his old truck. He let the back panel down to use as a seat and began munching on the corn. He looked out over the lake. It was a great view. There were still a few sailboats off in the distance out in the deep, middle part of the lake and a few speedboats with skiers carving S-shaped curves behind them, but the lake was beginning to quiet down in the early evening. It was one of his favorite times of the day. He watched a small boat pass down directly below the bluff, carrying a couple of fishermen on their way over to the east cove for some evening fishing.

He decided to get up early one morning soon and go out for some fishing himself. It was one of his favorite pastimes and he hadn't done much of it lately. His dad, him, and his brother used to fish all the time, and that thought, along with all the talk earlier, had made him miss Duke. He resolved to write him a letter and to spend some more time with his dad. It seemed like he hardly even saw his old man anymore, let alone spend any time with him. They still got along okay, it was just that things were changing big-time for Jack. He was having fun with his growing independence, but every now and then he caught a glimpse of his life of not so long ago when his family was his world. It had been a nice world, and sometimes he missed it.

Something in a Hendrix song playing in the background brought his thoughts back to the present, and he started thinking about her again. He had struggled with his thoughts and the overwhelming feelings he had for her all week. He had called her one night. Just hearing her cheerful voice with her thick Spanish accent had slayed him all over again, and as exhausted as he was, he hadn't slept well that night. Her voice had told him how happy she was that he had called her. There was a sweetness in it as she told him how much she had liked meeting him. Perhaps, she had said, with good fortune they would meet again at the Note, and again perhaps they might dance together and walk in the gardens. She had liked that very much.

"You gonna put that new Holley four-barrel carburetor in the Cherry this summer?" asked Big Schuler, walking up to Jack and holding an ear of the roasted corn.

"Huh? Oh yeah, sure would like to. Make a big difference wouldn't it?"

"Hell, yes. You get it, we'll all help put that baby in. Mr. Hansen said we could use the school's shop. He'd help us too. Be cool," said Big Schuler. "Jimmy's right, you could smoke Fletch, especially with that four-barrel. That GTO is fine, but it's all showroom floor shine. You'd take ol' Fletch with that new carb."

"Thanks, Schul," said Jack, staring at the ear of corn he was working on. "But I doubt it. I know what's under that Goat's hood. Stock or not, that's one big beast. Mr. Hansen's cool, man. Sure knows his cars. It would be great of him to help us too. Shoot, if I didn't know better, I'd say Mr. Hansen's been grooming the Cherry for this all along. You know, he helped me bigtime with refurbishing the motor, putting in that new competition clutch and the manifold and exhaust. He's the greatest, man."

"Hey Schul, by the way," Jack continued, "we all squared away for working the fair next week? I sure can use the extra bucks to buy that carb, even with the discount Mr. Hansen gets."

"Yep. Got it all set up," Big Schuler said. "They need us all. Couple of bucks an hour for mostly just standin' around and checkin' out the chicks. Shoot, we'd be doin' that anyway, and this way we get paid to do it. Be easier money than that balin' work. But you know, I sure do like those people. Jimmy's cool, man. I'd help his folks out anytime they need us again. Swear I'm ripped now for ball this year. Only a few weeks away now. Can't wait. We got a great shot at winnin' state this year."

That night they all hung around the cabin. Some played cards and others lounged around the smoldering fire pit to see who could make the best s'mores or brown a marshmallow to perfection.

Fletch was still seated on a stump pensively staring into the fire. "You know he did get gobbled up," he said softly.

"Who did?" asked Bobby.

"That bouncer over at the Note. Bust Up, he was called. The one Jack and Jimmy said tried to scare them when they were kids about the place eatin' up people's souls, and that was how it got its name and all."

"What about him?" Jimmy asked. "We never saw him again after that night."

"Well," Fletch continued in the same soft voice, "probably wasn't long after that night, he got himself what he thought was a better job over at the steel mill workin' in the foundry. That's hard, dangerous work I know all too damn well. Anyway, from what I remember hearin', somehow one of the big overhead suction augers broke loose. Came swoopin' down right over on top of him and sucked him up! Sucked him up and spit him out into a giant blast furnace before anyone could do anythin'. They just heard him screamin'. My boss says those furnaces get over nine thousand degrees." Fletch paused for a moment and inspected a well burnt marshmallow he'd been patiently holding over the flames at the end of a long stick. "They never found any pieces of him or nothin'. So, I guess you could say he'd got gobbled up by fires as hot as hell itself."

"Aw, Fletch, you're full of it!" Bobby exclaimed. "I never heard nothin' like that could ever even happen! Sucked him up into a big oven? Come on!"

"Sorry, Bobby, didn't mean to scare you none over it. Just what I heard happened to him over at the mill," Fletch responded with a wry smile, adding a spooky look to his face for added effect.

"Didn't scare me none, Fletch!" Bobby shot back. "Just sounds too strange that here he was tryin' to scare Jack and

Jimmy when they were kids about souls gettin' sucked up if they went into the Note, and then here he goes and gets sucked up into a furnace. Now that's too weird!"

"Well, that's just what they say happened, Bobby," Fletch responded, still keeping his voice low. "They still talk about it over at the mill. Is strange, though, I'll grant you that... Hey, maybe you can get a job over there someday too," Fletch chided. "I'll put in a good word for you with my boss. But you'll have to promise me you won't go and get sucked up into one of those big ovens too!" he chuckled, lightening the mood.

The fire had now dwindled down to just hot embers. Jack and Jimmy were seated opposite one another across the fire pit, and even though Fletch's story did sound far-fetched, they could not help but exchange incredulous glances at each other from across the glowing coals.

The next day there were chores to do back at their own homes, but later they all migrated again back to the cabin where they piled into the Cherry and headed out to the Note. They wound cautiously down the twisting, narrow roads that curled snakelike around the lakeshore. The new Borla exhaust and the ostentatious chrome exhaust pipes made a distinct guttural sound as they prowled into the Note's circus parade and looked for a place to park. Heads turned along with shouts and whistles to welcome them as they cruised by. After at least one obligatory pass through, Jack found a spot toward the back of the rapidly filling lot and quickly grabbed it and took up their routine positions in the truck's bed. It was a prime place to be to take in the whole scene. It wasn't long before they saw Fletch cruise by in his GTO with the same pretty blond curled up next to him. He smiled and winked as he passed by. *Man*, they all thought with envy, *Fletch sure has it made.*

Not Jack, though. He was so preoccupied looking over the scene for Alejandra that he hardly noticed Fletch. He thought he caught a glimpse of her in a crowd of girls heading into the Note, and his heart leaped. But she was too far away, and he caught himself before he bellowed out her name and looked like a clown. He didn't care, though, he just wanted to see her again. "Let's go on in," he said.

"Naw, not yet. This is the best part of the whole thing," said Bobby.

"Are you kiddin'? Meetin' chicks is what it's all about, man!" said Big Schuler. "This is all just part of the prelims."

"Amen, brother, it's gettin' dark. Let's go on in," Joe quipped.

Just as Jack was about to jump down out of the truck's bed, he heard the rumble of the big bikes. As was their custom now, they cruised through the lot loud and slow. Jimmy was in front with Rafe, Randy, and a couple of others strung out behind. Jimmy looked surly. He had a look, and Jack knew that look better than anybody. He had seen it since they were kids. Jimmy wanted a fight. Not just a fight, but a real bad butt-kickin', beat-the-livin'-crap-out-of-someone kind of fight, and that someone better hide. Jack watched as the bikers cruised past a beat-up old Oldsmobile. There was maybe a half-dozen other run-down beaters parked around it.

There was a rough-looking group of kids milling around who looked a lot like their cars, and there were people in an Olds sedan with the doors shut and the windows rolled up.

Someone rolled down one of the windows to throw out an empty beer can. A thick cloud of smoke rolled out as well, the pungent smell of reefer wafting out over the crowd. Jimmy idled, watching. No one inside got out. After a little while, Jimmy moved on toward the back of the lot. There they pulled up and hovered, still watching like a pack of wolves.

Ol' Jimmy was a patient wolf—real patient—but he was a hungry one too, thought Jack, keeping a wary eye on it all as they made their way into the Note.

Remo and some of his buddies were inside. He and Jack greeted each other with big smiles. Jack liked big Remo. He was a good judge of character and felt Remo and his buddies were good guys. Had they gone to the same school and played on the same team, they would have been good friends.

"Hey, brother Hayseed!" Remo said to Jack with a wide smile. "Man! What you been doin'? You boys are brownin' up this summer! Almost catchin' up with big brother Remo. For real, man!" He held up a thick forearm, comparing it with Jack's. He was just about right. Jack's tan was so dark after two solid weeks out in the sun that the skin shades weren't much different. "Hey, man, there's your woman." Remo nodded toward the dance floor just as Jolly Rogers spun up Iron Butterfly's "In-A-Gadda-Da-Vida."

There she was... and she had seen him. She looked every bit as beautiful as she had two weeks before. She wore a light purple silk blouse and blue jeans that fit her as tightly as a leather glove. When she smiled and waved at him, Jack felt himself fall about a thousand feet, no parachute and no bottom in sight. He smiled and held a hand up as if in total surrender. If her just being—living and breathing—wasn't enough, the song seemed to fit her movements like her jeans, accentuating her allure. Her sensuality was infectious. Other girls, including Cassie Kay, Dawn, and Sherrie, had started moving a little more, letting their bodies react more naturally to the intensity of the vibrations. The place was heating up.

"Man, that fine mama's sure got your number, Hayseed. She's movin' like she been takin' lessons from ol' Remo!" Remo exclaimed, laughing as he moved off with a girl of his own on his arm, making his way onto the dance floor.

Jack had barely retained consciousness through it all. Again, he had been mesmerized by her. She maintained eye contact with him as she moved. No matter what the rhythm, she could react to it and move in innocently provocative ways that were all part of her feminine DNA. And despite her appeal and fascination by all the boys, her infectious personality had made her popular with the girls, too, and they had all surrounded her on the floor, laughing, getting loose, and trying their best to move like her. None could, not even the attractive Dawn or Sherrie or even the athletic Cassie Kay, but they were all having a good time, and it was spilling out over the rest of the crowd.

Jack was enjoying watching her, along with everyone else too. She flirted with him, flashing her smile and tossing her hair. Even with her exotic movements, there was a controlled grace to her. But it was the fun she was having, her sheer joy, that was so infectious to everyone—everyone except that group from Torville. They stood around off on their own and kept to themselves.

Jack had taken notice and kept an eye on them, including the one he had had the run-in with two weeks before. Like Fletch had warned, things could happen fast, and if you were caught off guard or were on your own, you could be in trouble. Jack had learned to be aware of his surroundings out on the playgrounds as a kid. Learned to watch his back and keep track of where trouble was moving around.

There was the time not too long after they had been redistricted into the town school. It was a cold, gray winter day. They were having a snowball fight, and Jack had just thrown one and was watching its flight path when one of his friends had shouted, "Look out!" Instinctively, he ducked just as a big hoodlum flew over his back from behind him. He'd gotten back up quickly, but so had the hood. There was a fire and meanness in the kid's face, enraged that his plan to jump Jack had been foiled. Jack got his footing in the snow as best he could and balled up his fists, readying to take the hood on.

Just then, Jimmy stepped in between them. Nobody knew what was going to happen next, but then the bell rang and kids started making a dash for the school. No one wanted to be late getting back into class and lose out on lunch break the next day. But Jack and the hoodlum just held their ground, staring hard at each other. The other kid was bigger than Jack, but Jack still would have fought him. He wasn't bigger than Jimmy, though, and when Jimmy turned on him the boy had backed down and walked off.

Later that day, Jimmy caught the hood hanging out and smoking in the bathroom. Without any trepidation, he walked right up to the kid and pushed him hard. The hood slipped where the floor was wet from melted snow or a broken urinal, and as he tried to get his balance, Jimmy hit him hard with his fist right on the bridge of his nose. Blood spurted everywhere as the hood went down, holding his face. That was it. Jimmy had made his point. "Don't mess with me or any of my buddies, or you'll end up holdin' your bloody face, wallowin' on a filthy, stinkin' bathroom floor," Jimmy had warned. The hoods stayed away from Jimmy from then on, except when Jimmy went looking for them, which he often did. Jack never had any problems with them again, either.

Now Alejandra was walking toward Jack, swaying her hips, pushing her long black hair back, and locking her eyes on his. As she came up to him, she held out her hands, and he took them as she pulled him out onto the dance floor. Oh yes, she was his. She was Jack Dean's girl. He was the luckiest guy in the world.

They spent the evening in the back garden on the bench by the little fountain. They talked and kissed and laughed. Her eyes, her smile, her smell, her feel... her laugh... it was rich and warm. Just one more sweet blessing, like the topping on a beautiful cake, a rich, ripe cherry.

And so the night went. Jack was oblivious to the undercurrents going on in and around them now, but not Jimmy, who was where he liked it, right in the middle of the eye of the storm. In fact, Jimmy *was* the eye of the storm. He had a handle on it all now. He knew the good, the bad and the ugly. The Torville crowd was in his sights. He had been watching them for weeks now, knew they were the ones that had tried to take out Rafe, and knew after the fights a couple of weeks back that they were circling around Jack, and probably Bobby too.

Like a young buck in rut, Jack was distracted and vulnerable, and they were waiting to jump him, just like Fletch had warned. Jimmy had sized it up and knew they were outnumbered. The Torville crowd had continued to grow. They were smelling blood, and up until now, it had been their own. These were low-life people, and sometimes it seemed like their kind grew like flies on a rotting carcass... and right now it looked like Jack was the rotting carcass. He had embarrassed one of their own and they wanted revenge.

The only thing keeping a lid on things was Jimmy. The Torville crowd was well aware of him. They were putting things together too. They knew this living, breathing, brooding nightmare was watching them. They heard the rumbling of his chopper, saw the smoke of his cigarette swirling in their headlights. They knew his reputation. Some of them had known him back in his early football days when he'd annihilated them and left them crawling around on the field, clawing at the grass and looking for their helmets. It was Jimmy Meeks all right, wrong guy to get on the wrong side of. But it was too late as they realized they'd already made their play and hadn't figured out that this Jimmy dude and his crew were connected to those pissant Lake County wusses. Oh well, tough shit for him, man.

Too much fun playing chicken and making his uppity disciples learn to fly as they go careening off some back road.

But Jimmy wasn't alone in his watchfulness. Jack had left Alejandra sitting with Cassie Kay and the other girls while he went to go get some Cokes and popcorn. As he did he saw some of the Torville group meandering around behind him as he stepped up to the counter to place his order.

"Hi Jack," said a familiar voice.

Jack turned to his side and looked up at the large figure, flashing a smile. "Hi, Tom, how are you, man? Good to see you!"

It was Tom Morris from Carlyle, a nearby small town that Jack and his Lake County teammates knew well. The schools were in the same conference and played each other every year in virtually every sport. Tom Morris was one of their best ball players and Jack had heard he had already accepted a scholarship to play college ball. He was a big kid, almost as big as Big Schuler and Jimmy. And like them, he was no one to mess with.

"Good to see you, too, Jack. Dang, you been workin' out? You keep gettin' bigger every time I see you. Hey, you know my buds, don't you?" said Tom, gesturing toward his buddies behind him. Jack reached over and greeted several of the other Carlyle gang with a smile and a firm handshake. "You know any of those jerks over there, Jack?" Tom nodded toward the handful of the Torville crowd milling about nearby.

"No, and I don't want to," said Jack. "Fact is, though, I've had some bad run-ins with them. So have some of my buddies."

"Know what you mean. So have we. They're a bunch of low-lifes if there ever were any. We hate 'em, man. Bunch of drunks and shitheads!" Tom said, raising his voice over the music. "We're not the only ones. So have the guys from over in Easton, and I heard the River Ridge guys have had some run-ins with them too. We all hate 'em. Just want you to know, Jack, that if anythin' goes down with them and you guys, we're in it with you. We'll be around all summer, so we'll be here. We hang out a lot with the Easton guys when we're here, too, so let your buddy Jimmy know we're in on it with you guys."

"Thanks, Tom. Sure can use your help. Every time I see them, there are more of them. Something's gonna happen for sure. Jimmy's going to make it happen. They've been going after his guys, too, and he's going to do something serious about them, and he'll be glad to have you guys helping us out."

Maybe that helped to keep the lid on the pot that night. All was bliss. Jack had told Jimmy about his talk with Tom Morris, and Jimmy started to mix a little more with the Carlyle crew, and even joked around with the guys from Easton and River Ridge too. They all knew who Jimmy was, but not that well, so they welcomed getting to know him. If they were going to all be in a big brawl, it would be good for everyone to know who was who; who all were on the same side and who the friendlies were, even though they all knew who were the bad guys.

Nice girls from nice homes eyed the big biker as he socialized throughout the crowded nightclub. They dreamily crushed on him, wishing he were making social overtures with them. Not-so-nice girls watched him, too, and dreamed how they would crush on him, proper social protocol be damned. But Jimmy wasn't Jack. Socializing wasn't his thing. He wasn't so friendly and didn't have Jack's easygoing nature, or that smile. No girl was going to get Jimmy to dance, not even that pretty Cassie Kay. Jimmy was no dancer, but that didn't matter. They still swooned, but he didn't even seem to notice. He was on a mission. A red alert mission.

What was that old saying about Coral snakes? Red on yellow can kill a fellow, and red on black, good for Jack. So let Jack be. Jimmy would watch his friend's back. Just like old times. Good old buddy Jack. In the worst of it, Jack would be there with him. He could count on that. After all, it was Duke who taught them about that, about having each other's backs, and Jimmy never forgot that lesson. And he could count on his boys, along with Big Schuler, Bobby, Joe, and Fletch, and now, thankfully, it looked like some of these other guys were stand-up dudes and could be counted on as well. But when it did explode—and it would—by the looks of things they would still be way outnumbered. He just wanted to make sure, like Fletch had warned, that they were all together when it happened. Right there at the Note so they could ball themselves up like a fist and not be strung out around the county where they could be taken out piece-meal. Safety in numbers, that was for sure. That's why it had to go down here at the Note. Because when it did, it was going to go down hard.

Everyone lingered late in the parking lot, finishing off warm beers, smoking a last joint or two, or futilely trying to air out the odor of cigarette smoke that had permeated their clothes before going home. The Torville crowd cruised off slowly, warily watching the choppers parked in the back of the lot and out of the lights. Jimmy and the other riders just idled there, cigarettes glowing, sending their message: *Not tonight, pricks, not tonight. But it's gonna happen. We're gonna get you punks one of these days when the time's just right.*

Jack was unaware of all the undercurrents going on in the parking lot, and they had to pull him away from Alejandra as he was far away in la-la land. The two had walked out into the parking lot holding hands and were sitting on the bed of the old truck. They were kissing, laughing and holding each other close. Their innocent kissing had grown more intimate, seeming as natural as if they had always known how to, with Jack naively and awkwardly touching her, exploring her boundaries. They were both oblivious to the revving engines, the bright lights, the loud conversations, and the blaring music. They could have been on another planet, content to stay there until Jack's own buddies came upon them, pulling at him.

"Give it up, Jack!" said Big Schuler, tugging Jack off the truck.

"Say good night, Jack!" Joe laughed.

Jack walked Alejandra over to Cassie Kay's car, where Cassie Kay, Dawn and Sherrie were gathered, patiently waiting for her.

"Nice of you to escort her back to us, Jack, you are such the gentleman!" Cassie Kay teased.

"And we know you were behaving yourself," Dawn teased, wearing a devilish grin and adding a rakish wink of an eye.

"Gee, what have you two been up to anyway?" Sherrie questioned, continuing with the innocent teasing. "You sweet young things!"

"Okay, okay," Jack smiled. "Thanks for waiting on us. Sorry for stealing her away."

"Oh, no problem, sweet prince," Cassie Kay said.

"Yeah, we know she was in good hands!" Dawn exclaimed. They all laughed at Jack's expense as he sheepishly gave Alejandra an awkward good night kiss before she got into the car. He waved as the girls drove off and then walked back to his truck, his thoughts still out on Planet Nirvana.

"Hey, you the guys from Lake County? Which one of you is Jack? Jack Dean?" The voice came from out of the dark just as Jack had met back up with his friends.

"That's me," said Jack casually. The other boys standing around all had to admit that as cautious as they thought they had been, this guy had caught them off their guard and had just walked right up on them in their distraction, watching the Torville procession cruise away.

"We're from Central High. My brother is good buds with yours from back when they were in school. Somehow, I guess they ran into each other over in 'Nam. So my big bro asked me to look you up. He said it had something to do about a favor he owed Duke, something to do about him and his buddies helping my brother and his Central buds out in a big fight out here years ago."

"Yeah, great, good to meet you," Jack smiled at the newcomer and they shook hands. "Remember it well. I was just a kid but saw it all from the back of the truck right here. It was my brother's back then, and he let me and Jimmy Meeks tag along with him that night. Big rumble it was. Duke got his nose broken!"

"Looks timely that we met. We saw what went on out here earlier. Thought we were going to have to pitch in right then and none of you guys would even know who we were. Anyway, that crowd is a bunch of trash! We'd like to kick their ass too… so we'll be around, okay? Getting late and we're heading out but come on down and cruise the big town one of these nights and look me up. My brother said to get to know you guys better, meet some of my buddies."

"Sure, man, and thanks, sounds good," said Jack. They shook hands again before the boy turned and walked back to his car. "Hey!" Jack called after him. "What's your name?"

"Worley!" the kid shouted back before disappearing into the darkness.

Jolly Rogers had keenly watched it all too. He and his off-duty sheriff deputies had begun to figure it all out now. The Torville crowd was bad news. They had always been edgy and looking for trouble, and they had gotten away with a lot of their crap for a long time with no one seriously challenging them. Now there were a lot more of them. This bunch was different, and Jolly knew they were trouble, that big T, the thundercloud. He also knew Jimmy Meeks. He had known him since he was just a kid. He knew Jack Dean, too, and had been friends with Duke back when it was Duke coming to the Note, before he joined the army. Duke would watch out over those kids, keeping an eye on them when he'd have to sneak them out with him so that he could go to the Soul Note whenever he had to babysit on a Friday or Saturday night.

Jolly had lost touch with Jack and his friends after Duke left but had seen them off and on the previous couple of summers. Now they were all grown up and at the very center of it all under the thundercloud, a big thundercloud that was getting bigger and bigger, almost ready to burst. They were good kids, getting caught up in a bad thing. Jimmy, Jolly knew, had a tough-guy reputation and was not someone to mess with. Jack and their other friends could hold their own, too, but Jolly had seen this Torville crowd before. There had been a lot of other ruckuses over the past, just skirmishes really. They were a rough bunch, a big T, if there ever was one. Jolly took a deep breath and let out a long sigh, thankful all had stayed cool that night. *Close*, he thought, *close. Better beef up the security, big time.*

Chapter 11

In small towns and big cities, everyone cruised everywhere. It was just something people did. It was a large part of the social fabric of every community. It was a basic form of communication and interaction, not only within a community but also between communities, as cruising wasn't just limited to the hometown. Cruising in every other town was the custom too. The Beach Boys sang about it as they got around in the early sixties, and Smokey Robinson and The Miracles immortalized it with their hit "Cruisin Together," which everyone was listening to on their radios as they cruised the guts that summer. But cruising had been going on since the early Ford Model T's rolled off the assembly line by the thousands and paraded down Detroit's Woodward Avenue. Showing off the ride and checking out everyone else's was a huge part of it all. Cruising made the world go 'round.

Jack, Joe and Bobby did not waste any time taking Worley up on his offer to cruise the gut at Grand River.

They had cruised there before and were eager to do it again. After all, cruising Lake County's own small main street, while essential to meet up with friends and to see what folks were up to, could get a little mundane after a while. But not Grand River. Outside of the motor city, which was a long way away, Grand River more than held its own as far as size, the views and the action. The big plus was that it was nearby, only about thirty minutes from downtown Lake County.

Grand River's main drag was over twenty blocks long and it was packed, bumper to bumper, with cars of all description. Even the connector streets and the parking spaces lining the streets were packed. Horns and music blared throughout the gut as the Cherry crept along at a snail's pace. The boys were mesmerized at each passing vehicle. Whether it was one of the coveted muscle cars or a run of the mill four-door sedan filled with pretty girls, the boys were like kids in a candy store. At least Bobby and Joe were. Jack saw it as a business trip.

Since meeting Worley, Jack knew the least they could do was to accept the offer the kid had made and look him and his buddies up on their home turf. If they were going to get into a major rumble with some serious bad guys and ask these guys to get into it with them, then reaching out this way to get to know them better was the smart thing to do. Even though Jack would much rather have seen Alejandra that night, this just had to be done. It was part of Jimmy's grand plan: make friends and form an alliance, just like Grandpa Meeks had told them about. Even Jimmy was coming out of his surly shell. Folks were beginning to see a friendlier side of him that only Jack had known back when they were kids.

Grand River was different than other guts. The city council had determined that due to the large crowds and sheer number of vehicles that jammed the main street almost every night of the week now, some restrictions had to be put into place. In addition to bulking up the police force and creating a two o'clock in the morning curfew, all modes of transportation would only be allowed to pass through the main street three times in a row. After the three times, they had to leave the gut for at least thirty minutes. Then they were allowed to cruise again for another three passes.

At first, the three-pass ordinance met with a lot of opposition amongst the cruising crowd. There were also a lot of skeptics. Everyone wondered how the thing was going to be enforced or even if it could be enforced. But to everyone's amazement, it was, and strictly, as both the mobile police and those on foot became expertly adept at identifying each and every vehicle. Three times and you're out! Here's your warning, now here's your ticket. Then, after a while, everyone started to see the positives of it, if not the brilliance. For one thing, it opened the gut up to more cruisers so there was more flow, activity and variety. But what made it all the more interesting was that by being limited to pass through only three times, cruisers had to find something else to do for those thirty minutes they were banned. That basically meant getting out of their cars and going into restaurants, ice cream shops, and arcades. Not only was this profitable for merchant's, but it created a whole new social scene downtown for cruisers. They actually ended up meeting other cruisers instead of just staring at each other or making faces through their cars' windows as they passed by.

The boys were on their second pass when they cruised by an older model Chevy Bel Air heading in the opposite direction. The Cherry had been attracting attention with its gleaming dark red paint and brightly chromed exhaust pipes that curled up over and behind the cab of the truck. The sound the pipes made alone turned heads and this may have been what turned the heads of the three girls in the Bel Air as it passed by.

Bobby, on lookout, didn't hesitate to lean up and out over the passenger side window and blurt out, "Hey, hi! How you all doin'? Hey, we're on our number two. How about meetin' up with us?"

The girls all laughed loudly as one of them shouted back out of a lowered window, "Good for you! Better take care of your number twos by yourselves!"

"What? Bobby, that was the worst line ever, man!" Joe said as he and Jack just laughed and shook their heads. "Better let me have the window so you can take some notes."

"No way!" Bobby said, defending himself. "I'm just warmin' up. They were foxes! Let's look for them on the way back. I think they liked me!" Turning back around at the end of the main drag and heading back down the same street in the opposite direction, after a while they saw the same group of girls. "Hey, hi again! Okay, okay, good one. Ouch! Got me good! Here's your arrow. You're a good shot! Arrow got me good!" Bobby added an animated pouting expression on his face and faked tears. This seemed to catch the girls off guard and lowered their somewhat feigned antagonism.

"Oh, we're so sorry!" one of the girls hollered back. "Was funny, though! We like your truck!" *And you guys are kind of cute too,* the girls thought. "Okay, meet us over at the Green Onion. It's on North Capitol!"

Jack knew right where the Green Onion was. He'd been to it several times before with his family on visits to the city. It was well known for its malts and cheeseburgers and had been at the same location for many years. While a quaint and casual place to take the family for a burger in the evening, later in the night it became a popular hangout for the younger crowd and was generally packed by cruisers, especially on the weekends. But they got lucky this night. Magically a parking spot opened up just down the street, and as they entered the crowded restaurant the girls were already seated in a large, round booth near the front, waiting for them. Bobby took the initiative and handled the introductions as the boys slid themselves into the booth.

They were pretty girls, or "foxes", like Bobby had said, and friendly, too, thankfully, as the boys were definitely feeling as though these girls were out of their league. And they were.

"Where are you boys from? We haven't seen you around here before," said Sheila, one of the blonds.

"Lake County," Bobby piped up, eager to have the opening for a conversation and get over his nervousness. All the boys were feeling the nerves, too, and even though the girls were being friendly and all smiles, there was an underlying coolness to them which added to the boys' uneasiness.

"Lake County? Is that why you drive a truck?" Sheila asked in a teasing tone. The girls all giggled at the cutting insinuation that the boys were from a small farm town. This really hit a nerve with the boys, and while they laughed right along with the girls, it still stung. But it served the purpose of putting the boys in their place, tempering their enthusiasm and adding even more to their awkwardness.

"It's my truck," Jack spoke up, a little offended by the girl's remark. "I like it just fine. Gets us where we want to go, and I think it looks good doing it too."

"Oh, Sheila's just giving you guys a hard time," said Donna, the intriguing brunette sitting opposite to Jack. "I like your truck too. We all do. It's what caught our eye," she added, glancing slyly at Bobby. "Something you don't see or hear every day around here. It certainly stands out in a crowd." Her eyes remained fixed on Bobby.

This attention emboldened Bobby and helped him regain some of his composure. But just as he was about to chime back into the awkward conversation, the waitress made her appearance and asked what they would all like to order. The boys gentlemanly let the girls order first, all of them ordering cheeseburgers and Cokes. Jack and Bobby both ordered the same, making the order easy for the waitress.

Everyone was bemused over her feigned concentration, which she next directed at Joe. "And how about you, big fella?" she asked.

"Well," Joe said, hesitating slightly, still unsure about what he wanted to order. "I think I'll have the cheeseburger too... and a glass of milk, please."

"Milk?" the waitress asked, almost in shock. "Milk..." she repeated before plastering on an exaggerated smile and adding, "Uh, okay, I'm sure we still have some. Large or small?"

"Uh, large, please." Joe smiled widely, his cheeks flushed.

After the waitress left to place their orders, the booth remained silent. No one knew what to say. The girls just looked stunned. *Milk? Did he just order a glass of milk?* they all thought. On the verge of bursting into laughter, they couldn't quite comprehend if the guy was serious or just being a prankster.

Jack and Bobby were speechless as they stared blankly over at Joe. *Milk? Joe, are you kidding, milk? Oh, come on, Joe! Milk? Look at these chicks, Joe. Milk? You want to go out and find a cow and milk it too? Better yet, Farmer Joe, how about we just bring one along with us in the back of our old farm truck?* both boys thought.

"What? So I like milk." Joe shrugged.

"Yeah, good for you, Joe," said Patty, the other blond. "And it *is* good for you. Keep you nice and healthy. It helps to build strong bones and muscles too. You look like a nice, healthy, clean-cut kind of boy too." She winked at him.

Jack couldn't tell if she was sincere, or just being facetious and playing with Joe, but there was that "boy" word again, as if to emphasize "little boy." But it didn't seem to bother Joe. He was so smitten by her looks, he just sat there and grinned at her, starry-eyed.

It wasn't long before their order came, with the waitress making a dramatic deliverance in placing everyone's cheeseburgers and Cokes down in front of them. Joe's was last, and she seemed to take a particular pleasure in making a ceremony of placing the tall glass of milk down in front of him and offering him an extra napkin, silently gesturing he use it to wipe off any residue he might get on top of his lip. With an exaggerated wink of an eye, she walked off, and everyone laughed again, which helped to further ease the tension. Everyone enjoyed their meal as they engaged in small talk and friendly banter.

"So, what brings you guys down here to our fair city?" asked Sheila, sipping at the remains of her Coke.

Bobby, swallowing the last bite of his burger, responded quickly and, he thought, gallantly, "To meet you nice ladies."

"Oh, that's sweet, but don't you guys have any girlfriends back in Lake County?"

"Oh, yeah," Bobby spouted back. "Jack here does. A real pretty girl, too, almost as pretty as you girls. Ain't that right, Jack?"

"Well, actually, we're down here looking for a guy named Worley. He goes to Central," said Jack, looking directly at Bobby.

"You mean BTW or BMW?" asked Patty. "Are you looking to meet up with him as a friendly thing or a not so friendly thing?"

"Oh?" Jack wasn't sure what she meant by BTW or BMW. However, one did sound familiar to him. "No, as a friendly thing. I mean… we're friends of his and just wanted to look him up while we're here. He said to if we got down this way sometime."

"Okay, had to ask, they're friends of ours too. BTW is over in Vietnam and BMW, the younger one, just walked in the door behind you," Patty said.

BMW? Jack thought, turning to see the big Worley kid and his friends as they entered the restaurant. They recognized him right off.

"Hey, Jack! Cool, man, didn't take you guys long to come on down here. See you met some of our nice local lady friends. They have a way of attracting attention," Worley said.

"Yeah, man, they sure do, been real friendly to us. We've enjoyed meeting them," said Jack. The girls all smiled as they worked themselves out from the booth.

"Excuse us, we're going to go powder our noses now and let you boys be boys. It was very nice to have met you gentlemen. You all come back now, you hear?" Sheila teased in a mock Southern belle accent. As the girls passed by, a strong smell of perfume wafted around the boys.

"Yeah, and thanks for the dinner, too, boys. Nice meeting you and hope to see you around sometime. Don't be strangers now, you hear?" Donna added, mimicking Sheila.

With the girls out of sight, the boys all glanced at each other, miffed by the whole thing. They wondered at how adroitly they had been bedeviled by these pretty city girls and their sweet smiles. *Foxy for sure, and in more ways than one*, the boys all realized.

"Now you see what we have to deal with? That's why we head out to the Soul Note. Meet some nice homespun girls for a change… city girls, man. Anyway, cool you guys came down and we could meet up. I'm Big Mac Worley, friends call me BMW, and these are my buddies." Worley, or now "BMW," gestured to the boys beside him. "Good to meet you guys. So, looks like we have some things in common, like those Torville jerks. But hey, I'm starving, let's grab a seat."

As they meeted and greeted over a burger session, Jack told the story again about how his older brother, Duke, had given in and started taking him and his friend Jimmy to the Soul Note on the rare occasion he had to play the babysitter. BMW already knew most of the story from his brother BTW, so it was mostly for the benefit of the other Central High guys. Jack realized this and emphasized the friendship between Duke's Lake County and BTW's Central High buds, and that it was Lake County that night that had backed up the Central High guys in the brawl. Duke had said that someone from Torville back then had said something disrespectful to one of the Central High guys' girlfriend, and that was how it all started.

With the groundwork laid, the Central High guys agreed that they were all on the same side, and that throwing in with the Lake County guys was the right thing to do. They wanted to return the support their older brothers had welcomed and needed in that long-ago brawl. Plus, they'd had enough of their own issues with the "Torville trash," as BMW called them. Now was the time to pitch in and put them down once and for all, so a new ally was gained. Jimmy would be pleased.

Chapter 12

The Lake County fair was the event of the summer. Everyone went to the fair. It had it all: animals, 4-H'ers, tractor pulling, harness racing, and of course, the carnival. The loud, garishly lighted midway with its variety of food stands, game booths, and rides was the centerpiece. An exciting and mysterious world onto itself, the carnival was, for young and old alike, akin to Christmas in July.

With Big Schuler's connections, Jack and his buddies were among the fortunate few who got part-time jobs working for the fairgrounds during the couple of weeks in July when the fair took place. They worked the entry gates and directed parking, as well as hawked Cokes, popcorn, and cotton candy in the grandstands. It wasn't much money, but to them it was the best job in the world. They got to see all their friends, hang around the midway, get free rides, and check out all the girls. All the things they would be doing anyway, but this way they got paid for it. It sure beat baling more hay, and for at least a couple weeks, they were local rock stars. Plus, they needed the extra cash to help make up for all the dough they dropped picking up the tab for the Grand River girls, and as it ended up, Big Mac Worley and his buddies too.

The carnival always fascinated folks and being a part of its action and its backstage was an experience in itself for the boys: the lights, the sounds, the smells, the screams, the blaring music, and the rides that reached up into the heavens. These were the carnivals of old. The stage shows were an alluring mixture of forbidden no-no peep shows under large tents, and various exotic oddities of all sorts.

Barkers were on outdoor stages, gathering their crowds with their booming, obnoxious microphones. "She can walk, she can talk, she can do it all, if ya know what I mean! Hey, fella! Yeah, you there with your hands in your pockets. What're you playing with in there? Does your wife know you do that? Ha, ha, ha! Well, don't worry, I won't tell, will we, right, everybody?" He added an exaggerated wink with one of his eyes and waggled an index finger back and forth. An old farmer wearing faded bib overalls walked by. "Hey, pardner, want to borrow my mule? He's got five legs, and his butt is where his head's supposed to be. Know what his name is?" The farmer, his attention grabbed, chuckled and shook his head. "His name's Butthead!" the barker exclaimed. Loud laughter and gestures followed as the farmer meandered on down the midway, smiling, laughing, and shaking his head.

There was the obligatory three-headed pony, and the five-footed rabbit that could hop over a horse. For a quarter, you could walk behind a curtain and see the famous Annie, the biggest cow in the world. Then there were the human stars of the show: Big Jubal the Giant, Wanda the Tattooed Lady, Lavenia the Snake Lady, and a variety of hardened show girls. They were all an intriguing and welcomed distraction to the hot, boring, work-a-day midsummer. The boys got to know them all. Inevitably, during their work shifts, they would share a stool next to them in the food tents or take a break with them out in the back under a shade tree by their trailers.

The Snake Lady captivated them the most. Her gig was to sit on a stool under the floor of a flatbed trailer with a hole for her pretty head to stick up through. Ingeniously, an amazingly lifelike but altogether fake anaconda body was coiled up around her neck, creating the illusion of a giant snake with the head of a beautiful woman. Adding to the illusion and surreal effect, an arm was inserted into the end of the snake's body, enabling it to be swirled slowly around. For only a quarter, the curious and gullible could file by her, amazed and shocked at how real she appeared. All were taken aback by her exotic Cleopatra-like beauty. Lavenia would occasionally engage the onlookers in conversation, asking them if they would care to dance or light a cigarette for her. Even when everyone realized it was all a very sly ruse and that they had been cleverly parted from their quarter, most were so captivated by the apparition no one seemed to mind very much.

The boys interacted with and got to know all the carnival folks throughout the two weeks the fair operated and developed a friendly association with them. The boys eagerly earned some extra cash helping out with various chores around the rides and booths, and the ride operators gave them all the free rides they could handle.

One night, after the carnival had closed down, Jack was raking up debris from the day around the Snake Lady's trailer when he noticed something shiny glinting off one of the muted overhead lights. He bent down and picked up the object. It was a silver cigarette lighter with a yellow emblem that looked like a shield with a small black horse and prominent black stripe embossed on it. At first, he thought he would turn it in to the lost and found at the fairgrounds, but then noticed the lights were still on at the backside of the trailer behind the high canvas mural advertisement of the Snake Lady, so he decided to walk around and see if anyone had lost it. The Eagles' "Witchy Woman" was blaring out over the empty fairgrounds as he ducked under the canvas. Tables and lawn chairs had been arranged haphazardly under the canopy of some large shade trees. Big Jubal the Giant and Wanda the Tattooed Lady were playing a hand of double solitaire at one of the tables.

Lavenia the Snake Lady was leisurely filing her fingernails on one of the reclining lawn chairs. "Well hi, Jack," she said, upon noticing his presence. "Welcome. Like some iced tea, dear? I declare, it's still as hot here tonight as it gets back down in Tennessee. Help yourself." He poured himself some in a paper cup and sat down under the shade.

"You boys work here every year?" Wanda asked. "Sure is a friendly place. We always like our stay here. No one seems to mind too much us takin' their money." She giggled.

Lavenia just smiled. Her eyes looked glassy to Jack, but they always seemed to. She wore tight sequin blue jeans and red cowboy boots, a long-sleeved white shirt, and a matching sequin blue jean vest. She was a distinctively beautiful brunette, and she wore her hair in a bouffant style, more in fitting with the fifties or early sixties.

"I was just doing some raking up out front and found this lighter there in the pile," Jack said, holding up the lighter. "Just thought I'd check to see if any of you might have lost it?"

Lavenia's eyes lit up in amazement. "Oh, Jack, you found it! My lighter! Oh, we've all been looking over the whole place for it! Oh, my lighter! Oh, you found it! Bless your heart! Oh, gosh, here I am doing my nails, but let me give you a great big hug. That's all right, you come on over here, I don't bite!"

"Oh, yes, she does!" piped up Wanda.

"Well, okay, maybe I do, just a little, but just out of affection," said Lavenia, trying to hug Jack without touching him with her still wet fingernails. "Here, with my nails all wet, Jack, would you be so kind as to light me a cigarette with my new found lighter?" She nodded toward a pack of cigarettes on a table next to her. Jack didn't smoke but somehow managed to light it for her. She giggled as she saw how nervously he did so. "You boys are so cute," she teased him. "You're all such innocent darlings. It must be nice to be so innocent. I was once, you know?"

"That sure must've been a while ago," Big Jubal chimed in, with a roar befitting the giant he was.

"Oh, hush now, Big. I don't want young Jack here to get the wrong impression of me." She giggled demurely.

"Oh, somehow I don't think he will." Big Jubal winked and grinned.

"Well, you be nice," she scolded, exhaling and blowing little smoke rings upwards. Everyone watched as they floated up into the lower branches overhead and just seemed to hover there. "Bet you can't do that, can you, Big Jubal? All you do is just put your lips together and blow, gently like." She pursed her ruby red lips seductively. "I wish you would come back to Tennessee with us, Jack. I believe I'd like to get to know you better. You got a girl?" Jack nodded. "I bet she's real pretty. I hope she's sweet to you, Jack. You're such a nice boy. You know, there are women out there in the world who'd just love to take advantage of a nice boy like you, if you know what I mean." She winked wickedly at him and giggled again. "I just hope she's sweet. Just like little ol' me… once upon a time."

"Well, then, don't go corruptin' him and makin' him start smokin' just so he can light your cigarettes," said Wanda.

"Oh, fiddle, Wanda. Jack's not going to start smoking. He's an athlete. He's as pure and sweet as hive honey, aren't you, Jack? But he should learn how to light a girl's cigarette. It's just part of him being a gentleman, which he is, for gosh sakes."

"Well, you just let him go on stayin' as pure and sweet as hive honey, Lavenia. Folks here won't be so friendly toward us if we come up here every year and start corruptin' their sweet, innocent young boys before they ever get a chance to corrupt their sweet, innocent young daughters."

"Oh, land's sake, Wanda. Sometimes the thoughts that come out of that pretty head of yours are truly shocking, truly shocking." Lavenia turned her attention back to polishing her nails. "Jack, anyone ever call you 'Jackie'?" she asked softly, almost in a whisper. "I've always liked that name. I had me a Jackie once. He was my high school sweetheart. He was so sweet too. We got hitched right after graduation. Then he got drafted and went off to Vietnam. I kissed him goodbye real nice and long. I still remember that kiss as my best one ever. God, I loved my Jackie. He was so good and fine. Then he got killed over there and he never came back to me."

It all went silent for a moment. Even the background carnival rock music that seemed to always be blaring had shut down. "I gave him that lighter just before he left, bought it for him out there in Texas, at Fort Hood," Lavenia continued. "See, look here, it's got his old group on it, 1st Cavalry. Pretty, isn't it? The gold shield with the little horse head and big black stripe on it. It's so shiny. They gave it back to me with some of his other things, like letters I'd written to him... and such," she said softly. Tears welled up in her big brown eyes and silently trickled down her cheeks and onto her blouse. Her hands began to shake as she concentrated on putting the brush back into the bottle before the tears overwhelmed her and began to flow freely.

Wanda came over and put her arms around Lavenia and handed her a handkerchief. "There, there," Wanda said. "Just let 'em flow, honey, let 'em flow. They been needin' to flow again for a long time now, so you just let 'em go now."

Jack didn't know what to do, so he just stood there, listening to the Snake Lady weep. He started to leave quietly, but stopped and managed to mumble, "I'm sorry for your loss, Lavenia. I'm sure he was a really great guy. If you ask me, he was a real lucky guy too."

She looked up as he turned to walk away. "You're a nice, sweet boy, Jackie. He was too. You stay that way now, you hear? And thank you so much for finding my—his—lighter for me."

The next day Jack was working one of the main grandstand gates. It was actually just a rope that kept people from just casually walking back and forth across the dirt racetrack from the infield parking lot to get to the grandstands. When there was nothing going on, people just casually walked across the track, but when the harness races were running, or a tractor pull was going on, one of the boys—this time it was Bobby—worked the gate or the rope by the stands, and another worked the rope directly across the track. Mostly it was a routine and boring job. A better job was working the grandstands selling Cokes, popcorn and hot dogs. Doing this, on top of their two dollars an hour, they could make some tips.

The day had grown even hotter and Jack wished there was some shade. The trotters were out warming up. They made a big clatter as they rampaged past, their hooves kicking up dirt with their awkward prancing. When a group of them would clear on by, the boys would open the gate or lower the rope and let folks cross. It was usually routine, but sometimes the horses came up unpredictably fast as they came from around a blind spot where one of the big carnival trailers was parked too close to the tracks fence in the infield. It was getting near race time and the stands were filling up. There were more people having to wait at the gates to cross over the track. They were getting antsy as they waited, worried they wouldn't get a good seat.

"*Hola*, Jack, *como esta*?" It was Alejandra, and she looked stunning in a red and blue plaid blouse with snug blue jeans.

Lord, what a pretty girl, Jack thought, just staring helplessly at her. His face lit up. "What a pleasant surprise," he said, and then thought to himself how much he sounded like a lady at a church circle. His nervous system was ramping up into overdrive, choking out any rational thinking on his part. He just stood there marveling at her. Her black hair was pulled back into a ponytail, showing off those high cheekbones, those dark eyes, that smile with those white teeth, those lips…

"Jack! Jack Dean!" called a familiar girlish voice. Jack managed to take his eyes off Alejandra to look over across the track to Bobby's gate. There was a crowd gathered on that side, waiting to cross on over the track when the coast was clear. They were pressing against Bobby's rope, figuring to get a good start out of the gate. When Bobby decided it was safe, he would let the rope down, but before doing so, he turned and bent down to pick up a woman's hat that had blown off. It was Jessie Meeks, Jimmy's little sister. She had wormed her way right up to the front and was waving around a big blue ribbon.

"Look what Flower won! She won first place!" she exclaimed. Before Jack could answer, Jessie, in all her excitement, darted under the rope and out onto the track, running toward him, Flower's blue ribbon flapping in the wind.

Jack knew the trotters were swiftly bearing down the track toward her and that the harness drivers on their sulkies being pulled behind the horses could not see clearly in front of them, if at all. Realizing Jessie's peril, he dashed toward her. He could hear the horses galloping and feel the ground rumbling from their flailing hoofs. Jessie suddenly stopped and screamed as Jack dove desperately toward her, tackling her and rolling out of the way just as one of the big horses splattered by, its deadly hooves thrashing perilously close around them, yet miraculously sparing them any harm.

Jessie was crying now. Jack was afraid he had crushed her or that the horse had stomped on her after all. He gently started to lift her up as Bobby ran over to help. Everyone around them, including the crowd packing the stands, cheered when Jessie appeared to just be shaken up and not injured. As Jack stood and lifted her up gingerly, she held on tightly to him, shaking and crying. The blue ribbon was still out on the track, crushed by a hoof. Bobby darted out and grabbed it before another one of the trotters could further pulverize it. He tried to clean it off and smooth it out as best as he could before he handed it back to Jessie. Someone handed Jack a clean hankie, and he did his best to wipe her tears and calm her down.

She was still clinging to him when Grandma Meeks and Katie ran frantically up to them. Jessie cried even harder when she saw them and reached out to Grandma Meeks' outstretched arms. The two women were visibly shaken. They had been walking with Jessie when Grandma Meeks stopped by the Grange tent to buy a cherry pie and chat with old friends. Jessie, still excited about her ribbon, saw Jack and just took off running toward him.

Grandma Meeks' hug had a calming effect. "Everything's all right now. There, there," she said. The crowd was still applauding, but Jack was oblivious to it all.

"Jack Dean saved me Grandma!" Jessie sobbed. "I didn't even see that big horse. When I did, I thought he was gonna knock me down and run over me, just like Grandpa getting run over in that war."

Tears welled up in Grandma Meeks' own eyes now. "Oh, Jack, thank you! Thank you!" She hugged him tightly. Katie thanked and hugged him too.

He smiled. "Shoot, that's okay. I'm just glad you're all right, Jessie." They all thanked him again and gave him another big hug. Then Grandma Meeks said they needed to go wash Jessie's face and clean her up some.

"Bye-bye, Jack Dean," Jessie said, waving back at him and Bobby from Katie's arms. "Thanks for saving me! And thanks, Bobby, for saving Flower's ribbon!"

"Oh, Jack, that was the most amazing thing I have ever seen!" Jack heard her voice before he saw her and turned around just as Alejandra ran up to him. "You are a hero! You are just so wonderful!" She hugged him tightly, tears in her eyes. "I was just frozen. I couldn't move. I thought that big horse was going to run over that little girl, and then there you were!"

"Oh, heck," Jack said, still trying to catch his breath as he brushed the dirt off and tucked in his T-shirt. "Everything's all right now. I'll be getting off work in a little while. How about we go hit the midway and do some rides? I'll meet you at that tent right over there in thirty minutes, okay?" Jack pointed to the Grange tent near the stands.

When he met back up with her, they had both calmed down quite a bit and were ready to have some fun and just enjoy each other's company. Jack knew the midway pretty well by now. The boys helped out the carnies when they weren't working for the fairgrounds, just doing odd jobs. It got them free rides and gave them a chance to get to know the traveling carnival workers.

Word of Jack's heroics had spread. Several people came up and shook his hand or yelled "Atta boy!" or "Way to go!" as they walked along. Many of the "Game of Chance" booths that had already taken a good amount of Jack's and his friends' money, somehow worked it out so that Jack seemed like the luckiest guy in world, and it wasn't too long before Jack and Alejandra were swamped with stuffed animals.

They were having the time of their lives. With Creedence Clearwater Revival, The Doors, The Rolling Stones, Three Dog Night, War, and Mountain blaring in the background, they held onto each other, spinning and laughing from one ride to the next. It was the most fun he'd ever had. Later in the evening, after they had found their friends and deposited the stuffed animals in Cassie Kay's car, they had quietly wandered off behind one of the livestock barns. They sat down on a hay bale, holding hands and talking. He asked questions, wanting to know more about her. What her life was like back in Spain, her school, her friends, her classes, and her family. He wanted to know everything about her.

She responded eagerly with answers both in English and Spanish. In between, she asked those same questions of Jack. Off in the distance, the midway was winding down, and so was the music, as the slow, sad, melancholy Smokey Robinson and The Miracles song "Ooo Baby Baby" wafted over the fairgrounds. The remorseful ballad of love mistreated and lost were soulfully embodied in the haunting lyrics.

"Is love always so sad?" Alejandra asked, looking into his eyes.

Jack didn't know what to say. He'd never been in love before, nor had he ever thought much about it. He just stared back into those large inviting eyes.

"Are you afraid of love, Jack?" she asked, pronouncing the "J" much more distinctly now.

Again, he was speechless, still lost, gazing into those dark pools. Spontaneously, he kissed her, and she kissed him back. After a little while, she brought things under control. She leaned back away from him, smiled softly, and throatily said that she needed to go find Cassie Kay. It wasn't what Jack wanted to hear, but he knew the reality of the situation. What he really wanted to hear was, "I'm yours, all yours, forever, you and me. We'll be all alone someday. You can take me then, and never give me up... forever." But this was now, and he respected her wishes, so he stood up and helped brush the hay chaff off her, while she brushed her hair and straightened herself up. They held hands, laughed, and teased each other as he walked her to Cassie Kay's car.

Cassie Kay, Dawn, and Sherrie were placidly hanging out around her big Ford Crown Victoria with about a half-dozen boys around them, including Bobby, Joe, and Big Schuler. The girls were all holding several stuffed animals that their admirers had won for them. They probably just spent a good portion of their summer's earnings, all of them futilely vying for each lady's affections.

Jack kissed Alejandra lightly and waved her goodbye. He watched her go. One of these nights, one of these nights... he couldn't help himself from daydreaming. And then he wondered if it was all just a dream. That *she* was only a dream, but a real life one that he could touch, kiss, dream of... A real sweet dream.

He had managed to get his nerve up, sitting there on the hay bale with her, the horses looking on, and asked her if she would like to go to a movie or something. She had smiled and looked him straight in his eyes with those big brown ones of hers. "Thank you, Jack. You are very sweet to ask me, and I would love to go with you very much. But would it be nice if Cassie Kay could go with us too? You see, my parents have not given me their permission yet to go out with a boy without my friends to go with me. I hope they will meet you someday. I know they will like you and approve of my seeing you. It would be so very nice."

Unbeknownst to Jack, Lavenia had seen his heroics. She had been at the Grange tent and was walking back to the trailers when she glanced over at the track and watched the whole scene in disbelief: the little girl's horrific screams, Jack running and tackling her, the horse's hooves flailing and almost trampling over them, clumps of dirt flying everywhere... and then the little girl and Jack standing up somehow unscathed. She watched as he picked up and held the frantic, crying child, and then swiftly carried her off the track, while a throng of people had rushed up and surrounded them. Soon an elderly woman, who had been standing right next to Lavenia, ran over, crying out the child's name. The crowd parted to let her through and she wrapped the little girl in her arms, tears rolling down her face. "A miracle!" someone near Lavenia exclaimed. "A dadgum miracle it is!"

Lavenia recognized the elderly woman working in the Grange tent the next day. Surmising there was a familial relationship between the older woman and the young girl, she felt herself compelled to want to speak with her. "Excuse me, ma'am," she began, "I just wanted to say that I saw the entire event yesterday, and I believe I witnessed a miracle. Is that little girl your granddaughter? You must have been in a terrible state of fright."

"Oh, goodness me, yes, I surely was, dear. I believe it was a miracle too! The good Lord was watching out over my little darling, and His angels worked their miracle with Jack being there to save her. That Jack... he never even thought about his own self at all, not for a split second."

"Do you really believe it was God's doing?"

"Oh, *yes*," the elderly woman said. "It was His doing all right, without any doubt in the whole wide world."

"I wish I could believe like that," Lavenia said quietly, almost to herself, shaking her head slowly.

"Oh, but you can, dear, you can!" She reached into her purse and pulled out a small Bible. "Here, you take this, dear. Read about Him. He'll know you're searching for Him, and He'll find you. Trust me. He will find you, and then you will know how to believe in His miracles too."

Lavenia took the little book and held it reverently in both her hands. "Why, thank you, ma'am. You are very kind, but I couldn't take your own Bible."

As she started to hand it back, the elderly woman wrapped her own two hands gently around Lavenia's. "It's yours now. I know it by heart, and I'd like you to have it for your own. It has been a great comfort to me. You know, we lost little Jessie's mother, my wonderful daughter-in-law, a little while back. I just don't know what I would have done if I didn't have Him in my life to reach out to and be loved and embraced by. I just don't know how I could have gotten through."

Lavenia saw the lasting hurt and glow of love in the elderly woman's eyes. They glistened with a fine layer of tears as she seemed to look deep into Lavenia's soul. "I can tell you have a good and kind soul. I can see it in your eyes. You'll find it all in the book. And when you do, you'll find Him too."

"Thank you so much, ma'am. I will treasure it, and I will read it. I will. I promise you for your kindness."

"Bless you, child, and He will too. Trust me and trust in Him."

Jack didn't see much of Lavenia, Big Jubal, or Wanda again for the next few days. One afternoon he'd gone over to the Grange tent on his lunch break and sat down on a stool just a couple of the stools down from Big Jubal, who took up practically two of the stools on his own. The large man was just about halfway through a large piece of cherry pie. Jack could see by an empty plate, which had yet to be cleared away, that Big Jubal had ordered the special, an impressive dish of roast beef, mashed potatoes and green beans, and was now eating his dessert.

"How's business?" Jack asked pleasantly.

"Not bad, Jack, my friend, not bad at all! You know, there are pluses for a plus-size guy like me," he said, laughing. "Say, can't beat the special today! No way I'll ever lose an ounce in this gig. Every one of these county fair deals we do, there's always these Grange tents, and it's the best cookin' for the best price you'll ever find. That roast beef is fabulous, and I believe this cherry pie is the best I've ever had. They say it won the blue ribbon and I can see why. My lord, it's good!" He took another bite and stared off down toward the midway. Jack ordered a cheeseburger during the lull in the conversation.

"You know, Jack, Lavenia… she's really not as much of a vixen as she makes out to be. It's just her way of kiddin' around, I think, lightenin' up things, so to speak. She mostly keeps pretty quiet and stays to herself. Reads a lot, you know? She was one of the prettiest gals anyone's ever seen back when she first started up with us. People say that, at one time, she was a shoo-in for Miss Tennessee. 'Course I'm from Alabama, and everybody knows Alabama girls are the prettiest there is in the whole world, but I gotta admit, Lavenia could sure hold her own with any of 'em, maybe even more so. But that's been a little while back now."

"She was pretty messed up. One of those small town high school things, you know? Cheerleader and homecomin' queen. He was a mister all-star everythin', a real good guy, too, from what I hear. His gettin' killed over in 'Nam really shook her up bad, as it would anyone. Sent her to a real deep place. One thing not too many folks knew was that she was expectin'. She lost the baby and that crushed her up even more. You know, she reached out for somethin', and it was some bad stuff she got ahold of or that got ahold of her. She's still strugglin' with it all, dealin' with loss, and then the demons, man. Lot of us have 'em. When ol' Beelzebub gets hold of you, he don't ever like to let go. It's a fearful thing, you know, when he's got ahold of you. But he ain't never got to her heart—or her soul, neither. Not really, she just comes off as the bad girl 'cause I think that way she's maybe lookin' like she's bad like 'em, like she's on the dark side with 'em, too, you know? It's so the demons will be nice to her, I suppose, maybe leave her alone some."

"But, you know, she came to Sunday mornin' service, even had a little bitty Bible in her hand someone had given to her. She told everyone she saw you rescue that little girl. Said it was some kind of a miracle what you did. You did damn good, Jack. Who knows? You may have saved more than one soul with what you did." Big Jubal paused, still staring down at his plate and the last few remnants of the pie. "Anyway, you can tell she's wantin' to get straight somehow, but it's just awful damn hard to do, you know?" He finished his pie just as Jack's cheeseburger arrived, and with some gyrating, he managed to work himself up off the stool. He stretched, and as he started to walk off, he put his massive hand down heavily on Jack's shoulder. "You're a good kid, Jack, and your gal, she's awful pretty too. Seems real sweet. You be good to her, you hear? Not hard to see that she's got a big heart, too, just like our Lavenia."

Chapter 13

The long hot days made the week pass slowly. The next most exciting event occurred on one steaming night down on the crowded midway. Like at many county fairs, one of the most popular sideshows was the water tank dunk. For charity, a local celebrity—maybe the mayor or the sheriff or a popular teacher or coach—would sit precariously on a narrow ledge above a large tank of water. There they would do their best to entice onlookers and passersby to donate a dollar to a good cause and take their chances throwing three baseball size balls at a bullseye target. If the ball hit its mark, the ledge would give way and, with much commotion, in would plunge the sitting duck celebrity.

An enthusiastic crowd had gathered around the tank as one of the high school's most popular teachers, Mr. Hansen, was doing his best to antagonize anyone within earshot. He was still sitting high and dry despite the many unsuccessful attempts to dunk him. He was good at his job, drawing in a large crowd and the attention of other passersby with his invectives. "Hey, chubby! Yeah, you! Can you do the twist? Come on, give it a try, what's a buck? You're gonna lose all that baby fat come two-a-days! Think you'll be a real ladies man, don't you? Gonna get all the girls, are you?" Just then, Jimmy, Rafe, and Randy were strolling by and the hapless coach saw his next victims. "Hey! You there, Mr. Cool! You, too, little man. How about you, Dumbo? You could fly with those ears, I bet! How about it? Come on, now, give it a shot. Are you all chicken? Come on, now. *Brawk, brawk!* Yeah, you there, Stretch Gumby! I'll bet your arms could touch the ground! Better duck so your head doesn't bump into a cloud!" Muted chuckles came from a feeble few of bystanders in the large crowd.

All three boys stopped and stared incredulously at Mr. Hansen, who was precariously perched on the little board above the vat of water. Without hesitating, Jimmy walked through the crowd and grabbed a ball.

"Well, lookee here! A yuk yuk! Stretch Gumby, the farm boy, is gonna give it a go, are ya now, Stretch? A yuk, yuk!" Mr. Hansen teased. "Know how you can always tell who's a farmer? 'Cause they just pretend the ball's a potato! Har, har, har!"

Jimmy whipped what everyone swore was a hundred-mile-an-hour fastball. It hit the bullseye dead center with a *thunk* that could be heard all down the midway. "Potato" was the shop teacher's last word as he plunged into the icy water, drawing a roar of laughter from the crowd. As Jimmy started to walk off, he reached into his pocket and handed the ball boy a dollar. The crowd's applause followed the boys as they sauntered off down the Midway with Creedence Clearwater's "Sweet Hitch-Hiker" echoing from the loudspeakers down by the double Ferris wheel.

Jack's thoughts were always on Alejandra. Eventually the long week passed, and the boys finally had a weekend off. Jack had hurried home to grab some clothes for later in the evening after he met up with his buddies back at Old Mik Point. Even with the long hours at the fairgrounds, he had a chance to come home at night and visit with his folks and catch up with how his older brother was doing. Jack's parents and the entire town had heard about his heroic deed in saving little Jessie. Grandma Meeks had called to thank Jack again and had told his mother how wonderful Jack was and that they all thought the world of him. Even Jimmy had looked Jack up the next day while he was taking tickets at one of the gates to shake hands and thank him. "Good ol' Jack. If you need anythin', buddy, just let me know."

An envelope had come for Jack. He rarely got any mail. At first, he thought it might be from Alejandra, but after inspecting the handwriting he knew it wasn't from her, and he felt disappointed. He opened the note inside. In neat cursive handwriting was written:

Dear Jack Dean,
    I just wanted to write you this note to thank you again for saving my life. I could have been squashed

real bad by that big horse if you hadn't saved me.
You are so brave. You will always be my hero.

Love,
Jessie Meeks

P.S. Flower thinks you are wonderful too

He couldn't help but smile at her thoughtful note and placed the sheet down on a shelf by his bed. He then grabbed his clothes, kissed his mom goodbye, and headed out in the Cherry. When he got to Old Mik Point, the boys were down on the dock swimming, bathing, and drinking a few cold beers some older buddy had bought for them. Jack melted right in with his cutoffs, sun-bleached hair, and dark tan. He walked to the end of the dock and dove in, descending deep into the darker water. It was cold even now this long into the summer, and it felt invigorating. They spent the evening like this, along with listening to music, talking, and playing some cards. No Soul Note tonight. Alejandra wasn't going to be there. Tomorrow night, though, maybe…

Jack woke early the next morning, feeling rested. Quietly he grabbed a fishing pole and made his way down the stairs and out to the dock on Lake Kit. He smoothly rowed the wooden boat around the point. Birds were just now waking and starting their morning croons. He rowed into one of the small back inlets. The mist was still heavy on the surface, making it feel like he was fishing in a cloud as he made his first cast. The lure plunked heavily on the smooth surface, producing ripples across the lake. *It's a mystical time of day*, Jack thought, slowly reeling the line in.

He caught a movement out of the corner of his eye. Something was rooting about on shore near the water's edge. He continued to keep an eye on the commotion as he casted again and slowly reeled back in his line. He watched as the creature, an otter, gathered a mouthful of grass and disappeared under the water. It reappeared in the inlet, looking as if it were a clump of grass caught up in a current, heading toward the far shore. Once there, it would disappear under the surface again. Then the otter poked the tip of its nose out of the water as it swam back across the inlet to the other side once more. Jack refocused on his fishing. There was a monster old bass in this place that he had heard stories about for years. Big Harness, as the beast was known, was legendary, and Jack had been wanting to get a closeup look at him.

—⚏—

One day as kids, Jack and Jimmy were in the Meeks' big barn helping Grandpa Meeks with some chores in the tack room where all the saddles, bridles, and halters were kept. "Look here, boys," Grandpa Meeks had said, pointing to a large black leather harness hung on a wall. He took out his hanky and slowly wiped a light film of dust off it. "Used to be a lot of these around in here. Back when I was a kid and we didn't have all these combustion machines around; these things were pretty damn important. They were different sizes, you see, so they fit the horses just right.

They didn't chafe or hinder their movements or their pullin' leverage. See here?" He polished a small silver plate.
"What's that say, Jack?"

"Um, Big Har... Big Harness! Hey, that's the name of
that big fish over in the lake!"

"Yep, and was the name of my ol' horse," Grandpa
Meeks said. "I gave him that name. Big Harness was one of
the best draft horses we ever had around here. His mama
was called Peach. She was somethin' pretty and a good
fine mama. She was mostly Percheron and probably had
some Belgian in her too. They were like those giants you
see at the fair pullin' those sleds with the lead bars stacked
on 'em. Percherons come from around the south of France
and the Belgians from, well, Belgium. They were probably
always used for hard workin', but the Roman army used
them for fightin', and so did those knights back durin' the
Crusades and King Arthur's time. Boy, he was somethin',
big and strong. A workin' horse he was, but as gentle as a
lamb. All those big ones we had back then were, though he
was the biggest. Probably over seven feet tall at the withers
and weighed well over twenty-five hundred pounds. That's
some big horse. Dad said my grandpa had to have that harness special made for him.

"He broke down plowin' out in one of the south fields
one of the springs I was away for durin' the war. My ol'
man took it pretty hard, probably why I still keep the thing
in here. He wouldn't have thought much about my namin'
that big fish yonder after his favorite ol' workhorse, but to
me it was just some kind of tribute. And I don't think Big
Harness would have minded much at all... Sure do still

miss him and all those big fellers. This here ol' barn's a lot lonelier without 'em all too…"

—⁓—

Suddenly, Jack felt a thump on the port bow and the boat moved slightly as if being nudged. Looking over the edge to see what the heck had happened, he saw a little mound of grass pushing up against the side of the boat. Jack reached down and knocked loudly on the hull. The mound of grass stopped pushing and backed up. Jack looked down at it and could see little brown eyes in a furry face staring back up at him as if to say, "Sorry, old chap, but would you mind terribly moving a bit so I can get by?" He grabbed an oar and carefully used it to move the boat sideways so the little fur creature could pass on by. As it did, Jack could have sworn it nodded in gratitude as it went about its task. It crossed to the other bank where Jack watched it work busily on a burrow under an old oak that had partially grown out over the edge of the lake.

The early morning fog had lifted slightly from the surface of the lake by now. Jack thought he felt a sharp tug on the lure. He soon felt a whoosh of air right over the top of his head. He instinctively ducked his head, and as he did, whatever he had on his line decided it'd better let go. Jack looked up to see a pair of geese land just past his boat. They landed so smoothly and quietly that had he not felt them right over his head, he probably would have missed them altogether. He knew they mated for life, and he wondered if they were young and on their first elopement, or had they been together for years, spending a few peaceful moments in this small quiet cove for a long time. Gradually they floated off, disappearing into the mist, which was heavier on down the cove from him.

His next cast was a beauty, landing the hula popper amongst the reeds and water lilies near the water's edge. As he reeled in, the lure popped through cleanly, and just as it did, a giant, shadowy figure from the dark depths hit it. Jack watched the scene as if in slow motion. He reeled in and felt the tug, a solid tug that bent his fishing rod over, as if he'd snagged a snapping turtle. Then the line slackened as the big fish flew up and broke out of the surface. *Oh... my God! He's a big one! Has to be Big Harness!* Jack thought. It smacked back down on the water, like a fat man doing a belly flop.

Jack kept reeling and the massive creature kept fighting and jumping and thrashing its body. And then, just as Jack had reeled the monster in close, as if the giant finally had all the fun it had wanted, with one last death-defying leap, it suspended itself into the air, turning and writhing one more majestic time. When its mouth was angled toward Jack, out came the hook! He watched in pure amazement and disbelief as the big fish and the lure pirouetted in opposite directions while in midair, as if they were some kind of trapeze circus act. The fish gracefully splashed back down and disappeared beneath the surface.

Any other day, Jack might have been upset as all heck that the biggest bass he'd ever almost caught had gotten away, but not today. For some reason, he felt like the gods of fishing had blessed him with just the experience alone, and the knowledge that old Big Harness was still out there meant that maybe there would be another time. *It'd be a good story to tell Grandpa Meeks*, Jack thought, and then he would still have his hopes of catching old Big Harness himself.

Jack's luck picked up after that. Drifting farther out into the cove, Jack reverted to his old never-fail standby of worms and a cork float. With a lot of patience, he reeled in a stringer full of fat perch and lake trout that had been keeping their distance from the big bass's territory. Later, as he motored back to the dock, he glanced back toward the little cove. All was peaceful, back to normal now that the human intruder was gone.

As he neared the cabin, he saw a familiar figure dive off the end of the dock and come up out of the deep water, lifting himself easily onto the dock as Jack drew closer. Joe, good old Joe, with that shock of blond hair, almost white against his ruddy complexion. He was one of Jack's oldest buddies, and probably his closest since Jimmy had dropped out of school.

—◊◊—

Jack's dad had dropped him off at the high school base-ball field on the first day of Little League when he was just nine years old. No one was around. Jack just stood there wondering what he was going to do, when a kid his own age came riding up on a Stingray bicycle with the long banana seat and high-rise handlebars with his mitt dangling. As he rode in a circle around Jack near home plate, he asked,

"Lookin' for baseball sign ups, aren't you? Ain't here. Sign-ups are over at the middle school." Jack had no idea where the middle school was. He was still going to a one-room elementary school out in the country. Joe saw the forlorn look on Jack's face, and said, "Here, kid, get on. You can ride on over with me. Just don't go fallin' off and smashin' your head."

Jack propped himself up precariously on the handle-bars and away they went. As they rode up onto the middle school's ball field, where there were about a hundred kids milling around, everyone took notice. A big kid, who everyone called Schuler, yelled, "Hey, Joe. What gives? Some new kid shows up and you go chauffeurin' him around like he was your long-lost brother, man? Judas Priest, kid, how do you rate? How come the best ball player in town is ridin' you around on his handlebars like you're Mickey Mantle? What's your name, kid, anyway? Son of a gun, you better be good!"

After that first game, Jack had formed friendships with Schuler, before the word "Big" became part of his nickname, and a dark-haired boy named Bobby.

"Hey, you're not a bad player, kid," said Bobby. "Glad Joe picked you right off to be on our team, new kid and all. You can really smack the ball! Made some great plays at shortstop too. Joe, man, how'd you know this kid could play? Hey, want to come over to my house and shoot some hoops? My mom will make us some lunch and you can call home and tell 'em you're gonna be a town kid from now on! Hey, who's your favorite player, anyway? Mine's Rocky Colavito, he's the best, man."

"Yeah, I like him, too, but Al Kaline's my all-time favorite," Jack said.

"Yeah, he's good, but I still go with Rocky."

"Mine's Willie Horton," Schuler said. "The big guy can send it, man!"

—⟋⟍—

"Any luck?" asked Joe as Jack eased the boat up against the dock.

"Not bad." Jack held up the full stringer.

"Shit! Not bad? Not bad at all! I should've gone with you, man. Heard you ramblin' about early and thought about gettin' up and going out with you. Then I just thought if you wanted anyone to go along, you would have said so. You're kind of a loner sometimes, you know, Jack? Me too... occasionally. Just wanted to laze around out here on the dock by myself this mornin', I guess."

"Well, I got a little lucky. Let's clean them up and have some breakfast. Put them on the grill. Plenty for everyone. Had a little run-in with that old Big Harness too. One of those 'he got away' stories, though."

"Let's fry 'em up and you can entertain us with your adventures, man. Maybe we got some eggs, too, and slice up some potatoes. Hey, we still headin' out to the track tonight? You racin' Fletch and that new goat of his?"

"Yep, I sure am," Jack said.

They hung out by the dock for a while longer before heading up the stairs to the grill.

Chapter 14

As soon as they passed through Darden's entrance gate, it all seemed to hit every one of the body's senses all at once: the unearthly screams of the big engines, the vibrations of the ground beneath their feet, the acrid smell of burning rubber, the drag strip's heat waves, the lingering exhaust fumes, and the Top Fuels exploding down the drag strip like fire-breathing dragons hellishly riding Apollo rockets.

This was it, the biggest day of the year to the boys. They had been looking forward to it the way children look forward to Christmas morning. This was their Christmas morning—a sultry evening in late July. Jack drove the Cherry slowly down the pit row where all the backstage pre-race action took place. This was hallowed ground, like passing through the sacred halls of Valhalla. In awe, they slowly passed by the legendary Don "Big Daddy" Garlits and his crew, who were hovering around his infamous Top Fuel "Swamp Rat." As the boys inched along, they recognized more of their legendary favorites readying their dragsters: Don "The Snake" Prudhomme, Tommy Ivo, Kenny Stafford, and Shirley "Cha Cha" Muldowney, who was also known as the "First Lady of Drag Racing." There was also Tom "Mongoose" McEwen, and further along in the pit was one of the boys' homegrown all-time favorites, Conrad "Connie" Kalitta, or "The Bounty Hunter."

These icons of drag racing were their heroes. As much, if not more, than any of their other sport heroes growing up, like Mickey Mantle, Johnny Unitas, and Bart Starr. They were the idols of a sport as raw, bold, and dangerous as any on the planet. Like baseball and football, drag racing was an All-American sport, having incubated and evolved all around the country, its grassroots beginning in the thirties and forties. But its popularity exploded after World War II with racing clubs popping up across the country, from Los Angeles down to Tampa and on up to Philadelphia and Detroit. Commercial drag strip venues opened to give the clubs places where they could legally gas out, and maybe, with a fast car and steely nerves, win enough to make a little cash too.

It was all about speed. The machismo of the daring Craig Breedlove and Chuck Yeager said, "My monster is faster than yours—faster than anything else on the face of the earth." The space race was on. Man was riding monster rockets to the moon, and also down a quarter-mile stretch of tarmac out at Darden Dragway.

Jack didn't think the Cherry was going to set any speed records, but the five dollars it cost to enter the Street Stock grudge race, which included the privilege of entering the pit area, was worth every penny. After a while, they found their way back to the lineup of other awestruck amateur hot-rodders patiently waiting their turn to punch the pedal, burn the rubber, and see what really was under the hood of their own machismo's pride and joy.

The stands were packed, everyone on pins and needles awaiting the finals of the Top Fuels. These menacing low-slung machines with their long "rails," and their gargantuan rocket engines strapped on their backs were the stars of the show. While the fans loved the funny cars, custom Pro Streets, and the local Street Stock grudge runs, it was the Top Fuels they lived for. For what seemed like months now, the local radio stations had been blaring out advertisements of what they all had been waiting patiently to see. The beasts were now running on the volatile nitromethane, which was recently approved for the first time in many years since it had been disallowed as too dangerous by the National Hot Rod Association, or the NHRA, the governing authority of drag racing.

After they found a place to park out in the back of the pit area, Jack and the boys wandered wide-eyed past the pit crews working diligently on their machines, hoping to catch a glimpse of Big Daddy, Mongoose, or The Snake. They made their way over to the entry booth where Jack stood in line to pay his entry fee.

"How ya doin', Jack?" It was Mr. Hansen. Jack's face lit up with a big smile. He was truly glad to see his teacher. As far as the boys were concerned, Mr. Hansen was "the man." He was the coolest of all their teachers, but to them, he wasn't just a teacher, he was their friend, and when it came to all things auto, he was their mentor too.

It was Mr. Hansen who had encouraged Jack to try to buy the old truck from Duke when Jack had told him about Duke's proposition. He offered to help Jack turn it into what Jack had envisioned for it to look like all along, and even allowed Jack to bring it into the school's auto shop the previous semester and make it his class project. All the boys in the class, while working on their own cars, helped Jack patiently disassemble the engine and rebore the cylinders, then painstakingly reassemble it with all new parts: a manual transmission, brakes, shocks, wiring, and an exhaust system. Just the past week he let Jack bring it into the school's shop during his summer technology class to help him install the new carburetor.

Lamar Hansen had found a home in Lake County. He'd had a promising racing career himself until his new bride had begged and pleaded with him to give it up. He'd finally relented and opened up his own shop instead, building the beasts for other racers. Then tragedy struck. On a cold, wet evening, his beautiful young wife was hit by a drunk driver while driving back from the grocery store. She was killed instantly, and the drunk driver, whose license had been suspended for previous drunk driving convictions, was also killed in the collision. It had devastated Lamar, and as if to take out his vengeance, he'd gone back into racing, back into riding the fire breathing dragons down the quarter from racetrack to racetrack around the country. Then on one hot and humid night, right there at Darden a few years back, the beast had caught an updraft, and in a split second, it had taken flight, careening over backward. Lamar "Glory Boy" Hansen had a glimpse of glory as the long rails crumpled agonizingly around him and the flames engulfed the tumbling mass of steel.

His death wish was almost fulfilled and would have been except for the amazingly fast response of the rescue team. His roll cage had miraculously remained intact, cocooning him securely as he tumbled over and over down the track. They got him out just before the flames caught up to them and caused the car to explode. As though protected by the arms of an angel, Lamar had emerged relatively unscathed, but the horrific experience was enough, and Glory Boy hung up his scarred helmet for the last time. He applied for the auto shop teacher's position at Lake County High and had found a new passion: teaching. He also taught driver's education during the summers and took great pride in heavily stressing upon developing safe young drivers with a healthy respect for the dangerous machines they would now control.

A grease monkey kid from a little town out in the California desert, Lamar had hot rods and racing in his blood. As a kid growing up in the fifties and early sixties, cars, hot rods, and drag racing were a fact of life. Rodding and drag racing were hugely popular out in the desert and valley towns of California, and Lamar Hansen loved it. Now, even though he had officially retired, he was still a frequent visitor to Darden, enjoying the chance to see old friends and keep up on the latest racing technologies. He still carried the call of the wild in him, but now he took solace in coaching young kids like Jack on the sport as a safer and more controlled venue than a country road to shake out their "need for speed," as he called it.

After they installed the new carb and tuned the engine and made sure the brakes, hoses, and tires were all good, Mr. Hansen had Jack meet him one late afternoon at the drag strip. He wanted to give Jack some practice runs down the track. It was a great opportunity for Jack to get a feel of the slick tarmac, learn how the Christmas Tree worked, and get an overall feel for how the Cherry would respond when pushed to her full throttle.

Mr. Hansen coached Jack throughout all his runs. He explained to Jack how races were often won right at the start by the driver with the best reaction time, the one who could "cut the light," or launch the fastest. Then it was just a matter of keeping the tires on the pavement, working smoothly through the gear progressions, and holding the line down the track straighter than the other guy.

The Christmas Tree, or "the Tree," as it was also called, was a set of vertical lights that gave the drivers a visual countdown to the start of the race. Jack had seen the Tree many times over the years and thought he knew how it worked, but Mr. Hansen patiently described how the pre-stage indicator lights were the yellow bulbs that told the driver he was getting close to the line and the starting position. The second stage of lights were also yellow and told the driver his front wheels were on the line and ready to race. Afterwards, there were the amber countdown lights, and then the green lights—the "go" signal. This was the most crucial time. If the driver hit the gas too quickly, the red light would flash and the driver would be disqualified.

Mr. Hansen knew how important it was for Jack to practice his staging and launching techniques, so he had Jack do these many times over. He also coached Jack on all the other aspects of the drag strip: the miles per hour timer, the ET clock at the finish line, the shutdown area at the end of the quarter, the time slip, the burnout box, the sixty-foot timer, the 330-foot timer and the 660-foot timer, and the halfway point of the quarter-mile race. Jack was amazed at how much he really didn't know about drag racing than he thought he did after all the races he'd seen. He saw how much Mr. Hansen enjoyed it all, how much more animated and alive he seemed here at the track than back in the auto shop. Everyone at the track seemed to know Mr. Hansen too. They all called him Lamar and would shake his hand and smile, seeming genuinely glad to see him.

Finally, Jack and Fletch's numbers were called. While still nervous, Jack felt under control and ready for the long-awaited launch. All through the evening he had looked for Alejandra. He didn't expect that he would see her with the thousand or so spectators cramming in the stands, but he knew she was there with Cassie Kay and the other girls. Bobby, Joe, and Big Schuler all reported they had seen them. They had wished Jack good fortune and to remain cool. It was their way of saying "be safe." The thought of personal injury, or worse, had really not occurred much to Jack up until then. There had been a few crashes and mishaps that evening, and the fire and ambulance crews had been active. But he was so confident after Mr. Hansen's coaching sessions that he had not factored in or questioned his own mortality or well-being.

Now, fortunately, there wasn't any time to dwell on the possibility as he pulled the Cherry forward into the burnout box. Expertly, he pushed his left foot down on the clutch, shifted into first, and with his right foot, he pressed down on the gas pedal. He quickly released his foot off the clutch and mashed it down on the brake pedal. With the engine revving loudly, the rear tires screamed even louder as they spun in place against the tarmac, the friction burning their rubber and heating them so that they would hopefully enhance their grip on the track's greasy surface. Through the thick smoke he glanced briefly over at Fletch, who was completing his own burnout. Remarkably, Fletch was looking directly at Jack, grinning confidently as he gave Jack a thumbs-up. Jack smiled, too, and with equal confidence, he returned the thumbs-up.

Then it all seemed to happen in a split second, just as Mr. Hansen had said it would. The yellow lights flashed, then the amber lights, and finally the green lights. Jack smashed down on the gas pedal and felt the truck jump and ignite like never before. He kept her in low gear as she launched true and sure off the starting line. Jack confidently and smoothly began putting her through the higher gear progressions—just as Mr. Hansen had coached him. For an instant, he saw the timer lights as he flew past them faster than he had ever thought possible. It was all a blur. The stands, the crowds... and Fletch, were all one big, loud smoke-engulfed blur. And then it was over. He'd flown past the finish line and now slowed down and looked for the turnout into the time slip booth.

Coming to a stop, Jack sat for a moment just wanting to collect all his senses, gather his nerves, and absorb all his built-up adrenaline. He was alive after all—more alive than he had ever been. His body was saturated with the same kind of sensations he felt when he was with Alejandra, and whatever it was, he didn't want it to fade.

He saw Mr. Hansen standing next to the booth with a wide grin, pumping his fist. Then he saw Fletch jump up in exaltation, and he knew he had lost. But even this realization didn't dampen his spirits. He had raced, and raced well, and his Cherry—his grand old truck—had run a gallant race, and he was proud of her. Fletch was proud, too, and when he walked over to shake hands with Jack, he gave him a big brotherly bear hug.

"Way to go, my man! You're one cool dude, Jack. Man, was that cool or what? Holy shit, that was close! What the shit you got in that truck anyway? Man, you damn near got me. Damn!" Fletch exclaimed.

"Well, actually Fletch," Mr. Hansen chimed in, "if we factor in the dial-in times from each of your practice run times, he *did* get you. After all, nice as it looks, that is a 1949 F1 and that '67 GTO of yours is in a slightly different bracket. That still a 389 under the hood, Fletch?" he asked, half in jest, referring to the GTO's powerful stock engine.

"Oh, yeah…heck, you're right, Mr. Hanson. But I'm not so sure that flathead V8 of Jack's isn't burning nitro the way it stroked down the track!" Fletch joked good-naturedly. "Well, Jack, guess you won, brother. Congratulations!"

"How about we call it a draw?" Jack said, and with that they shook hands again.

"You're the man, Jack," Fletch said as they turned to leave.

"No, you are, Fletch," said Jack.

Both knew they had shared an experience and a thrill like no other, and they were both whole and alive as ever to tell about it. And that is just what Fletch started to do as soon as they met up with everyone back in the grandstand.

Before Jack climbed back into the Cherry to slowly move her back to the pit area, he thanked Mr. Hansen for all his help. "Happy to do it, Jack. I enjoyed being back out here. It's what I love. It's been in my blood since I was just a kid and I can't seem to give it up entirely. Smell of that nitro, I guess," Mr. Hansen said, laughing. "That was a heck of a race, Jack. Glad you and Fletch had some fun. You launched her great and took her down that track as smooth and straight as any seasoned 'Fuelie' out here. Your brother Duke sure would've been proud to have seen you."

"Yeah, he sure would've. I'm gonna write and tell him all about it. Thank you, Mr. Hansen. You're the best."

"Say, I saw your friend Jimmy Meeks looking on. Heard his choppers down at the far end. I know he's not a hood, Jack, 'cause I don't see him or his buddies wearing any gang colors. I remember him in my class before he dropped out. He seemed like a good kid going through a raw deal. Sometime, when you get the chance, tell him I like bikes too. And if he'd want to bring them into the class sometime or if he needs anything in the shop, that would be cool."

"Thanks, Mr. Hansen. You're the coolest. I'll tell him. Who knows? Maybe we can get him to come back to school and back on the team too."

"Well, no strings attached. Besides, I do dig bikes. Take care, Jack. And hey, drive safe!"

Jack's adrenaline was still lit up as he navigated the Cherry back to her parking spot at the far end of the pit. The big boys, the Top Fuels, were firing up the nitro for their finals and getting into their assigned positions and lane assignments. Now that Jack had a real run under his belt, he felt like a kindred spirit with these "Fuelies," as Mr. Hansen had called them.

By the time Jack reached the stands, he heard his name being called by the familiar, thickly accented voice that he would never grow tired of hearing. He looked up to see Alejandra smiling and waving joyfully to him. "Oh, Jack, I was so frightened by all this for you. I am so happy you are good and nothing bad happened to you. This car racing is so new to me. Never have I seen such an event. Oh, I was hoping for you to win, but I was so hoping you would not crash too. I am still shaking so much, I almost spilled all my popcorn. Would you like some?"

The rest of the evening he and Alejandra enjoyed just sitting together, talking, sharing popcorn, drinking Cokes, and eating hot dogs, which since the fair, she had become so fond of. The Fuelies were as exciting as advertised. Alejandra could barely watch as they roared past the stands. They all sat close enough to feel the intense heat of the fiery, nitromethane burning, four hundred horsepower engines as they blasted by in the blink of an eye. She didn't know what to cover, either her eyes from the dust and track grime the dragsters kicked up, or her ears from their deafening sound. And the smell of the burning rubber, fuel, and grease made her nostrils feel sensitive and prickly. Despite this, she enjoyed herself now that she knew Jack was safe and sitting next to her. She found it all exciting, letting herself get caught up in the thrill as the dragsters roared by, spewing their flames and smoke so loud the grandstands shook.

Eventually drivers were eliminated until the final pairing. As expected and as advertised, two of the best and most famous of the drivers, Don "The Snake" Prudhomme and Don "Big Daddy" Garlits, faced off in the last race of the night. Big Daddy was running his famed Swamp Rat, the sixteenth version of it. But this one was radically different than all the others. With this Swamp Rat, Big Daddy and his team had repositioned the huge engine from the front of the cockpit to the rear of the dragster, adding weight nearer to the rear wheels and providing better vision for the driver. They had also configured a spoiler above and behind the driver's head. These new changes were not without big risks. But that was drag racing. Like Lamar Hanson, they all knew the risks, especially Big Daddy as he had crashed badly the year before. But the risks paid off this night as the Swamp Rat worked up to more than two hundred and thirty miles per hour, hitting the finish line in a winning time of just over five-and-a-half seconds, setting a new record.

Afterwards, the boys walked the girls back to Cassie Kay's car. Everyone was in a jovial mood, having had a great time. Jack held Alejandra's hand as they walked slow and brushed up against each other. The vibrations they had felt in the stands were still lingering, and Jack put his arm around her as they neared the car. The parking lot had thinned out and quieted down by now.

Even with their ears still numb and ringing, the loud rumbling of the bikers as they pulled up and circled the car was deafening. Jimmy turned his bike off and the others idled more slowly. "Hey, nice run, Jack boy. Have to say, I was real impressed. You looked as cool as that Steve McQueen guy out there. I'll bet ol' Fletch was sweatin' it, man," Jimmy said.

Suddenly, down the middle of the parking lot, a line of those old beaters from Torville roared by, barely missing people walking to their cars. Gravel and dust kicked up all around them and flying beer cans just missed hitting them. The now common flashing of middle fingers, flying cigarette butts, and accompanying expletives echoed out from their windows as they passed by.

"What is with those idiots?" shouted the normally passive Cassie Kay. "One of these days they're going to hurt someone bad. Assholes!" she screamed after them.

"One of these days they're goin' to *get* hurt bad," Jimmy snarled. He kicked down on his starter and roared the bike to life. "You all be safe. Looks like they're headin' back to Torville so they're goin' the other way. Let's go try to catch up with those pricks. See if they really want to rumble or if they're just chicken shits. I'm gettin' tired of their shit. Later." And with that, he and the other bikers roared off after the Torville beaters, already speeding out of sight. Cassie Kay wanted to yell out after Jimmy, *"Beat the living crap out of those pricks for me too!"* but she didn't.

Just then, Fletch, with the beautiful blond next to him, pulled up in the GTO. There was another couple in the backseat, but Jack didn't recognize them. Behind Fletch, a glistening yellow and black Dodge Challenger pulled up. As the driver's side window rolled down, the boys could see that it was Mr. Hansen.

"Everything all right?" he asked, sticking his head out the window. "I saw that group of old beat-up junks go flying by out of here like numbskulls. No one got hurt, did they? I just had Hank back at the track call them in to the highway patrol and the sheriff's office. They're drinking and they're dangerous. You guys know those jerks?"

"Well, we don't know them, and we don't want to, but we've had some run-ins with them. We think they're from Torville," Jack said.

"Yeah, I've heard some things about that place—none good," Mr. Hansen said. "Well, how about we all just kind of form a convoy and head back into town? It's getting late and who knows what that crowd will do. Everyone be safe and remember this isn't the quarter anymore."

Everyone made it back to their homes safe that night. Mr. Hansen made sure of that as everyone cautiously and slowly—for them—followed him back into town, including Fletch, who graciously brought up the rear.

Jimmy never caught up with the Torville beaters, either. They had to stop at a traffic light down the road, and as they did, a contingent of sheriff's deputies, state troopers, fire trucks, and ambulances with sirens blaring sped past them. Farther ahead there had been an accident. Jimmy and the other bikers cruised by slowly, trying to get a glimpse of what had crashed and gone off the road and down into a steep ravine. They couldn't tell if any were the Torville cars and didn't see others pulled over. Even if they weren't the ones down in the ravine, Jimmy was sure they had been involved somehow, and had probably caused whoever was down there to lose control or be forced off the road. By the time they pulled over to wait to go around the accident scene, Jimmy knew the chase was over.

Back at the cabin later that night, Jack thought he heard the growl of the bikers as they passed by out on the main road, heading in the direction of Jimmy's farm. He rolled out his sleeping bag on one of the picnic tables and daydreamed of Alejandra as he stared up at the starlit sky. Hearing the bikes, he hoped it was Jimmy and that they would pull in so he could hear if they had caught up with the Torville group, but they just cruised on past. *Must not have been too exciting. If it was, they probably would pull in and tell everyone what happened*, he thought.

He did hear a lone bike turn down the lane the next morning. It was Jimmy, and he looked as low as when his mother had died. "It was Charley, man. They got Charley. The pricks!"

"What? What happened?" Jack asked. The other boys gathered around.

"We came up on a crash when we were after them. I'd forgotten Charley had split before we had, said he was gonna head over to Grand River to meet up with some dudes over there. That's the same road over to Torville, man. Anyway, we came up on this accident that had closed down the whole road and backed up traffic for miles. We decided to give it up and head back. Had no idea who it was in the crash, man. Come to find out it was Charley. Hank called the farm this mornin'. He'd just found out from one of Charley's brothers, 'cause he was supposed to be workin' down at the shop this mornin'. Damn it, man! The cops said it looked like he'd lost it on a curve. I mean, it was slick, man, but Charley knew his bike and he knew how to ride. Sure as shit, those pricks came up on him fast and just took him out. Bet the barn on it, man! Damn it!" He walked over to one of the picnic tables and rested on it, looking up into the shaded canopy. He lay there for a long time until finally standing up and quietly mounting his chopper, roaring off.

The next week passed slowly. Jack went back to work at Feed 'n' Seed and was kept busy taking inventory, sweeping the floors, stacking fence posts, and organizing sacks of fertilizer and bags of feed. He missed the excitement and activity of the fair. The boys had all said their farewells to their friends in the carnival crew after helping them fold up and pack away their various tents, food stands, and massive rides, preparing to move on to their next venue, which was probably just down the road in the next county.

They milled about with a crowd that had gathered to see them off. Lavenia was one of the last to pass by on her way to board a bus idling nearby. She spotted Jack and walked over to him. "Well, Jackie, my dear," Lavenia began, batting her long, dark eyelashes as she sidled up close to him, "I believe I am going to miss all of you handsome young boys. I suspect y'all are the cutest boys we'll see all summer. You stay innocent now, Jackie, you hear? Don't go letting some ravishing vixen steal it away from you. You all save yourselves up for that special one and only," she teased, using her sweetest Southern belle charm. She pursed her ruby red lips as she reached up and lightly kissed Jack on his cheek, giving him a big goodbye hug, her sweet jasmine perfume wafting up his nostrils. "There now. You stay sweet now, Jackie, you hear? Y'all stay sweet and be good boys now, and grow up and be fine, good men." They all marveled at her as they watched her walk away in that sultry swaying way of hers. She glanced back, and as she did, she held up the little Bible that Grandma Meeks had given her and smiled wistfully with one last wave.

"My Lord," said someone in the crowd.

"Damn," someone else said, "that's the prettiest lookin' Snake Lady I ever did see!"

Another man in the crowd said, "Harv, now I'll grant you, she's as pretty as a grand prize peach, but how many Snake Ladies have you ever seen anyway?"

"Well, I've seen me plenty…" Harv said as he shuffled away slowly, shaking his head.

And then the carnival crew was gone. As Jack sat alone in the shade on the loading dock during his break, eating a bologna sandwich, he still felt that kiss and faint smell of Lavenia's jasmine perfume. But it was Alejandra's kisses and fragrances his thoughts wanted to dwell on.

In a way, it does feel good to get back to the feed store and back to a familiar work routine, Jack thought. Earlier in the week they had all gathered and gone to Charley's funeral. Jack was surprised at all the mourners there. He knew Charley had a large family, but it looked like half the town was there too. It was a sad scene, as all funerals are. But Charley's death was a tragic shock to everyone. Even though Charley had his faults, youth had been taken away, and the grief and shock of seeing Charley's corpse resting in the open casket had a profound effect on everyone.

Jimmy and his family also attended. Jimmy wore a dark suit and tie, and never said a word. After it was over, he left, and no one saw him again the rest of the week, except for Jack when he pulled into Feed 'n' Seed in one of the farm's big half-ton trucks to pick up a load of feed and salt blocks. But he didn't say much as he and Jack loaded the truck's bed up. When they were done, they knocked fists, and Jimmy gave Jack one of those "I'll get those sons of bitches" looks as he drove off.

Throughout the week everyone rolled by Feed 'n' Seed at one time or another. Friends and acquaintances just wanted to come by and share a Cola, as if to be with each other and verify that they were still around. Life continued, and the world kept turning. And for Jack, the hard, familiar work was good for him. It helped to take his mind off Charley and all the sadness of the funeral.

Finally, the weekend rolled around. The boys spent Saturday at the cabin doing odd jobs, working out, and working on their cars. Jack was just finishing up lazily washing and polishing the Cherry, listening to Santana on the truck's eight track, when they heard the sound of choppers down the lane. It was Jimmy with Randy and Rafe trailing along. Jimmy didn't look very sociable. "Had another run-in with that Torville bunch. Tried to run off Randy this time," he said.

"That's right, man," Randy echoed when Jimmy looked his way. "Came right at me. Tried to make me chicken. And I did, or they would have taken me right out. Threw some beer cans at me too. After I got my shit together some, I turned around and went after 'em. Man, was I pissed! They were hightailin' it, though. Finally, I gave it up. Almost lost it more than once goin' around those curves. Don't know what I would have done if I'd caught up with 'em, but I know what I will do to 'em if they show up tonight."

"Same assholes who tried to take out Rafe," Jimmy said. "Same pricks that I bet anythin' *did* take out poor Charley, damn it. If they're at the Note tonight, somethin' is goin' to go down. They've been pullin' this shit and gettin' away with it all summer. If we just keep lettin' it go on, someone else is gonna get killed. It could have just been Randy. We kick their ass good, they'll stop, man. Just like that rumble Duke had that time years ago out at the Note, Jack. Just a different bunch of assholes we got to deal with this time." He backed the Harley Fat Boy around and kicked down on the starter. "Later," he said as they all headed back down the lane. Everyone just stood there for a few minutes and watched silently until they were out of sight.

"Holy Shit!" Bobby finally said. "Holy shit."

"Well, just so you all know, that was Jimmy's way of asking for our help," Jack said. "No way would he come right out and ask us."

"Jesus, I didn't think Jimmy Meeks ever needed help with anythin' or anybody," Bobby said.

"He don't even need to ask me for any help—ever," Big Schuler chimed in. "'Specially when it comes to helpin' him kick some low-life ass."

"Jimmy'll bust 'em up bad!" Bobby said.

"Yeah, but there'll be a bunch of them there tonight," Jack lamented. "But Jimmy's right, they've been working this up. This thing's gotten way crazy, man, and we're all in on this. I've had my run-in with 'em, and so has Bobby. If anything, it's Jimmy who's got our backs, yours and mine. He's figuring this thing with them will just keep going on 'cause he knows it's us they want too. If Jimmy lights it up with 'em tonight, I'll be right there with him."

"Oh, shit," Bobby said. "We all will. At least it looks like we'll have some help. Like Jimmy says, we got us some allies now, and it looks like they've all got axes to grind with those pricks too."

"Oh, yeah." Jack sighed, looking up into the high tree branches. "So you guys have all heard that story of Duke taking me and Jimmy to the Note back when we were kids, and how Duke and his buddies threw in with the Central High guys in a big brawl with Torville back then, too, right? Well, so Bobby, Joe, and I went and got Central on our side now. They look at it as they owe it to us 'cause of back then, kind of a return of a favor, but they're pissed at them, too, for their own reasons…" Jack paused as if re-calculating the odds. "Tom Morris and his guys are in with us, and Jimmy's got the Easton and Grand River guys in with us too. We'll still probably be outnumbered, but they're gonna freak out when they see all of us. They're still thinking it's just us, so we've got to stay alert 'cause it can all happen fast. Just one wrong look was all it took back then. But it had probably been brewing for a long time, just like now.

"When it did light up, though, things just got crazy. Girls screaming—everyone screaming and yelling and fists flying. I mean, there's thumping and crunching going on everywhere. I remember seeing this one guy who had a guy's head down on the pavement and he just kept pounding on him. We lost track of Duke, but I saw this guy who was Duke's buddy from Central, BTW, just walking around with some guy in a headlock with one arm and swinging away at another guy with the other. I don't know how they knew who was who, but I guess they did."

"Wait a minute, who was BTW?" Big Schuler asked.

"Oh, that was Big Tough Worley! He's the big brother of that Central dude that came up to us in the parking lot at the Note a few weeks ago, remember? Turns out, somehow he and Duke met up over in 'Nam, and he must have told his brother to look me up. So he did and said to come down to Grand River some time. So me, Bobby, and Joe went down there and met up with him. They call him BMW, Big Mac Worley. Cool, huh?

"Yeah, real cool. Take that big guy's help any day," said Bobby. "He and his buddies all looked like rough dudes. Anyway, so go on with your story, man."

"Okay, so it seemed like it just kept going on everywhere, all over the whole parking lot. Seemed like it lasted forever, even after the sheriff's showed up they had a hard time breaking it all up. It wasn't good, lots of guys got hurt real bad. I mean no one got shot or knifed or hit with any chains, not like that, just went down mano-a-mano. Duke took some good shots, but I'm thinking he dished out a lot of 'em too. He ended up with a cracked nose and I think he might have needed some stitches too.

"Afterwards, he drove us back home with blood drooling out of his nose, and his knuckles were all bloody and swelling up. He told us it was all about backing up his buddies from Central. He said they'd gotten to be friends with them there at the Note. I remember him telling us those Torville guys should have learned two lessons that night. One was to mind their manners, and the other was that some lessons get learned the hard way. He doubted they'd ever have any problems with 'em again…" Jack's voice trailed off. Everyone was quiet, lost in their own thoughts.

"Welp, guess he figured that wrong," said Joe.

"Guess so," said Jack. "Who knows? Maybe that's why he asked BTW to have his brother tag up with us, but Jimmy knows what we're getting into. He saw that brawl back then too. Thing is, times have changed. Things aren't as sweet and as innocent as they used to be. This Torville crowd don't look like any honorable cracker heads to me. Jimmy just wants a good old-fashioned rumble to settle things out, but I don't think that's what we're in for. Oh well, it is what it is, man. We just happen to be the lucky ones in on it this time. We're Jimmy's pards, man. That means he'd fight all hell for us, but it works both ways… We fight all hell for him too."

Joe groaned. "Sure feels good to be so lucky, don't it?"

Chapter 15

It was a typical sunset scene in the parking lot outside the Note. The Chevelles, Camaros, GTOs, and Mustangs were all on parade. Girls were combing their hair and touching up their makeup as they waved and flirted. Guys were polishing off beers and an occasional last toke. Strains of hundreds of different radios and eight tracks wafted all through the lot. Summer was drawing to an end. School would be starting in a couple of weeks. Football practice, the dreaded "two-a-days," began on Monday. In a few weeks, it would be Labor Day, which meant docks would be pulled in and the lake would close down. Summer's end was near, so this would be one of the Note's last big weekends.

Over on the back side of the lot, the Torville contingent was much larger than usual. Everyone knew who they were. They weren't hard to spot as their cars were dumps and their looks were just as rough. For some warped reason, this was their MO. Their cars all looked like they had been in a junkyard derby, which was the big pastime in Torville.

And they all looked like slobs: dirty jeans and T-shirts with long scraggly hair. It seemed like the same with their girls. They were a crowd that stood out. Nobody understood why they were the way they were, and around the old Soul Note, nobody wanted to anymore. Everybody just wanted to keep their distance from them.

But not Jimmy, Rafe, Randy, or half a dozen other biker pals of Jimmy's, who thundered into the lot that hot and muggy evening. Jack and the boys had pulled and settled in about fifteen minutes earlier. Most of them had gathered around the Cherry, sitting up in the bed or on the lowered tailgate, listening to Jack's Santana's *Abraxas* tape. Jack was scanning for Alejandra. Maybe she was already inside dancing, warming the place up.

"Hey, Hayseed! What's up, man?" It was Remo, who wore a wide smile and was in good cheer, as usual. He was with Henry English and Ernie Rauls, two other ballplayers Jack liked and got along well with. "Ready for two-a-days, man? You been workin' out? All you hayseeds still be lookin' little compared to ol' big Remo," he chided, with a big wink and a laugh.

Alejandra was not inside. She, Cassie Kay, Dawn, Sherrie, and some of their other friends were standing near the front door when the big choppers rumbled by and turned into the lot. Alejandra had been feeling the tension for weeks now too. She was more perceptive about things than most young women her age. Centuries of conflict in her bloodlines had given her an intuitive sense of her surroundings. When she saw the bikers and noticed that there were a couple more than usual, she walked around to watch where they went.

Cassie Kay was watching too. She knew Jimmy, not as well as Jack, Rafe, and Randy did, but she had known of him since the seventh grade. She'd never had any classes with him, but she would notice him in the hallways. He was one of the few boys taller than she was at the time. Even back then he was imposing. She didn't know his name until one morning when she was walking into the school. A group of kids had gathered just outside the entrance. Everyone was staring and pointing at a little dog that some hood had kicked in the head. Its eye was a swollen mass of blood and tissue. No one did anything. They were all just frozen in shock, standing and staring at the poor, whining, shivering little thing.

Then the crowd parted as a big boy in a plain white T-shirt and denim jeans pushed through. Without hesitating, he'd bent down and picked up the small dog, gently cradling the terrified animal in his arms, petting and speaking to it softly, vainly trying to soothe it. She remembered the look on the boy's face as he stood up and looked around at the crowd. It was a look of hopelessness, which quickly turned to one of anger and resolve. Someone held the door open as he walked into the building and down to the principal's office, still cradling the dog. Cassie Kay didn't fully realize it, nor was she anywhere near ready to admit it, but she had fallen for that big farm boy right then and there.

Somebody said, "That's Jimmy Meeks! Oh, boy, is he mad. Somebody better watch out. If he finds out who did that, he's gonna give 'em an eye just like that dog's!" Later she'd heard that Jimmy did find out who did it and had busted them up good—real good. She'd also heard that Jimmy's mom had driven into town and taken the little dog to the vet. It had lost the eye but found a home on the Meeks' big farm. She then heard that his younger sister, Jessie, had nursed it and that it wasn't long before he'd become a barn dog and a favorite of their Grandfather's. Jessie had named him Little Pete after Peter Pan, because she'd said he was like a pirate dog, having only one eye.

The girls watched as the bikers rumbled and weaved their way through the crowded lot. The evening was sizzling, and the dust and exhaust seemed to hover in their wake, giving the scene a surrealistic air. Jimmy nodded as he made his way by Jack. He was on the hunt and he knew right where his prey was. It was a nasty, filthy prey, but it was Jimmy's kind of prey—low-life prey—and his blood was up. They made their way toward the back where the Torville crowd had gathered. Jimmy slowed his chopped Fat Boy to a crawl as he passed. He ripped the throttle loudly for effect as the bikers slowly circled the Torville cars.

When he stopped his bike, Jimmy had everyone's undivided attention. "Rafe, do you see the pricks who tried to run you over? You, Randy?" Both bikers shook their heads in unison. The big Olds with the roughed in Bondo job wasn't there. Jimmy looked hard at the crowd. He kicked the stand down on his bike and stood up. He left the bike growling as he took several steps toward the Torville crowd, many of them backing away as he did. He stopped and straightened himself tall. He wore a leather vest, a white T-shirt with the sleeves rolled up, denim jeans, and black steel-toed work boots. Dust swirled up around the bronzed mass of muscle and veins coiled for action. "You all know who we're lookin' for! I don't like assholes killin' my buds!"

The Torville crowd just stared at him. No one had ever confronted them like this before. Jack and Bobby had been the first in recent memory to take on any one of them, but here was this one big nightmare again, wanting to take on the whole bunch. "You're all a bunch of low-life sons of bitches if you don't give the pricks up that killed my buddy Charley Taggert out on M39 and had just tried to take out another one of us!" Jimmy glanced over his shoulder toward Randy.

Jack, Bobby, Big Schuler, Joe, Fletch, and the others watched intently, like everyone else, at the encounter. They moved up and nearer to the bikers. If something was going to flare up, they would be there. Jack couldn't just stand there. He knew how quickly it could all break loose, and when it did, his friend would need him there by his side quickly, so he made his way over close to where Jimmy was standing, and the others followed him. He realized, though, that this was Jimmy's action, so he stood a few feet away yet close enough so that there was no doubt that they were there—not that Jimmy needed any backup.

Alejandra had moved nearer, too, watching, mesmerized by these wild, raw American boys. She was fascinated yet wary of the big biker, who was willing to confront a nasty looking mob to defend and protect his friends. She had kept a shrewd eye on him, as he was not only Jack's very good friend, but he could also get Jack and a lot of others hurt, or worse, like the one who had been killed.

"That's one bad dude!" It was Remo, who seemed to have appeared out of thin air next to Alejandra. He, too, had watched the surreal scene and was trying to make sense of it, appreciating the intensity of the biker. Tough as Jimmy was, there was a large and growing swarm of the Torville crowd, and even with his buddies backing him up, Remo could see they were still far outnumbered.

Alejandra turned and looked up at Remo. "Is he a bad boy, Remo? He's Jack's friend."

"Oh, I know. I mean, he's a bad dude, all right. Not like *bad* bad. That Torville crowd—now those are bad people, real bad people. That big dude, he's bad like 'watch out for him, dude' bad. Hey, hey… he's somethin', though, I like his style. I surely do."

"Yes," she agreed. "But I hope Jack does not get hurt. Those are bad people, but Jack, he is good."

Tom Morris and his Carlyle buddies all saw it, too, and so did the River Ridge and the Easton guys. They watched, impressed with the boldness of that Jimmy guy. *One cool dude*, they all thought. *Standing up for his buddies like that. Bold, man. Bold! Kind of dude I'd fight along with anytime. Go to war with, that kind of dude, for sure. And look at Jack and those other Lake County dudes. They're right there. Right up there backing him up. Dang! Not near enough of them, though. Bold, yes, but they're way outnumbered, man. I'm in on this—we're all in. Had plenty of our own problems with those Torville pricks, too, and we didn't do anything. We'd just let it slide. But not this time. Not this time, damn it!*

Jimmy just stood there, daring any of them—or all of them—to step out on him. No one did. They just stood there looking at him, cigarette smoke hanging in the air. One of them passed a joint and another swigged the last of a beer, crushed the can, and threw it to the ground. "Bunch of fuckin' low-lifes!" Jimmy said as he turned and walked back to his bike. Mounting it, he stood it up, kicked it into gear, and roared off. Rafe, Randy, and the others followed, looking surly, and kicking up a cloud of dust and exhaust in their wake.

"Whoa!" Bobby said. "Was that somethin' or what? Man, somethin' is gonna hit the fan royally here tonight for sure."

"Holy shit!" Big Schuler said. "I thought it was gonna bust wide open right here and now. Man, that Jimmy is wild, man, wild. I'm sure as shit glad I'm on his side!"

Jack relaxed and uncoiled a bit. He, too, had thought it was going to bust loose, and he had gotten all wound up for it.

"*Hola*, Jack!" He turned to see Alejandra walking up behind him. His heart leaped, and his body ramped up again with a different set of endorphins raging.

"You look great!" he said, and she did, dressed in a black blouse and denim jeans.

"Somehow I thought I would find you gentlemen around here somewhere. *Hola*, everyone," she said

"Hi, Alejandra," the boys said in unison as they started to head toward the Note's entrance, their attention now focused on Cassie Kay. She had watched it all from farther away and was walking into the building. Even from a distance, her fluid figure was a sight to behold.

Jack and Alejandra danced a little that night, mostly to the slower tunes. They just wanted to hold and touch each other. They sat on the little bench by the fountain, again, talking and kissing and touching. The night was winding down inside the Note. The last song was by Santana.

"Oh, Jack, this one is my favorite! It was our first slow dance, remember? Come, let's dance to it again, please."

They held onto each other as closely as they could. Jack was better at it now, more secure in being so close to her, her smell, her feel. "You've become such a good dancer now, Jack, so very nice. So this will be our song… for always and forever, our song. Wherever we are in the world, our souls will always be together when we hear this song. Your soul will always be mine, and mine will always be yours. Always we will be like we are now, here at the Soul Note." She whispered softly into his ear, "*Te amo, Jacinto, te amo. Te amo con todo mi corazón y alma.*" She pulled back and met his puzzled gaze. Despite the darkness, Jack noticed how her eyes appeared teary. He had wanted to hear those words from her since the beginning, and though her final ones he did not understand, he knew they were meaningful to her.

"*Te amo*, Alejandra, *te amo*," he said back. She kissed him then, lightly, preciously, and he kissed her back more firmly than he ever had, not caring if anyone around him noticed, and even if they had, no one would have cared. They wanted to kiss like that too.

Too soon the song ended, and after a little while they found Cassie Kay with Big Schuler. Joe and Bobby had paired up with Dawn and Sherrie again. Upon meeting up, they all walked outside to their cars. A light rain had started and there was a slight misty wind. There were crowds moving all through the parking lot and the roar of Jimmy's bikes shattered the eerie silence as they pulled up and slid to a stop just as they had all reached Cassie Kay's car. "It's goin' down! Now!" he shouted. They hurriedly ushered the girls into the car just as it was about to erupt.

Jimmy hadn't gone into the club that night. He, Rafe, Randy, and a group of some of his other biker friends had dropped their stands down on the edge of the lot and waited as even more of the old Torville heaps continued to pull in. They watched the drunks toss out their beer cans and liquor bottles and stumble out of their vehicles, laughing and pissing on other cars, or on themselves.

It had started raining when Rafe saw the car, the Olds Ninety-Eight with the raw Bondo patches all over it. It was the one that had tried to run him off the road, the same one that had sped past them in the parking lot at Darden Dragway and had maybe caused Charley's accident. It was the very same one that Randy said had tried to make him hit the ditch as well. It was them all right.

The boys watched as the Torville group piled out of the heap and stumbled around drunkenly, trying to get their bearings. They heard the swearing and laughter as one of them crushed a half-filled beer can against his forehead, the liquid splashing all over him. "Shithead," the boys heard, along with someone by one of the other cars puking. "Asshole," they also heard. They saw another group pass a joint around, giggling and dancing some kind of silly jig to whatever music it was they were listening to.

BMW and the Central guys were watching now, too, as well as Tom Morris and his Carlyle buddies, and the Easton and Grand River guys. They were all watching quietly after having stealthily exited the Note earlier, one group at a time, and had gathered themselves around their cars or just around the corner of the building, out of sight in the darkness. Jimmy was watching them closely, sizing them up, calculating their numbers and deciding which ones he wanted the most. They had all seen Jack, his girl, and the other Lake County contingent leave the Note together, knew the Torville crowd had, too, and knew that now it would happen. Jimmy had made sure of it.

From the darkness, the boy that Jack had the short-lived fight with weeks ago lunged at him but slipped in the muddy lot. This gave Jack time to lunge back, slipping as well but able to grab the kid and land a punch before they went sprawling, both swinging wildly. Jack could hear screams but was oblivious to everything else as he groped for an opening to land another blow. He felt someone else, who was nearly on top of him, try to grab at him, and then felt more missed punches just over his head.

Just then, a big hand grabbed whoever it was by the back of the collar, and like a big crane lifting up a sack of manure, Jimmy pulled the boy up. With his fist clenched like a big ball-peen hammer, he brought it down on the boy's face. The crane dropped the sack of manure, letting it crumple into the mud.

All hell had broken out around Jack by then. Rafe had grabbed someone and was wailing away on him. It was the boy who had flipped him off. Good-natured Rafe who rarely lost his cool. His long hair was whirling every which direction, his white T-shirt was wet with blood, mud and sweat. Out of the corner of his eye, Jack briefly saw Randy rolling around with someone, flailing his fists to try to get one in.

Jack bounded up quickly, still slipping and sliding, trying to gain his footing on the rain slicked ground, flailing his fists at the one he'd been tangled up with. In a split second, he took it all in: crowds of other guys running toward the commotion, Tom Morris grabbing someone and throwing him down hard right in front of Jack, and BMW running head on into some big Torville dude in a mud-splattered T-shirt, blood now splattering from his face. Jack could hear the yelling, grunting, and groaning of the combatants as the brawl grew throughout the parking lot.

Someone had pulled out a chain and there was a dull repetitive thud of a fist on someone's skull. Jack jumped on one of them, who looked like a giant wet rat as it ran by, knocking him down and slipping in the mud as he did, the chain just barely missing his head. He got back up and, gaining his balance, lunged at the place the chain had come from. He was all rage now, no longer the easygoing guy he was moments before the fight. It felt good to get his hands on the boy, or rat, or whatever it was—a big hay bale! Jack wailed on him before he felt something hard across his head, making him even more enraged. He felt his hair being pulled, his fist melting into the soft flesh of someone's face, and warm blood oozing over the hand gripping the boy's collar.

Jack felt a jolt on his left side and pain ripped through him. That one hurt, and even in his rage he felt it. Someone had kicked him hard in the ribs. He rolled right into another kick that just missed his other side. He knew he had to get up somehow, but before he made a move to someone fell down beside him, holding their groin and face at the same time. Jack looked up and saw Jimmy with his long arms and giant fists flailing, smashing what looked like shrunken heads. He looked wild, like something out of some kind of *Night of the Living Dead* movie. Jimmy, surrounded by mere mortals, looked like Achilles or Zeus. Outnumbered, it was Jimmy's kind of fight. He was in full glory, grabbing, smashing, and pounding away. "Got your back, Jack boy! Here's another!" he barked out, throwing another clump down next to Jack.

Finally, Jack managed to stagger to his feet. It seemed like there were hundreds of Torville's. Where did they all come from? And they were mean fighters, dirty fighters. He caught a glimpse of Bobby rolling over on the ground with one of them, getting punches in where he could. Big Schuler was next to Rafe, their backs against a car, looking like two gladiators wailing and crashing and roaring. Rafe, his long hair now just wet strings flying loose, grabbed a kid and slammed him down on the car's hood, smashing his fists down and down again.

More of the Torville crowd jumped in and Big Schuler, wild with rage, clawed at them, throwing them off like ragdolls. Jack, still managing to stay on his feet, threw an overhead punch that landed solidly against someone's ear. Readying to throw another, he saw Fletch on the other side of the car throwing wild punches at an elusive, greasy-looking head that was bobbing and weaving. Somehow

Jack could hear BMW and the Grand River guys off to one side in their own wild melee, and he caught glimpses of the Carlisle and Easton gangs on his other side, closer to him, everyone thick in the mayhem.

Then Jack saw him. *There he is! That one with the chain again! Gonna hit Jimmy from behind! Ah!* he thought and grabbed hold of the kid and rolled him to the ground. The boy somehow managed to swing the chain up at Jack, but Jack ducked just as it whizzed over him. He smashed his fist into the kid's face again and again, and even as someone pulled him down and away, he managed to land a hard punch to the kid's gut before being thrown to the side by someone.

The fight seemed to last forever, growing with a life of its own. There were just so many of them. Every time Jack had a chance to catch his breath, he would see another one right in front of him and would just barely have the chance to dodge an oncoming fist or that chain or get a punch in himself. Then Jack heard a booming voice, a *big* booming voice—a roar! The looming shadow above him revealed itself. It was Remo! He had two of the Torville's in headlocks and was roaring as he lifted them up and down, trying to pop their heads off, letting them fall away like limp little dolls. Jack pounced on the chain with his fists flailing, some landing, some missing. Somehow, he managed to grab hold of the chain with one hand during his rampage and was able to keep it from doing more damage.

In the midst of all the chaos, the sudden shriek of fog-horns—the same ones Jack had heard years ago in Duke's fight—echoed throughout the parking lot. In an instant, the chain pulled back and slithered out of Jack's grasp. He felt someone running past him and heard someone else groaning on the ground next to him. Jack bounded up quickly, wary of stragglers trying to get a last punch in. It was a chaotic scene: car horns were blaring, the blue and red lights of the sheriff cars were dancing, tires were screeching as they tried to catch a grip on the wet pavement. The sirens were louder now as they grew closer. Everything seemed like mush to Jack's senses. It all happened at warp speed, and he was desperately trying to slow it all back down and regain some kind of coherence.

Fortunately, Jolly Rogers had beefed up the security by adding more off-duty deputies. They had helped to break things up, but it had happened so fast and there had been so many more involved that night, far more than there had ever been. And it looked like it was more organized than these fights usually were. Jolly had seen it brewing—they all had. They had seen the ever-growing gatherings of the Torville contingent and knew they were the ones looking to start trouble. They also saw Jimmy, Jack, and their other Lake County friends hanging out more with the guys from the other schools, so they had a good idea of what was going on. The sheer size of the brawl and the intensity of it, though, had somehow caught them off guard that night.

Jolly had lost track of Jack in the large crowd, but fortunately Jimmy, Rafe, and Jack's other friends had managed to stay close together around Jack in order to prevent him or any of them from getting dragged off. If that had happened, it could have been far worse, especially for Jack and Bobby too.

As it was, the fight was bad enough, and even though the off-duty deputies had acted quickly with the sheriff's patrol being nearby, it had still gotten way out of hand. Fortunately, the blaring of the sirens and foghorns over the outdoor speakers, along with the illuminating display of the revolving red and blue lights that Jolly had installed overhead on several of the lamp posts around the parking lot, had helped to defuse the brawl... somewhat.

Jolly knew these kinds of eruptions were virtually inevitable. The kids from around these parts weren't from upper crust, namby-pamby households. Most of them were from rough-and-tumble blue-collar factory towns and neighborhoods, or from rural hardscrabble farms. Mixing them together, along with the added intoxicants of cheap wine, beer, pot, and girls, always made for a toxic brew. These boys, as he knew all too well, knew how to fight and would fight at the drop of a dime, mostly if provoked, but not always. Tonight, however, they had been provoked, and from the looks of things, the ones doing the provoking had got what they deserved. Thankfully, from what he could tell surveying the scene, there had been no knives or firearms involved.

On the other hand, Jack could have argued vociferously that the use of chains constituted as deadly weapons. He looked around him, still trying to gather himself and steady his nerves. The adrenaline that was once furiously coursing through his veins, and which had helped to mute the pain from any blows, was now dissipating.

"Jack! Jack!" Alejandra was suddenly next to him, holding him and helping him walk. "Are you all right? Are you all right?" she kept asking.

"Yeah... sure... I'm okay," Jack struggled to say, wincing from the onslaught of different pains. *No, not really*, he wanted to say, *I hurt like hell here, and this is burning here, and my hands are throbbing...*

Then he heard the sound of the big bikes as they roared by. Jimmy, though, slowed and pulled up next to him. Jack was standing with Alejandra, Bobby, Big Schuler, Joe, and some of the others. Jimmy eyed them all hard, nodded, and then looked directly at Jack. Briefly they looked at each other, eye to eye. Then Jimmy nodded again, an acknowledgment of gratitude, of a deed well done—of a brotherhood. He extended a bloodied fist and Jack met it with one of his own. He did the same in turn with the others, looking each of the boys in the eyes, even smiling slightly and nodding his head in thanks and approval for their actions Then he slowly and loudly eased the heavy bike away.

As Jimmy passed by Remo, he stopped and stared once more before nodding his head in thanks. Again, he stretched out a bloody fist and Remo stretched his out, too, and they knocked their fists together. Jimmy did the same with several of Remo's friends and with others that he recognized as allies that were still around. It was raining harder now, and the sirens were still growing louder as they grew closer to that side of the parking lot. Jimmy roared off with lightning crackling and thunderclaps pounding overhead. An 8-track tape player from someone's car was eerily playing "Riders on the Storm" by The Doors.

Blood was running down Jack's face from a small gash above his eye, and his left side had a sharp throb from that one hard kick he'd got. Still in a daze, Jack faintly heard Alejandra say that he needed to go to the hospital, that he might need stitches, and needed to have his ribs looked at. She opened the door to the backseat of Cassie Kay's Ford Crown Victoria. "Lie down here," she said gently, "Bobby will take care of your truck. Please, Jack, there is no way you should drive." He relented and laid down, gingerly holding his side, and rested his head on her lap.

Joe eagerly volunteered to drive. He had fared better in the fight than Jack but was still not in the greatest shape to be driving at night on a rain-soaked road. Cassie Kay hesitated, her instincts cautious. "Oh, come on, Cassie Kay," said Joe. "I'm fine, it's Jack that wound up wrestling with that chain. I'll be real careful, I promise. Besides, I know these roads out here like the back of my hand."

Cassie Kay relented and handed him the keys. She did trust Joe, knowing that he was a good driver and that he would be cautious. Besides, Cassie Kay was an intuitive young woman and thought it might be a blow to Joe's boyish pride to be seen riding shotgun while she drove, especially after that testosterone-laced brawl she had just witnessed.

It was pitch black and still raining hard as they headed down the narrow winding roads toward town. The curves were wet and treacherous, but Joe slowed to a crawl to navigate them. Joe was a mature driver and knew how to handle an automobile in all kinds of weather. It went with the territory in this part of the country. It also helped that Joe knew the road well, knew its imposing curves and switchbacks, and to anticipate their approach.

Suddenly there were headlights, bright, glaring lights coming up fast from behind, blinding Joe in the rearview mirror. The car was coming on fast, way too fast, and it couldn't slowdown in time to keep from slamming into them from the rear. It had to veer around the big Crown Vic. When it did, it went into a spin on the slick pavement, and as it came back around, it careened into the side of the Crown Vic on Joe's side and sent it spinning too.

Jack had faded out with his head on Alejandra's warm lap. It felt so good with her nursing his head and slowly running her fingers through his wet hair. Now he felt as if he were in a washing machine, tumbling over and over. He heard screams and tearing metal. For a split second, he felt himself flying through the air until suddenly hitting and rolling along a hard surface. Then it all stopped.

From somewhere nearby, Jack could hear a female voice scream and groan before shouting, "Oh, God! Oh, God!"

He was lying in wet leaves and could smell the dirt where he lay face down. The pain was incredible, shooting and stabbing from all over his body—all one giant pain. Delirious, he began to crawl, grabbing handfuls of dirt and leaves with his one working arm to pull his body toward the wreckage of the Crown Vic. He tried to push himself up but was unable to. One of his legs didn't seem to work right.

It was so dark. He could see one of the headlights of the Ford glaring off into the woods, but he couldn't make out the whole car. It all seemed so far away.

"Alejandra?" he croaked. There was no answer. He tried to call her name again, louder this time. Still, no reply. Panic suddenly engulfed him. "Oh, God!... Alejandra!"

1988

Chapter 16

"**Y**ou all right, mister?"

The bright glare of a spotlight blinded Jack as he turned to look at where the question came from. He put his hand above his eyes in a vain attempt to shield them and regain his vision. The snow was coming down hard still and had now completely covered Jack's long black overcoat. His cigar had burned out, but he still held onto it. The Santana cassette tape wined eerily from inside his car through the driver's side door that he had inadvertently left open.

"Yeah, I'm okay," Jack said, squinting his eyes to see who had interrupted his reflections.

"Well, that's good, mister. Little lonely out here tonight, though, ain't it? Cold as hell too."

"Yeah, sure is… Just checking out the old place."

"Oh yeah?" The deep voice moved closer, the light still in Jack's face, blinding him. "You from around here?"

"No—I mean, yes, I was. Been a while. Long time ago."

"That right?" said the stranger. "How long ago?"

"Well, this place was still open then. Would've had a big crowd this time of night. It was quite a place."

The man shut off the blinding light, engulfing Jack in total blackness. As his eyes adjusted to the darkness, Jack could make out the silhouette of a large, dark figure standing in front of a patrol car about fifty feet away. The apparition moved swiftly toward him. Then the smaller, less intense beam of a flashlight hit him up close. Jack flinched from its suddenness. "My God! Well, I'll be damned!" the stranger exclaimed. "Jack? That you, Jack? Jack Dean? It's me, Jimmy! Jimmy Meeks!"

"Jimmy?" Jack was in disbelief. Peering around the light, he instantly recognized the familiar face of his old friend. "I'll be damned! Yeah, Jimmy, it's me. Damn! Big ol' Jimmy Meeks!" he exclaimed in shock as they embraced in a bear hug.

"I'll be damned, Jack! Where the hell have you been? Damn! I can't believe it's you. Jack Dean! Damn!"

"Well, look at you, man. You a sheriff or something?"

"Yes, sir. Matter of fact, I *am* the sheriff. They call me Sheriff Meeks, now. Come on, get in the patrol car, I promise I won't arrest you for loiterin'." Jack turned off his car, cutting off a Santana riff, before climbing in next to Jimmy in his squad car. Jimmy had turned on the heater. "I can't believe it's you, man. Normally I never get out on patrol much anymore, but I let a couple of the boys take some time off tonight, so I decided to just take a ride over this way. Not that far from the farm anyway. It sure doesn't look like the ol' place, huh?"

"Nope, sure doesn't," Jack agreed. He welcomed the warmth inside the patrol car as he stared out the passenger side window at the dark parking lot. "What the hell happened? This used to be the most popular place around for a hundred miles on a Friday or Saturday night."

"I guess it was a combination of things," Jimmy replied. "A lot had to do with the state changin' the legal drinkin' age back then, remember. I think the feelin' was if an eighteen-year-old kid could get drafted and go off and get his butt shot to hell in Vietnam, then he ought to be allowed to come home and have a beer and vote too. So, why would anyone come all the way out here anymore for somethin' to do when you could go to the bars and nightclubs right in your own backyard? But all the fights and the accidents… just kind of killed it off, too, I guess."

Jack continued gazing out through the windshield at the long, vacant, dilapidated old structure with its peeling white paint, exposing the raw gray cinder blocks. "Well, at least it's not eating anymore souls," Jack mused, grinning, as he recalled the ominous warning the Note's bouncer, Bust Up, had used so devilishly years ago to scare him and Jimmy from sneaking into the nightclub when he wasn't looking.

"Nope. Nothin' much to feed off of out here anymore, that's for sure." Jimmy shook his head and smiled, too, remembering the warning as well. "Can still get a little spooky, though. Like tonight, seein' you standin' out there all covered in snow. Thought you might be a ghost or somethin'… and what the hell you doin' out here this time of night standin' out in a freezin' snow storm and after all this time, anyway?"

Jack didn't answer the questions. He just kept staring out the window into the darkness. After a moment, he looked over at Jimmy and then around the inside of the car. "Hey, this is pretty cool. I haven't been inside one of these in a while."

"Shit, I bet you never have, Jack," Jimmy responded, letting his questions go unanswered, at least for the moment.

"No, not like you. You probably knew your way around one of these pretty good back then. I can't believe it! Jimmy Meeks... Lake County Sheriff!"

"Well, you know, if you can't beat 'em, join 'em," Jimmy quipped. "Can't believe it's really you, Jack."

"It's really me, Jimmy, and I'm not a ghost. And it's sure good to see you, my friend. I've been wanting to come back here for a long time, but you know, busy, working a lot, you know... I always wanted to come back to see the old place... and say thank you. Don't know what I would've done back then without you helping me out like you did when you found us."

Jimmy stared off into the darkness thinking what a miracle it was that Jack was not a ghost and of how close he had come to being one. "Oh, hell, Jack, that's why you're out here? You were like one of the family to us, you know that. You were—still are—like a brother to me. We had a lot of good times, didn't we?"

And so they sat there in Jimmy's patrol car and talked and reminisced about all the old times... all the good times. But eventually it all had to come around to the bad times.

Both of them were taking deep breaths, staring out the windshield at the snow and the cold darkness.

It was Jimmy who finally spoke. "Still almost feels like yesterday, huh? I couldn't believe I found you lyin' out there in the pourin' rain. It was dark as shit! I just had a feelin'… I knew you were with them. It was such a bad scene, Jack. I've seen a lot of bad ones since then, but that was bad, *real* bad. It shocked the hell out of me, that's for sure. Rainin' like that, pullin' bodies out… Joe all crumpled up… poor Cassie Kay, screamin' like she was… all the cryin'." He paused, remembering the nightmare. "Me, Randy, and Rafe headed out of here like bats out of hell when we heard the law comin'. Kind of left you all hangin' here, didn't we? So, after a few miles I said, 'Screw it. If anyone ought to hang for it, it ought to be me.' We pulled off and we were goin' to turn around when you all went passed us. Then a bunch of those Torville idiots came flyin' along in one of their old beaters and I knew somethin' bad was goin' to happen, so we peeled out after them. That's when we came up to it…

"Damn. I'll never forget how sick that sight made me. It was so dark out there that night, but we could see one of the headlights of that Torville car still glarin' back off the road. Everythin' was smashed up bad. There was hardly anythin' left of that car, just pieces of it. There were pieces of people all over the place, and beer cans all around it too. I sent Randy back here to the Note to get help. Luckily, some of the deputies were still around. I found that Ford of Cassie Kay's way down back in the woods. It must have rolled over half a dozen times before it hit a big tree. It was all smashed up too. I was freaked, Jack. Cassie Kay was screamin' and cryin'…

"The foreign girl—your girl—was slumped over in the backseat. She wasn't all busted up or anythin', and at first I thought she was okay. But she wasn't movin', so I put my fingers up along her neck to find a pulse, like I'd seen them do on TV. My hands were shakin' and damn, I just couldn't find one. I remember closin' my eyes and as gently as I could, I kept tryin' to find her pulse, but there just wasn't one… and I realized that she must've broken her neck, and she was just… gone. When I opened my eyes, they must've adjusted to the dark because I was lookin' right at Joe. I could see how bad off he was and realized that there was nothin' I could do. Nothin' I could do…"

He lit a cigarette and took a deep drag, and then offered one to Jack, who was still staring out the windshield at nothing but the darkness. Jack shook his head. "I went back over to Cassie Kay. She had curled herself up and was shiverin' and sobbin'," Jimmy continued. "I didn't know what to do, and I only had my ol' vest to put around her. I just held her as gently as I could and tried to keep her warm in that pourin' rain. I kept tellin' her that everythin' was goin' to be all right, that big Jimmy's got her now. I just kept holdin' onto her like that, and it seemed like forever until that ambulance finally got there. She was tough, though. I could tell she was in a lot of pain, shiverin' and shakin', but she just gritted it out.

"Then I thought I heard someone moanin' back further in the woods, so Rafe and I started lookin' all over, but it was so dark, and I was slippin' and slidin' all over that I thought it was hopeless. Finally, the cops started showin' up, lights flashin' everywhere, sirens blarin'. One of their headlights was shinin' back into the woods. That's when I caught a glimpse of somethin', like a big lump movin', and I ran over to it to find that it was you! You were just kind of movin' with your face in the leaves and dirt, not really goin' anywhere. I reached down, not really knowin' what to do. Man, was I freaked. I didn't want to try and move you and make matters worse. I've had all kinds of trainin' since then, but back then, shit, I didn't know what to do, so I just kind of turned you over slowly. That's when I saw your leg and could see how busted up you were all over. Man! I just started bellowin' like an ol' hog for someone to come and help. I thought you were dyin' on me right there, and it seemed like it took them forever to put you on that stretcher. You looked like a broken doll. I thought for sure you were a goner.

"It was a bad scene at the hospital too. Bad, man. We all left our bikes right out there under a tree. I rode in with one of the deputies. He was pretty cool—they all were. They knew us—had to know it was us. But they didn't hassle us at all. Said it was good that we helped out. They were just tryin' to figure out what the hell had happened. After a while, though, they could tell. It didn't take much imagination to figure it out. Anyway, it was all a nightmare, everyone there at the hospital cryin'. I didn't know what to do. I called my grandma and she called your mom and dad. They all showed up there about the same time. I don't know who called Joe's people. His poor ol' grandma was there cryin'. Everyone was cryin'. Cassie Kay's parents just cryin' all quiet like. Your mom and dad tryin' to hold up, but you could see how worried and upset they were.

"You were in and out of it for a long time. Came to see how you were doin' most every passin' day. Brought the whole family some days—even little Jessie. She begged us to let her come see you. Said you had saved her life, and she wanted to help save yours too. All that hospital staff didn't seem to bother her none, but one day she started to cry. I saw these big tears well up. Said she couldn't do much to help save you, but Grandma said sure she could, we all could if we prayed. So, all of us prayed together. And she said that if you left this life, even if you didn't live, you'd keep on livin' in Heaven with God, like Mom, and that God would hear Jessie's prayer and all of our prayers. So, we all kept on prayin', even me. Big, chip-on-the-shoulder, hard-ass me.

"Some days you were better than others, but for a long time we still didn't know if you were goin' to make it. It was a miracle you did. One time I came to see you, you were semiconscious. You recognized me, though. You made me promise to go back and play ball again. Said the team was really goin' to need me. That we still needed to win state. I still can't believe I shook your hand on it. I had to go back to school and everythin'. Turned out to be the best thing I ever did. Even ol' Rafe came back with me. Remember we dedicated the season to you and Joe?"

"Yeah," Jack mumbled, before turning to Jimmy and smiling slightly. "And you guys won it all."

"Yep, we were all pullin' for you. We prayed for you every day. I hadn't prayed since my mom died. I didn't even like God anymore after that. Then, with you all busted up, there was no one else to turn to. Only Him. And I did, man. I prayed hard. I've been prayin' hard ever since…" Jimmy was quiet for a moment, then he smiled. "Somehow, we did win it all. Beat Remo's team in the championship. They played me everywhere. Made all-state. That's how I got that college scholarship, earned my degree, and how I became Sheriff Meeks. It straightened me out. Guess that night changed us all in a way, didn't it, Jack?"

"Yeah, it sure did," Jack agreed. "I always wanted to thank you for all you did for me, Jimmy. The way you went after that bunch that summer. It was me and Bobby they really wanted, yet you were the one that got us all to stand up to them. Then all you did for me out in the woods there… I would've been a goner for sure if it weren't for you finding me that night."

"Are you kiddin'?" said Jimmy. "It's me that ought to be thankin' you for all you did for me! Hey, we did have quite a row with that Torville crowd, though, didn't we? Wasn't much of a plan, though. You were innocent, so we all were lookin' out for you, and it all just kind of fell into place. We knew somethin' was goin' to happen that night, so we all just hid out and watched for them. Sure enough, they did just what we thought they would do, try to take you down like they did. Then *wham*! We got 'em. Good thing we had all the help we did, though. Had even more than we expected with Remo chippin' in. We needed it too!" Jimmy laughed, breaking the tension. "All I can remember is seein' you duckin' from some guy swingin' a chain all over. But you know somethin'? We never did have a problem with them after that. Still don't. All those kids killed... I guess that night changed them too."

Jack nodded, staring off into the blackness, and said, "Nightmare changed us all, for sure. Taken me a long time to get over it, don't think I ever really will. Joe and Alejandra... I tried to stay in touch with her folks. They came all the way from Spain to bring her body home. I vaguely remember them by my bed, holding my hand. They left me their address back in Spain. I wrote to them when I finally could, and they wrote back. They wanted me to go and visit them, and I wanted to. Man, I missed her. Took a long time, but I knew I had to somehow, someday... deal with it all... somehow move on."

And so there, during a snowstorm and in a sheriff's squad car in the abandoned parking lot of the place where so many lives had been changed so many years ago, two old friends reminisced about it all. Summers spent fishing, baling hay, camping out, schoolyard fights, football and baseball games, girls, and all the old pals. Bobby had moved away. He lived out in California somewhere and had a sales job of some kind. Big Schuler played college ball at Western and was coaching and teaching school right over in Easton. Rafe joined the army and was still in it. He was a sergeant stationed over in Germany now. Randy managed a Harley shop in town and was still good friends with Jimmy.

"And Remo, man, he's the sheriff over in East Lake County," Jimmy said. "See him all the time. Him, me, and some of the other sheriffs around here set up a youth camp program. We take kids from tough situations and bring them out to the farms to help with balin' and different stuff.

It's great for 'em, just like it was for us. Really helps keep 'em out of trouble—they're too tired most of the time. Just like it did for us, huh? Teaches the kids what hard work's all about. Most of them really get a lot out of it."

"That's great, Jimmy," Jack said. "And good old Remo. Last time I saw him he was cracking heads. That was something! We sure needed them and all those other guys too."

"Speak for yourself, man, I was lovin' it. But it was great of Remo to help us out like he did. He can still crack some heads if he needs to, though. Hey, where you stayin'?"

"Over at The Lodge at Camp Kit down the road. I didn't even know the place was there. Just saw it as I drove by. I still can't believe it was that old fish camp. I was lucky they had a vacancy and got a nice cottage down by the lake. Their main lodge was all booked up. You wouldn't think there would be a lot of demand this time of year, but it's a great place, and a lot of folks want to get away for the weekend, I guess," Jack said.

"Did Carla cook up her meatloaf specialty tonight? I love that meatloaf of hers."

"How'd you know?" asked Jack. "Yeah, and it was great."

"That little bit of sausage in it... Taste familiar at all? You probably don't remember, but Carla's my older cousin. She's got my aunt's old recipe. Remember? We used to have it at least once every year when we were balin'. Grandpa loved it. When Carla and Nick moved back here and fixed up the old camp, it was one of the first things on the menu."

"Unbelievable! You know, I did think it tasted familiar, but I just couldn't think of where I'd eaten it before."

"Hey, tomorrow's Saturday. Why don't you come on over to the farm for dinner? We all still get together. Grandpa's gone now, but Grandma's still with us. You could meet my wife and kids. Katie will be there too. I bet you haven't had a good home-cooked meal like Grandma's in a long time, except for Carla's meatloaf! It'd be great to have you back out to the farm again. There're some things I'd like to show you too."

Chapter 17

Saturday turned out to be a beautiful day. The storm had moved out and a brilliant sun highlighted the glittering snow and crystal blue sky. In the daylight, Jack felt that he could have found his way to the farm blindfolded. He pulled into the old familiar driveway, passing by the big walnut and oak trees lining the lane, their branches bare now that winter had been officially ushered in.

As he parked and turned off the car, he took a deep breath and let it out slowly. Even though he looked forward to seeing Jimmy's family again, there was still the apprehension of seeing folks he had left in his wake years ago so abruptly when he had moved away for his first job in the radio business. But it had been more than just the job. He knew that, even then, he had needed to leave so that he could try to work it all out. He believed he could push all the bad memories away, or take them away with him so that, with time, he could find the strength to resolve them, or at the very least, keep them at bay in the hope that the good memories would come back, and in return, the good old Jack could come back too.

He wanted this to be that day and realized now that these good people, the Meeks', were a big part of the good memories. He knew he needed them to help him finally put what had happened into some kind of perspective, to reflect, to reconcile, and to get him, as Crush would say, "all whole again." If he was ever going to live his life like it should be lived, ever to enjoy and live life to its fullest again, this was what he needed, and they were who he needed. He hoped they would understand his reasonings as to why he left and why he came back.

As soon as he got out of the car, there was Jimmy—tall and athletic-looking as ever, and maybe even a little thicker—welcoming him with a wide grin on his face as he wrapped Jack in a big bear hug. "Good to see ya, buddy! Glad you could come over. Cold out here today, isn't it? Beautiful day, though. Come in, come in!"

When Jack entered the house, a room full of people greeted him warmly. Before Jimmy began introducing him to everyone, Jack handed him a paper bag with a couple bottles of champagne he had bought from the little grocery store Carla had suggested.

Jimmy started the introductions first with his wife, Cassie Kay. As beautiful as ever to Jack, she wore her blond hair pulled back, a pretty printed dress, and a welcoming smile. She was about to offer Jack her hand, but instead gave him a heartfelt embrace. "It's so wonderful to see you again, Jack. It's been too long."

"H-how? W-when?" Jack stammered, momentarily baffled. "I knew you two had gotten to be good friends after—"

"We'll tell you all about it," she interrupted, smiling widely. "Your old buddy Jimmy here turned out to be quite the romancer."

Katie looked as beautiful as ever too. Tears welled in her bright blue eyes as she hugged him.

Then there was Grandma Meeks, older and frail now, but still with those same warm eyes that had first greeted him years ago when she had offered him a slice of her Rhubarb pie. They were watering now. "Jack. Oh, Jack. We've missed you so," she said, opening her arms to him. Jack hugged her tightly, moved more than he could have anticipated. When he pulled back, he handed her the large bouquet of flowers he had been holding. "Oh, how beautiful, Jack, thank you so much!"

Taking a deep breath and recovering his composure quickly, he continued to greet all the other family members. Jimmy's dad had remarried a nice lady. He looked a lot older, but seemed more like his old, jovial, relaxed self from before Jimmy's mother passed. Cassie Kay and Jimmy's two sons and daughter were nicely groomed and well-mannered. The boys looked to be about ten and eleven, and the youngest, a Cassie Kay look-alike with her blond curls and bright blue eyes, looked about seven.

Jack was feeling somewhat overwhelmed when he glanced up from bending down to greet the children. She had entered from an adjacent room, and as he rose up he looked directly into one of the most enchanting faces he had ever seen. It was highlighted with an inviting smile and framed by a shock of wavy honey-colored hair. It was Jessie—little Jessie! But she certainly wasn't little anymore. She held his gaze with dazzlingly blue-green eyes as she walked toward him, every feature on her lovely face reflecting a genuine happiness at seeing him. As she neared him, Jack felt something like a big stone roll over and spread a ripple effect throughout his body. The entire room felt their energy, but neither noticed as they stared into each other's eyes.

"My gosh, Jessie, you look fantastic! My gosh!" Jack exclaimed. They hugged each other. As they did, Jack felt the most intense warmth he had not felt in a long time—a very long time.

"Oh, Jack, you look great! You haven't changed a bit—handsome and dashing as ever." They stood holding hands, just looking at each other, Jack marveling at her. "Gosh, Jack, we've missed you!" She hugged him tightly again. "It's so good to see you!"

"Y-you, too, Jessie," Jack stuttered, suddenly realizing there was a room full of people watching them. He looked around. "It's great to see all of you again. Sure feels great to be back here."

"Make yourself at home, Jack," said Jimmy. "The ol' place still look familiar to you?" He handed Jack a tall glass of dark liquid. "That's Grandpa's ol' brew. He really never drank that much of it himself, but remember how he used to let us have a sip or two of it back when we were balin'? Me and dad are kind of carryin' on the brewin' tradition."

Jack took a long swig of the cold, rich concoction. "Tastes great! Sure hits the spot. It always did," said Jack.

Jessie had gone back into the kitchen with the other women to help with dinner. He watched her from where he sat in the living room. Her laughter was as engaging as the rest of her. He watched as she tied an apron around her waist, still amazed at the transformation that had taken place over the last... how many years? Occasionally she would glance at him, and every time she caught his look she held him a moment with those eyes, making that stone flip over inside him again. Jack found it hard to believe that Jessie was now somewhere in her mid-twenties and had grown into such a beautiful young woman.

The champagne Jack brought made for a nice touch with the big platter of fried chicken and all the trimmings of mashed potatoes, green beans, peas, applesauce, and homemade buns. The food was delicious, and Jack complimented all the women for such a fabulous meal. He had not had one nearly as good since those dinners years ago when they were out baling hay.

"Anytime you'd like to get some good old-fashioned exercise again, you're more than welcome," Jimmy said. Everyone laughed.

"Sure could use some right now after this great meal," Jack replied. He had miraculously been seated next to Jessie. Even though he was excited, she had made him feel relaxed and at ease. He tried to stay tuned into the rest of the dinner conversation, but Jessie was so gracious and interesting he found himself mesmerized by her. He learned that she, too, had gone to State and was now a teacher at the local public school. She enjoyed her work very much and loved living right back here where she grew up, where the happiest days of her life had been. It helped her keep that connection in a spiritual way with her mother and grandfather, whom she still missed very much. But being here with the family, and helping out with Jimmy's children, kept her life full.

Jack didn't want to ask her about boyfriends, or fiancés, or anything that would crash the soaring emotions he hadn't felt in so long and may have never felt prior as a grown man. He had not wanted to feel anything ever again for so long. He had kept things simple, just for fun, with no attachments or serious consequences. And now he wanted whatever this was to last forever.

They talked throughout the meal. She seemed fascinated with his life and adventures, the radio business, his travels, and all the cities he'd lived in. As he spoke, she would watch him with all her attention, smiling, nodding, and occasionally laughing. She was enjoying his company as if she were reading for the first time what she knew would be her favorite novel, one she knew she would never want to end. And when it did, she would want to reread it many times over.

"Excuse me, Jessie," Jimmy butted in, "I wonder if I might pry ol' Jack here away for a few moments. There's somethin' I want to show him out in the shed."

Jack excused himself, repeating what a great meal it had been and how much he enjoyed visiting with her. He wondered if she had any idea just how much he truly had enjoyed it. Her look as he walked out the back door with Jimmy told him she did know, and she had enjoyed it too.

Jimmy led Jack to a large pole barn, one of several outbuildings that had been constructed since Jack had last been on the farm. He slid open a door and they entered a cavernous dark room. Jimmy switched on the lights to illuminate the area. The floor was paved, and it was relatively warm inside. There was a basketball hoop at one end and Jimmy's two sons, who had followed the men from the house, started shooting baskets.

"Come on over here, Jack. Take a look at this!" Jack's eyes immediately spotted the irregular shape covered by a large sheet. Jimmy grasped the sheet and pulled it back, unveiling his old chopper. It was beautiful now as it practically glistened with all the chrome Jimmy had added to it in recent years.

"Oh man, Jimmy, she sure looks great. You've really gussied her up nicely since the last time I saw this old Fat Boy," Jack said.

"Thanks. Know who helped me with it? Ol' Mr. Hansen—Lamar! He's still at the school auto shop teachin' the kids about their cars and how to fix 'em up and drive 'em. He asks about you from time to time too. I still take her out every now and then. Just to show her off. Fits like an ol' glove whenever I do. Sometimes I'll take her into his shop, or he may stop by out here. We've gotten to be good friends. Take a look over here, Jack."

Jack looked up and saw Jimmy standing over by a lineup of all the old tractors, there was the Allis Chalmers, the red Farmall, and the old, regal John Deere. They all were polished and looked to be in mint condition. "They're all pretty much retired now, but I just couldn't bring myself to part with any of 'em. Grandpa sure loved 'em, didn't he? So, I just work on 'em from time to time. They're classics, huh?"

Jack marveled at them, still as fascinated by the big machines just as he had been as a kid. "Yeah, they're great, Jimmy."

"Look at this, ol' buddy," said Jimmy as he walked behind the row of tractors. He pulled off another larger sheet, this time truly shocking Jack.

"I'll be damned!" Jack gasped. It was the Cherry, looking amazingly like her old self with the polished deep red paint and the chromed exhaust pipes that Jimmy himself had helped put on back then.

"Oh, man, Jimmy. She looks great!"

"Thanks. I've tried to keep her up. Well, Lamar's helped me work on her too."

Jack knew Jimmy had taken in the old truck after he had moved away, and his parents had sold their old place and moved, also. Jack hadn't been able to drive for a long time after the accident and so she had sat in an outbuilding. Jimmy had asked Jack's parents about the truck before they left. Unsure at the time just what to do with it, they asked him if he could take care of it, so he had agreed to do so for however long they wanted him to. "I wanted to keep her safe and under wraps in here, hopin' someday I could give her back to you as kind of a thank you for helpin' me turn my life around. I have a lot to be thankful for, and you're one of the biggest reasons it has all turned out the way it has."

"Aw, Jimmy…" Jack was still in shock and virtually speechless. The old Cherry! He just couldn't get over seeing the truck and how great she looked. He walked all around her, admiring her like the work of art she was. He opened the driver's door and peered in. Everything was the same, even the old 8-track tape player was still in the dash. He climbed in and sat behind the wheel. Like Jimmy had said about his Fat Boy, she still fit like an old leather glove. For a minute, Jack felt those emotions trying to engulf him again. All he could do was stare at the dash. "I'm sorry, Jimmy. Sorry I just split the way I did. And sorry I didn't keep in touch. I just got caught up in… life, but I… should have stayed in touch better. You… your family… were always great to me."

"Hey, Jack," Jimmy said, dropping a big paw on Jack's shoulder. "We're just glad to see you again. Yeah, we've missed you bein' around, but it's good to know you're doin' well and things have worked out good for you. Like I told you, I owe you a lot. Weren't for the curveball life hit you with… Should have been you back then makin' that all-state team, gettin' that scholarship, playin' for State… Instead, there you were practically dyin', thinkin' 'bout me, makin' me change my life. If I hadn't seen what all you went through back then, I never would've changed. Probably have ended up in the pen, the way I was so bitter about losin' my mom back then… How 'bout we just call it square, huh?" He offered the big paw and the two old friends shook hands. "What do you say we fire her up and take her for a spin?"

It felt great to get behind the old truck's wheel. Even though it sure wasn't his car's smooth ride, it felt as natural as ever working the clutch and seamlessly shifting her through her gears. The big 8-cylinder growled loud and purred just right. Even the heater worked. The years melted away as Jack drove down the familiar roads, down past Old Mik Point and the abandoned cabin of their old friend, Joe.

"Remember the old place, Jimmy?"

"Yeah, poor Joe. His grandma never did do much with it. She kept it up some, but she passed away a few years ago and it's just pretty much been abandoned ever since. They must be just tryin' to sell it to settle the estate because none of the rest of the family lives around here anymore. It's always been one of the best locations on the lake with that view from the bluff and that sandy beach it has. Someone would probably get a good buy on it right now too."

A little farther along they came up to The Lodge at Camp Kit and slowly passed by the entrance. "Sure is a big change from back when we were kids and it was just a rustic old fish camp. They've done an amazing job with it. Talk about having a vision!" Jack said.

"Yeah, who'd of thought anyone could've done what they have with that ol' place." Jimmy shook his head. "But everyone around here is sure thankful to have the lodge. We've stayed there several times just for a quick getaway."

"So, tell me about you and Cassie Kay," Jack asked. "How'd it happen, man?"

"Well, that night, before the cops got there, I found her. Like I told you last night, she was screamin' and cryin' and I just tried to hold her, calm her down, see how bad she was hurt. The cops and ambulances showed up, and I helped get her onto a stretcher. That's when I started lookin' around for you. At the hospital, I would look in on her, maybe bring her a flower or somethin'. She was banged up pretty bad, but every time I saw her she was cheerful and smilin' and seemed happy to see me. I liked that about her—her strength. It reminded me of Mama, how she was when it was so bad for her. Anyway, after she got out we just sort of started seein' each other, hangin' out together, you know, just good friends like. Then up at State, there she was! Studyin' to be a nurse, and the rest just happened, as they say…"

"That's great, Jimmy," said Jack. "Damn, I wish I'd known. I'm real happy for you, man. She was always the greatest. Your kids are terrific too. I'm sure glad it all turned out the way it did. What about all the old guys? You ever hear from any of them?"

Jimmy laughed. "Hell yes. Let's see, besides what I'd told you already, Rafe finally gave in when I did and decided to go back to school to play ball with me. Was damned good too. He even went up to State with me and played a couple years until he blew out his knee. He's still in the army, but I have an open invitation to him to come back here and work for me when he finally gets out. I think he'd make a damned good deputy, don't you?"

"Yeah, I'll bet he would. Little hard for me to picture, though, since the last time I saw him he had long hair down his back and a beard like a mountain man," Jack said, shaking his head. "That's great, though. Army! Good old Rafe. Always knew he was a stand-up guy and the real deal."

They talked again about all the old friends, including more about Randy, Bobby, and Big Schuler, and Jack welcomed hearing news of Fletch, married to Dawn now with three kids of their own. "And he's drivin' a minivan! Can you believe it? Lot of folks are still around. Some moved away for a while and then moved back. Guess they realized how great a place it really is here."

Jack kept his eyes on the road ahead. "Yeah, this always was a great place. I've never found anywhere else like it. And man, with all my moving around, I've tried."

"You know, Jack, come to think of it, it's interestin' that you went into the radio business. I mean, I know your dad was in the business, but I remember when Duke had come home on leave while you were in the hospital. He wasn't back for long, but he spent the whole time with you. He brought in one of those early boomboxes with detachable speakers. It had an AM/FM tuner and an 8-track player. I don't know how much of any of that you remember, but he made sure the music was playin' all the time. He had the nurses promise to have somethin' playin'—even when no one was there, even in the middle of the night. When we came to visit, we always brought along a new tape for you to listen to.

"You probably had about a hundred of 'em. Steppenwolf, Mountain, The Doors, Cream, that favorite Santana one of yours, and even one of Duke's Dick Dale surfin' tapes. Duke thought it was a way of reachin' you, always lettin' you know the world was out here for you when you came around. I think it might have been a big reason you're with us here and now. And that was when I promised him I'd take care of the truck for you, if your folks wanted me to, that is. Promised him I'd keep it here at the farm, both of us just prayin' you'd be drivin' it again someday."

Jack thought about Jimmy's theory for a little while, reaching back into the murkiness of whatever conscious memories he had of that darkness. "I think you may be right, Jimmy—no, you *are* right. I don't remember Duke being there much at all, and I don't know when it started, but I do remember hearing the music. Sometimes not very coherently, but I knew it was there. And when I did come out of it, it was Santana's tape that was on, that *Abraxas* one. I didn't want to come out of that dark place because I knew when I did, it wasn't going to be good. But I just couldn't fight it anymore. It was almost like being born, I think. I got pushed back out into the world, like it or not, like I was caught up in one of those big Pacific waves Duke used to surf. It was all loud, and instead of pulling me down and under, it kept pushing me up and onto the shore. Then afterwards, the music got me through all those months of that rehab hell too. So, you're right. Ever since then, somehow I've needed to keep close to it. I haven't thought about it that much, but maybe that music did have a lot to do with my being here right now. You know something? I still have all those old tapes... I always will."

Jimmy sat quietly, reflecting on the epiphany Jack had just described. He was about to respond when he noticed the wristband Jack wore in memory of imprisoned Vietnam War soldiers or of those still missing in action, even after all these years. He could see it had Duke's name engraved on it. "We sure were sorry to hear about Duke. Hit Grandpa real hard. He liked ol' Duke a lot. We all did. Have you had any news about what might've happened to him?"

"No, still nothing much. Just an occasional 'no news' from the war department and that they're still making concerted efforts... I don't know, I still want to believe he's out there surfing some big rhino wave somewhere, just like he always said he was going to do again someday."

"He sure was somethin', that Duke," Jimmy added. "Whatever happened, I'm sure he was in the thick of it, tryin' to help someone else out. Just the way he was. He sure was good to us, wasn't he?"

"Yeah, he was great... the best. Sure wish I'd had the chance to get to know him better. Not just as his little brother..."

After a while, Jack turned around and drove back to the farm. "Hey, what's that new building over there?" he asked, turning into the drive.

"Oh, that's our Farm Market. It was Katie's idea, the modern version of it anyway. It all started with Grandma's egg stand she set up out by the road years ago. She'd sell out of her eggs so fast she started sellin' her pies and any fresh fruit or vegetables we didn't need ourselves. Katie started helpin' her out and she just kept addin' all kinds of products to it. We've got everythin' now: fresh baked bread, churned butter, jams, jellies—you name it. But Grandma's pies are still the big draw. Folks come from all 'round, especially for her rhubarb! Jessie helps out all the time, too, when she's not teachin'. She does the bookkeepin' for both the market and the farm, which no one else, including me, wants to do. She calls it a 'labor of love'. It's amazin' how much it's grown. You should see the crowds we get when we open the pumpkin festival. We even give hayrides. Everyone has a great time. The cider business is bigger than ever, and we're even sellin' our own maple syrup now too. It's gotten to be a big profit-maker for the farm and it sure has helped to keep the farm goin' strong."

When they walked into the house, everything had settled down. Jessie greeted them with her warm smile. "You two looked like a couple of boys skipping school the way you took off in that old truck. I could hear the tires screeching! How about some pie and a cup of coffee?"

"Sounds great," Jack said, again mesmerized by her. "It's a little cold out there." They sat and visited in the comfort of the living room while a fire was crackling in the large stone fireplace. He felt at peace here with Jimmy and his family, just as he had when he was a boy and would eat popcorn and watch a Western film with them on a small black and white television.

After a while, it was time for Jack to leave. He had truly enjoyed his visit, and he gave thanks and heartfelt good-byes to all. When he got to Jimmy, they shook hands again. "Thanks for taking such great care of the old Cherry. Would you mind keeping her here a while longer? I promise I'll be getting back here a lot more often. Think I might even look into Joe's old place. Looks a little worn down now, but it still looks good to me."

"You bet, Jack. Best thing in the world seein' you again. Don't be a stranger anymore, okay? We need your smilin' face around here, and I can always use your help with the balin'! So if you get a longin' again for hearin' those ol' tractors workin' and need a good workout yourself, just come on out. You know when first cuttin' is. Cherry's yours whenever you want her, buddy. You can sell that Mercedes and roll in some real style with her in the big city." Jimmy chuckled and then in a serious tone, added, "And we'll always be keepin' Duke in our prayers too."

Jessie grabbed her jacket. "I'll walk out with you, Jack."

Jack said more goodbyes as they walked out into the growing darkness. "Sure was nice seeing you again, Jack." She looked up at him with those big blue-green eyes.

"It was great seeing you, too, Jessie. You all have been great to me. I sure appreciate it."

"We've missed you, Jack. I hope you'll come back and visit us again real soon." She stood close to him and the urge to reach out and pull her to him was almost overwhelming. He wanted to kiss her—and not with a goodbye kiss. "I hope to, Jessie. I owe your family a lot."

She smiled again. "No, Jack. We owe *you*. I saw how Jimmy's life turned around because of you. I remember how he was after Mama died. Everything that happened to you changed him. And you know, I'll always be your biggest fan for saving me from being crushed by that horse that day. I will never forget that. I was so scared! Remember the note I wrote you back then? I know I was just a little girl, but you were and always will be my hero." She kissed him softly on his cheek and hugged him tightly.

Both her closeness and her kiss had caught him off guard. There was something more to it than just a friendly peck on the cheek. It conveyed something more, and he wanted to learn what that meant. Regretfully, though, he had to say goodbye for now, but he knew that he'd be back again, and soon. He held her hands, not wanting to let go, and looked down into those eyes that seemed to offer so much compassion and promise. "Yes, I do remember that note, Jessie," he managed to say.

In the distance he heard a familiar sound, a cowbell, and they both turned toward its direction. "That's just old Sweetness, Jack. Remember her? I'm sure she was a bell cow even back then. She was Grandpa's favorite. Poor thing, she doesn't produce much anymore, not since Grandpa passed, but she's still top gal around here."

Jack watched as she made her way down the path from a far pasture with the whole herd following in a single file behind her. He heard a door slam and caught a glimpse of Jimmy's two boys running down to the barn to greet them. *The work goes on*, he thought.

"The world keeps turning and the cows still need to be milked." Jessie laughed. "Farm life. It's good for the soul, Jack. For mine anyway."

"I think I know what you mean, Jessie." With one last hug and a long look into those deep-water eyes, he climbed into his car. Turning out onto the long drive, he slowly made his way back down the lane. In his rear-view mirror, he saw she was still there, sending him one last wave goodbye.

Chapter 18

It was almost dark when Jack pulled into the parking lot back at the lodge. He was still in time for supper, but as much as Carla tried to convince him to join in, he was still too full from the dinner he had on the farm.

"Oh, I know what a wonderful meal you must have had," she said. "Grandma Meeks' fried chicken is legendary, and I'm always trying to get her to give me the recipe. The thing is, though, I don't think she's ever written it down. Hmm, maybe Jessie knows what it is? I'd love to put it on the menu, call it 'Grandma's Special Recipe'. That would really put us on the map."

"I'm sure it would, although Jimmy and I agree your meatloaf is something special."

"Why, thank you, Jack. That Jimmy still has quite the appetite, doesn't he? And not just for meatloaf. He seems to like my roast beef, too, which is what we are having for supper tonight. How about I make you up a nice sandwich? Nick can bring that and a little piece of my chocolate cake by the cabin for you later. We like to spoil our guests here, you know, 'cause we want everyone to keep coming back. Especially this time of year with this fabulous balmy weather and that sandy beach down by your cabin," she said facetiously.

It wasn't long before he heard a knock on the cabin's door. It was Nick with a couple of big slices of Carla's chocolate cake, a roast beef sandwich, and a bottle of Maker's Mark. His dogs, Elvis and Jerry, were standing by his feet, their tails wagging. "Carla figured this might hit the spot in case you get a little hungry later. Thought you might like to share a shot of this with me too?"

Jack grinned. "Thanks, Nick. I sure appreciate the room service. Thought I wouldn't get hungry again until next week, but this looks great. A nice bourbon, too! Happy to break bread and have a nip with you."

Nick found a couple of highball glasses in the cupboard and poured a shot in each. Handing one to Jack, he said, "How about a toast? Here's to homecomings!" They both smiled, clinked glasses, and drank the bourbon, grimacing at its stinging raw bite and shaking their heads. "Damn, that's smooth!" said Nick. "How about another?" With a quick nod from Jack, he swiftly refilled the glasses. "Here's to the Soul Note. May her memory live on forever!" Jack hesitated and did a double take at Nick, who smiled grandly as he downed his glass. With a wry smile, Jack did the same. "You don't recognize me, do you?" Nick asked. Jack furrowed his eyebrows, seemingly confused. "It's me, Jack, your old Soul Note deejay, Jolly Rogers!"

Breaking into a wide smile, Jack exclaimed, "Unbeliev-able! Jolly Rogers! Hey, where did that big 'fro you used to have go? And the gold chains and bell-bottoms?"

"All right, so I've changed a little. So has everyone! Everyone except you, that is! Once I put the name with the face, I knew it was you, Jack. You're looking great, and you're obviously doing well. Last time I saw you, you were still in rehab. It's good to know it's all worked out good for you, kid."

"Thanks, Jolly—Nick! Damn, it's good to see you too. Unbelievable! Jivin' Jolly Rogers."

"Still hip and flippin' the hits," Nick chimed in.

"I've got to sit down," Jack said. "I think I'll have a bit of that cake too. All this homecoming stuff is making me hungry!"

"Oh, what the heck, I'll have some too. I can't fit into those old bell-bottoms anymore anyway," Nick lamented as he took a bite of his cake. "I'm sorry, Jack, I couldn't help myself. When Carla said you were going over to see the Meeks' today and that you and Jimmy were old friends, it all just clicked. Right when you first came into the lodge, I thought I knew you from somewhere, but I just couldn't figure out where." He paused, lost in thought for a moment, and took another bite of cake. "The old place looks pretty forlorn, doesn't it? Been closed and run-down like that for a long time now ever since they made the legal drinking age eighteen back in '72 when you and Jimmy were just seniors in high school. The experiment didn't last very long. The state changed it right back to twenty-one a few years later. Too many accidents…" He went quiet for a minute. "Sorry,

Jack, I know you know that all too well. It's just good to see you."

"And you, too, Jolly! Just for old times, I'm still going to call you Jolly. So how did this all come about? How did you go from deejay to proprietor of this fine establishment?"

Nick just shook his head. "Being Jivin' Jolly Rogers was just a part-time gig for me back then. I was an accountant and I was keeping the books for the owners while I was working on getting my CPA license. But I liked being a deejay too. It was a lot of fun. Always loved the music, and hey, it wasn't a bad way to meet the ladies, either. I got the CPA about the same time they decided to close the place down, so I moved to the big city and got in with one of the big accounting firms there. Worked my way up. Along the way fortune smiled on me and I met Carla. Turns out that she was from here, so after we got married we'd come back here on vacations and somehow found this place, or more like it found us 'cause I sure wasn't looking for an old, run-down fish camp. Anyway, we took the plunge and poured our hearts, souls, and money into it. And it turned out to be one of the best decisions we've ever made. I love it all: the place, Carla, Elvis, Jerry, and just being plain old Nick."

It was late when Nick stood up and woke the dogs to leave. The cake, the sandwich, and most of the bottle of Maker's Mark had disappeared. Though before Nick left, Jack could not help but ask one more question that had been on his mind for a long time. "Jolly, do you remember a bouncer named Bust Up? He was at the Note back when Duke brought Jimmy and me with him one time back when we were just kids."

Jolly smiled, "Bust Up? Great big, scary-looking guy? Sure, but I think you mean George. Yeah, I got him the gig. I mean, he was as big as a horse, but even though he looked the part of big, bad bouncer and was actually pretty good at keeping the peace, the truth is that he was—and still is—the nicest, most mild-mannered guy you'd ever meet. He only lasted that one summer. He was studying accounting with me, got his degree, and got a great corporate job with National Motors."

Jack was shocked. "You mean he didn't get sucked up into an oven at the foundry back then?" he asked incredulously. "That's what we'd heard happened to him!"

"What? Where did you ever hear something like that?" Jolly asked, equally as shocked.

"Just some talk one night around a campfire back then, as I recall. Someone trying to spook a bunch of us gullible guys," Jack said smiling, slowly shaking his head still in disbelief.

"Heck no. Shoot. In fact, he's now a vice president in their finance department. Married with three kids and doing great!" Nick exclaimed before saying his goodbyes and heading back up to the main lodge. "Oh, hey, Jack," he said, turning around just outside the door. "Rock 'n Roll is in the Soul!" And with that he and the two dogs were gone down the path.

Jack slept soundly again that night. His small cabin was warm, and under the thick comforter he was downright toasty. A breeze had kicked up during the night, stirring up the lake. He had opened one of the windows slightly to listen to the lake's diminutive waves lapping hypnotically against the shore. Even still, morning came all too early. He woke to the sound of crows cawing off in the distance and lay in bed listening to a variety of early rising birds, squirrels, and chipmunks chattering and clattering around. After a bit, he roused himself and took a long, hot shower.

He made himself a cup of coffee in his cabin and carried it with him as he walked down to the lakeshore. The walk refreshed him, and it felt good to breathe in the lake's frosty air. As the early morning fog cleared, he could faintly make out Old Mik Point across the way. He thought about his conversation with Nick—or Jolly—which had turned into something more akin to a reminiscent jam session. After their own catching up, they had talked for hours just about the music. He had been amazed at how much Jolly knew of the music industry, especially of the vintage rock that Jack had built his successful radio career on. He thought he had learned a little of it over the years, especially through Crush, but Jolly's knowledge of the genre was truly impressive. Jolly was a veritable walking, talking Rock and Roll librarian. He knew all the groups, their players, their histories, their lineages, their hits, their flops, and what many were still doing. Just like Crush, it was a shared passion, and he knew Crush would find a Rock and Roll history soulmate were he ever to meet Jolly one day. Jolly was just as keen on what Jack had been doing to keep the old sound out there, alive and breathing, and garnering a legion of new fans and a giving it whole new life.

Jack found a small flat rock along the shoreline, pitched it out across the lake's surface, and watched as it skipped several times before sinking. He smiled to himself as he thought about what Jolly had said he recalled that night Duke had brought the young Jack and Jimmy to the Note. Jack's question about Bust Up had stirred his memory. The boys had perched themselves up on the wall outside the entrance, and Duke had asked Jolly if it was all right if the boys hung out there. Jolly had agreed so long as they stayed there on the wall and that it was cool with Bust Up. During one of the songs, he had stepped out to get some fresh air and have a smoke. Even though it was a steaming hot night and was like an oven inside the place, he wore a dark suit, a white shirt, and a narrow dark tie. "Some kid in there named Duke asked me if I would keep an eye on you kids while he danced. Said he was from California," Jolly had said to the two boys. "Tipped me a couple bucks to play that Beach Boys song he's dancing to now, "Little Surfer Girl." Jolly paused in his reminiscing and sipped his bourbon. "And then all hell broke loose! Another one of those combustible brawls the old place was notorious for. Just like the one you guys had back then. We tried to keep a lid on things but... anyways, I lost all track of you kids..."

Jack heard a faint bell tone back toward the lodge, signaling breakfast, and even though the roast beef sandwich and chocolate cake had been timely the night before, he was surprised that he was hungry again. As he walked back past his cabin and up the winding pathway to the main lodge, he consoled himself that the long, brisk morning walk had worked up his appetite and even burnt off a few calories.

He enjoyed Carla's big breakfast and visiting with the other guests. To Nick's amusement, Jack now referred to him as Jolly, and despite looking a little more rumpled than usual, he still had that "Jolly" smile and energy. They still had a lot of catching up to do, including all the questions Jolly still had about Duke. He'd been good friends with Duke and his buddies all those years ago. He was near to them in age and had just started his part-time deejay gig when they had all first started going to the Soul Note.

But it was Sunday, time to head back to the city. In his cabin, Jack changed into his dress slacks, a pressed white shirt, and tucked a tie into the sleeve of his navy blue sport coat. After packing, he stopped by the main lodge to check out and say goodbye to Jolly and Carla. He thanked them for their hospitality and promised he'd be back again soon. He chatted and laughed some more with Jolly and said that if he ever wanted to revive his deejay career, he could always use a "hip, hit-flippin' jock like Jivin' Jolly Rogers," and that he could use a good accountant too. "And I've got a program director I'd like you to meet. You two are rock music history kindred souls!"

Back down the main road, he pulled into the lane at Old Mik Point and looked around the abandoned cottage. Lake Kit looked cold and gray in the daylight. The lake hadn't iced up yet, and a stiff wind kicked up the waves, creating frosty, frothy caps as they rolled up on the shore. He stood there on the bluff, taking it all in.

Now November, summer was long gone, and the docks were all stored away. The recent snow storm gave notice that winter was ready to pounce, hard and unforgiving. But winter, too, would one day relent to the inevitable seasonal passage. The welcomed rebirth and renewal of warmer days would come again, and the drab gray shades would fade away and be replaced by the vibrant hues of nature's summer palette.

With a deep inhale and a long, slow exhale of breath, Jack knew he was ready. Driving back out onto the main road, he stopped to quickly jot down the phone number on the "For Sale" sign at the end of the lane.

The treacherous road was slick with the dust of even more snow flurries. He came up on the Soul Note, looking just as shabby and forlorn as it had the other night. He slowed down and passed by one last time.

Farther down the road, he pulled over. He left the car running but lowered the window and left the radio dial on his station. Shutting the door behind him, he walked up the road several yards or so until he saw it. The years and nature had tried to conceal it, to disguise the horror of it, but he knew he had found it. He had found the place where it had all changed, where young, precious lives full of promise and dreams were taken from the living world and from those who loved them, and where the ones who were spared were left to try to make some semblance of what used to be from the broken pieces that were still salvageable. It had taken what seemed like an eternity for Jack to put back those pieces, but time had to take its course and heal the deeper emotional wounds.

Somehow, he had needed to come back here. Not just to this place where the tragedy had happened, but to all of it. The Soul Note, the Meeks' farm, Jimmy and his family…

this entire place had brought him back to his life before, back to the people who had known and loved him then, who always had, and who always will. It had taken him so long to get his physical self back to being strong and healthy, all while trying to comprehend and work through the anguish of the nightmarish loss of Alejandra and Joe, and the bitterness of it all he still held inside him.

He realized he had run from it, moving from place to place, not wanting attachments, not letting anyone get too close for fear he'd wake up like that again. He had wanted it all to be just that, a nightmare, a horrible nightmare that would disappear when he woke up, and he had prayed that it was one. *Oh God, please make everything and everyone be okay! Please, God, take me, not them. Please don't make me wake up*, he had pleaded in his subconscious.

But he did wake up, pushed up out of the depths and regurgitated by the mighty waves that thrusted him back into the world of the living. He realized now that he had just been existing, putting one foot in front of the other day after day. He was wide awake now, though, and alive as ever, standing in the frosty woods on a quiet Sunday morning all these many years later, the crows still cawing in the distance. Nearly all remnants of what had happened here long ago were gone now, except for the scarred bark on several of the larger trees that had long since healed over.

Nature had renewed and restored itself. A familiar old tune from his car's radio drifted out into the still morning air. The Marshall Tucker Band's song "Heard It in a Love Song" brought his thoughts back to the present. It was another one of those greener-pastures-on-down-the-road mantra songs that he had identified with way too much over the years. *But how could I not have?* he wondered, pondering the irony of hearing that particular song just now recalling the tragic accident that had claimed the life of one of their founding band members, Tommy Caldwell.

And he had been there in Jacksonville when another tragedy, as shattering as his own, had happened. He was working at the radio station during that fateful October morning when a plane went down in a swamp in Mississippi and took so many lives of the Lynyrd Skynyrd band with it. Jacksonville's own, the shock and agony of that tragedy was felt profoundly by all at home and throughout the country.

Yet another of the Southern rock bands, The Allman Brothers Band, had suffered their own heart-wrenching losses back then, too, as had so many other groups from a variety of tragedies. Jack marveled at how the survivors had somehow kept going, had continued to struggle through their grief and play on. They kept struggling and playing on, and that was what he resolved he had to do as well. After what had happened here on that dark night, and then through the devastating news of Duke, he knew that he, too, had to keep struggling on. If these bands could pick up the pieces and carry on through their nightmares, he would too. And that was when it had all changed for him. He had found a mission and had vowed to keep that sound—their sound, their music—and all the other great rock music out on the airwaves for as long as he could, on any station he could, and with Crush's help, the mission had been a great success. Rock and Roll was here to stay. After all it had to be, he smiled as he thought to himself. *Rock 'n Roll is in the Soul.*

With one last look around, he turned and walked back to the warmth of the car. He sat there for a moment, staring out of the windshield, the song fading off. It made him recall, again, one of those late-night talks with Crush...

—〰—

"What was the name of that place, that ol' rock club you told me about where you and your buds used to hang out? The Soul Note? Yeah, I'd have liked that place. Where I grew up, us kids never had nothin' like that... a Soul Note." Crush paused briefly in thought as he sipped his whiskey, blissfully inhaling its vapors as he did so. "You know, Jack, that name's fittin' 'cause I bet it did have a lot of soul, a lot of spirit, and maybe it claimed a lot of 'em too. Maybe it's still got a good chunk of yours', too, you ever think of that? Maybe that whole place—that whole time back then—still does." Crush paused again, now deeper in thought. "I'm talkin' like that old Roman religious stuff, a *Genius loci*, you know? Back then they saw it more as the protective spirit of a place kind of thing, and that concept is cool to ponder, for sure. But it's more than that. It's more like the whole spirit of a place, man. Like what makes a place or a whole area tick, you know? I'm talkin' what makes it special, what makes it cool, you dig? And I'm thinkin' that whole place you're from has a good *Genius loci*, brother. And you need to go get yourself some of it man. And I'm talkin' like go take a whole bath in it!" he chuckled as he stared into his drink, the ice in the glass having nearly all melted.

"In case you haven't noticed, Jack," Crush continued, "I'm not just a weathered ol' hippie, I'm also a wise ol' sage of a Bodhisattva, too, and I say you need to pull your boots on and go back there and let what all happened set itself right with you, brother. That doc back then set your bones right so they could heal up, and they did good, but now it's gotta be you to go back, let that *Genius loci* of that place help you find that missin' piece of your inner spirit, your Ch'i, or soul, or whatever you want to call it, and get it back while you still can so you can really be whole again. Set your Tao right, man, and maybe find some real happiness in the life you were spared back then to have. So, damn it! Like I been gettin' after you all this time. Go boy! It will be good for ya!"

—⚘—

So Jack had finally heeded Crush's advice, and Crush had been right, it had been good for him. Now he knew what he needed to do. It was what he had needed to do for a long time. When the haze had cleared away from Old Mik Point earlier that morning, it seemed as though it had lifted from over him as well, and with stark clarity, he knew what it was he had hoped to find by coming back. Now he knew that he had found it. In this *"Genius loci,"* as Crush had called it, this place of soul, he had found that missing piece of his own soul.

As the Eagles ballad "Desperado" began playing on his radio, Jack turned the car around onto the highway and headed back into town. On the outskirts, he passed by the old Feed 'n' Seed, closed now on a Sunday morning. Entering the city limits he made his way down Main Street. Then he took a right on Tenth Avenue past Hank's Garage and another right on E Street. It felt good to him to be back once again on the familiar tree-lined streets. Just a left down Penny Lane and there it was, the large brick building with its bright white columns.

As Jack pulled into the parking lot, he could hear the church bells ringing and saw Jimmy and the family just starting to enter through the doors. Jessie saw him first, and he watched her face light up with a vibrant smile as she waved to him. Jimmy turned and saw him too. Smiling grandly, he greeted Jack with a handshake and a pat on the back. Grandma Meeks hugged him and took his hand. Jessie took his other hand as they all entered the sanctuary together, the organist welcoming them with the hymn "Amazing Grace." It was a hymn he remembered well from his youth, and as the organist struck and held that first note, that soul note, he knew that it had him. And there on a pew, seated between Jessie and Grandma Meeks, he felt the warmth of the sunlight as it filtered down like a refracting rainbow through the stained-glass windows of the cupola high above.

Grandma Meeks had felt it too. "It's His everlasting light," she whispered to him, smiling knowingly. She squeezed his hand. "He has found you, Jack. Look, it is right here in the Bible, Isaiah 60:20." She read softly aloud to him, and Jessie listened in. "Your sun will never set again, and your moon will wane no more; the Lord will be your everlasting light, and your days of sorrow will end."

Just then, the congregation began to read the 23rd Psalm in unison. Each verse offering comfort and strength, with one verse in particular striking a chord with Jack: "He restores my soul."